BETWEEN SHIFTS

The City Between: Book Two

W.R. GINGELL

Warning! Within the pages of this book, you will find murders, mayhem, and Australian spelling. My Korean skills are barely so-so, and romanisations may not always be searchable online. Don't say I didn't warn you...

The City Between Series

Between Jobs
Between Shifts
Between Floors (Av. Dec 31ˢᵗ)

Cover by Jenny at Seedlings Design Studio

With many thanks to the people at Kalbi in North Hobart,
who put up with my awkwardness on a weekly basis
while I take over one of their tables
and gorge myself on Bibimbap.

CHAPTER ONE

I woke to the softness of near dark. The bed was warm beneath my body, but my pillow felt cold against my cheek. Beside me, a weight pressed down on the bed.

Just a bit of weight. Just enough for someone to have their knee on the bed, leaning over me...

I turned my head slowly, eyes wide and frozen in the darkness, and the thing leaning over me—the massive thing with a real weight and presence to it—tilted its head. Inky black against the softer dark of my bedroom wall, it was broad-shouldered and human shaped.

When I turned my head, it lunged for my neck.

I woke with a yell, throwing wild punches; and this time I woke properly. But as I woke, still punching and kicking, I woke to a redux. A huge shadow loomed over me, utterly solid and real, shoulders broad against the lighter room.

I grabbed something, I don't know what, and swung wildly, blind and deaf to everything else in my fixation on that huge shadow.

It darted back instead of disappearing, and I followed, panting and crying all at once. The corner of one bedpost caught me near the hairline, knocking me back, and for a moment I saw a bright burst of light.

Through the light, a voice said, "Pet. *Pet.*"

What?

"Pet."

Zero. It was Zero.

I put down the thing I was holding with a shaking hand—what was it? A knife? Where the heck had that come from?—and panted rather than said, "Please don't stand next to me when I'm sleeping."

A small glow of light lit Zero's face; then softly, subtly, the entire room. "Why?"

"That's where the nightmare stands," I said. I sat up again, shivering, and rubbed the bump I could already feel forming on my head. There was a bit of dampness there. "Did I cut you?"

"No," he said, but I could see a faint trickle of midnight blue on one of his arms. "Do you always sleep with a knife under your pillow?"

"No," I said. Seriously, where the flaming heck had that come from?

"Do you always wake up swinging?"

"No," I said again. This was the first time I remembered waking up fighting. "Usually I wake up screaming."

Zero nodded, his eyes hooded and deep with thoughts while shadows flickered across his pale face. What was he thinking about? "Come out," he said, and vanished from the room.

I don't think I'll ever get used to that—the way they can appear and disappear around the house whenever they want.

After he left, I flopped onto my back in the bed with the sweat cold on my brow but relief coursing through me. They were back. My psychos were finally back. Maybe I could have a night without the Nightmare again, now.

That'd be nice.

I puffed a shaky breath of air at the ceiling, and saw a soft glow in my peripheral. It would have made me jump if I didn't already know what it was. Over on the bookshelf there was a tiny tree that was growing on a tiny rock, its roots wrapped around and around that rock as if it was trying to force nutrients from it.

A dryad, Athelas calls it.

Flaming heck. Zero must have seen it.

That was another thing Athelas had said—don't let Zero see the dryad if you can help it. Well, Zero must have seen it when he was in here; the thing was glowing like a nightlight.

The little fella had been glowing like that the last few nights, too. Don't ask me how a little tree on a rock can glow, because I don't know. I don't know how a tin of cat food can be a little tree on a rock, either; but the dryad had definitely started out as a tin of cat food.

Well, I kinda know.

There are layers to reality.

Like trifle, Athelas says, but it's not exactly like that. There's the real world—the *human* world, my three psychos call it, because to them the real world is the one underneath, or Behind, or wherever it is. Then there's the bit between, like custard but not quite.

Maybe I should try that again.

They call it Behind and Between, but that's not really right, either. They—

Man, this is *hard*.

There are layers to reality. There's the human world, of course; but if you know how to see it—if you know *where* to see it— there's a place called Between that's like reality *plus*. Reality plus a bit of fae around the edges. Reality plus an extra edge of danger. Somewhere that an umbrella can be an umbrella or a sword, depending on how you see it. Somewhere that a tin of cat food could be a little rock with a tree on it.

Somewhere creatures you didn't know were real outside the

pages of a book pass through, stealing away some unwary humans and stabbing the others with knockout needles.

If you know how to see it, you can go from the human world into Between; and from there to Behind.

If you're mad enough.

I don't really recommend it.

But if you've ever driven up to the crest of the southern outlet just before you get into Hobart and thought the skyline looked like a castle for just the blink of an eye before it turned back into a normal city skyline, and thought you'd just imagined it—

You didn't.

You just got a sight of Hobart Between.

Places aren't what they seem to be, and neither are things when it comes to Between.

Once you start seeing it, it's hard to stop. Worse, you start to attract the attention of Behindkind like fae and vampires, so it's better not to try to start with.

Unless you're me. Then you have to keep doing it.

Because nowadays there are three Behindkind living in my house: two fae and a vampire.

"*Pet*," said a voice with an edge of a growl to it.

"Heck," I said, flicking my legs out of bed. It was time to get up.

My owners were home.

THEY WERE ALL THERE WHEN I GOT DOWNSTAIRS: ZERO, FAE, white as snow—so white he almost glowed and almost as big as a horse—Athelas, also fae; sitting in his favourite leather chair with one leg crossed over the other, as tranquil and subtly amused as always, and Jin Yeong, vampire; the creases of his trousers sharper than his vampire teeth, his hands in his pockets and his mouth sulky as usual.

"Ah, Pet," said Athelas. He was smiling, but I felt a bit worried about this smile. "I see you're well. Are you responsible for the cut my lord is sporting?"

My eyes flicked over to Zero. There could have been the faintest gleam of amusement to his eyes, or maybe ruefulness.

I said, "You lot shouldn't come into my bedroom without knocking."

JinYeong hissed a small laugh and stalked away into the kitchen. Athelas chuckled, and I suddenly felt a lot less worried.

"Exactly what I told Zero," he said. "I did not, however, expect him to come out of the encounter with an injury."

"I didn't mean to," I muttered. I still felt bad about that, but it wasn't as if Zero couldn't kill me several times over. I'd seen him wandering around Hobart with worse injuries than I'd given him this morning. The knife wound I'd given him was only a scratch.

I could see it colouring the edges of the tear in his shirt, staining it bright blue at the edges and fainter indigo further in.

Oh. It was still bleeding pretty well, though.

"Sorry," I said.

"Don't sleep with a knife under your pillow," Zero said.

"Didn't mean to," I said gruffly. I wish I knew how the knife had gotten there. It wasn't like anyone else could sneak into the house these days. Not without a good amount of magic, anyway. Had I put it there ages ago, before the psychos came here to live, and forgotten about it while they scared the Nightmare away?

"I'll teach you how to use one later. Or perhaps a sword."

"Okay!" I said, before he could change his mind. He'd said he was going to teach me a couple weeks ago, but they'd been gone since then, and I didn't want to miss out again. "Later, when?"

"Soon," he said. "Coffee."

"Oh, yeah," I said. I'd almost forgotten part of my function as pet—make the tea and coffee. I'd been practising, too; tea didn't come naturally to me, so I'd been looking up a few things on the library computer. I'd found a loose-leaf earl grey tea for Athelas, too; he was the only one who drank tea, so I could have just skated by, but he was also the only one who regularly told me stuff, so I liked to keep him happy.

It was nice to hear the back and forth of Zero and Athelas' voices as I got out the tea things—it was even nice to hear the murmur of carpet as JinYeong crossed it; the house had been really quiet for the nearly two weeks they'd been gone. I'd just gotten used to having them in the house when they left again to take care of some changelings that had been taking over human lives, and it had seemed like a lot longer than two weeks. I'd gotten used to them very quickly.

And that reminded me, I thought, as I poured tea and prepared the coffee plunger. I hadn't seen the crazy old homeless bloke lately, either. He was the only survivor of a nasty murder scene over the road, and the survivor of a bloodbath of fae a bit later, so if anyone had reason to be slightly mad, he did.

I wouldn't blame him if he'd disappeared for a few years again —I'd probably do the same thing if I'd survived what he'd survived.

Actually, now that I came to think of it, I *had* survived that. I'd survived the murder of my parents and the murder of the guy across the road. I'd survived a few Behindkind attacks, too. But for me, running away had never seemed like an appealing prospect; before, because I desperately wanted to keep my parents' house; now, because I finally felt as though maybe I was safe for the first time in my life.

Which meant I was as completely troppo as the old bloke, because living with three otherworldly psychos was *definitely* not safe.

"You're cracked," I said to the broken tile above the sink, as I dropped the used teaspoons with a clatter.

"I'm sure you've already thought of it," said Athelas' voice as I balanced the tea and coffee tray to carry it out, "but I wonder if you've found a good source of moving water yet, Zero?"

"Are you feeling particularly weak?"

A brief pause. Athelas didn't sigh, but he might as well have. "Not particularly, but if you're intent upon keeping us in this hamlet for the next goodness-knows-how-long—"

"It's hardly a hamlet."

"—then we should consider finding a source to recharge."

"You lot got batteries, have you?" I asked, stepping down into the living room with my tray. It wouldn't surprise me. There was still a lot I didn't know about the fae—or vampires. Search engines were more helpful about vampires than fae, but they weren't that useful, either.

They ignored me.

Jin Yeong took his coffee from me with a slight lift of the lip to bare one tooth, but he didn't have a bloody look in his eyes, so I took it as a *good morning* more than a *watch out or you're dead* kind of thing.

Zero said, "There's a flowing body of water roughly forty kilometres away as the crow flies, and a waterfall roughly the same distance away in a different direction."

I passed Athelas his tea and made a mental note to figure out what they meant by recharging and water. I mean, water can recharge stuff if it's hydro-powered, but I didn't think Zero was hydro-powered. He was too active away from water—though mind you, his body was big enough to hold a pretty big charge if they really did run on water.

It was the stupidest thing I'd ever heard.

Dissatisfied, I sat down beside Jin Yeong with my own coffee, trying not to wrinkle my nose. Even if I hadn't known they were home because of Zero fetching me, I would have been able to tell by the smell of Jin Yeong's cologne hanging around the living room.

"Don't get comfortable, Pet," warned Athelas.

"What? Thought you wanted me here? Zero called me down."

"We did; but not merely for tea and coffee."

"Why have you got a dryad in your bedroom?" Zero asked. "Where did it come from?"

If I hadn't been focused on Athelas, I might have jumped. "You mean the little tree on a rock?"

"It's a dryad."

"Dunno, it's just sitting there. It always sits there."

That was actually true. It had been sitting there ever since I brought it home from the supermarket where I found it; but when I found it, it had been a tin of cat food. And the supermarket hadn't exactly been the supermarket at that point, either. Remember what I said about layers?

But it was a lie, too, even if I didn't actually lie; a lie Athelas had advised me to tell.

Zero said exactly what I'd hoped he would say, and he didn't seem surprised when he said it, either. "It was always in the house, I suppose?"

"Shouldn't it be here?"

He said, "Don't answer questions with questions," but he didn't follow up, either, so he must have believed me.

I felt a bit bad about that, but mostly I felt relieved. I'm a really bad liar, and I was just lucky he hadn't noticed. That's one good thing about the fae—they think of *all* humans as sort of slightly more intelligent pets, and that means they underestimate us a lot. If the stories I've researched online are right, they've been doing that for thousands of years.

You think they would have learned by now, but if my three psychos are any indicator they're just as superior as ever.

"Zero didn't call you down so you could sit down and make yourself comfortable with coffee and ask questions," Athelas said mildly.

"Fair point. What's up?"

Zero said, "First, do something about that dryad by the end of the month."

"Yeah," I said, glumly. Dunno what I was supposed to do

about it; it was a little tree on a rock. Was I supposed to plant it in the garden or something?

"And get some more food in the house. We'll need a big dinner before we go out."

I cupped my hands around my coffee, hunching my shoulders. "You're going out again already? Didn't you catch all the changelings?"

"We caught all the changelings," Athelas said, smiling faintly. "Never fear, we'll not be long. However, we've got to find a source of moving water nearby. If you're a good pet, perhaps we'll take you with us."

Zero opened his mouth, and I thought he was going to object, but he shut it again and ducked away into the alcove beneath my bedroom that he uses as a study and bedroom for the few hours per night that he sleeps.

Okay, so maybe I *was* going, too? I craned my neck to see Zero. "You want me to go shopping right now?"

"Not right now," Zero said. "There's some unpacking for you to do."

"What unpacking?" I asked. There were only two packs on the floor by the chairs; a black leather satchel type thing I'd seen slung over Zero's shoulder when he left, and the neat doctor's bag that Athelas used when he travelled. I pointed at them. "That?"

"Not mine," said Athelas. His eyes were gleaming with amusement. "You'll be busy enough with Zero's."

"Yeah?" I looked doubtfully at the satchel and grabbed the strap.

"I'll carry it," Zero told me, stepping briefly from the alcove again to pluck the satchel away from me.

It must have been pretty heavy, because I heard the slight grunt he gave as he picked it up, and Zero doesn't really grunt at much. He put the satchel over by the bookcase between the windows on the far side of the living room, and when he turned his back, I tugged at its handle cautiously to test the weight.

I nearly fell over. It didn't even *shift*. It just sat there, like it thought it was Thor's hammer or something.

"What's *in* there?" I asked in astonishment.

"Books," said Zero, turning back. There was a faint narrowing to his eyes that meant he knew I'd tried to lift the bag and was laughing at me.

"Yeah? A library full?"

"Very nearly."

"Hang on, what?"

Instead of answering me, Zero unlatched the front flap and flipped it over. I could see the spines of four books in the opening; not too bad, and definitely not a whole library. Why were they so heavy?

"Arrange them alphabetically," he said, and ducked into his alcove.

"Sure I'll manage that without help?" I asked him.

Athelas laughed softly into his tea, but Zero didn't answer me. I saw why when I took out those four books: there were another four books directly beneath the first layer, and when I took *that* four out and put them on the carpet, there were still four more there.

How many fours were *in* this satchel?

Lots. There were *lots* of fours in the satchel.

By the time I could move the satchel at all, there were nearly twenty me-sized stacks of books beside the bookcase. It was still pretty heavy, though, so there were probably a good few more piles of books to come out.

"You related to Mary Poppins?" I asked Zero, but he didn't answer that, either. "Where are they all gunna fit?"

"They'll all fit in the bookcase," he said. He stepped from the alcove once more, picked up two of the bigger books, and went over to the kitchen table with them.

Beats him sitting over there sharpening knives, I suppose; I don't know how, but he's somehow more approachable when he's sharpening knives than when he's studying his magic books. He just looks a bit thoughtful while he's sharpening knives, and you feel like you might be able to talk to him. When he's studying, there's a deep frown between his brows and what feels like a thin layer of ice all around him. Dunno what he's studying, but when he studies, he studies *hard*.

I went back to the impossible satchel of books and started propping up books in the shelves. I didn't notice until I'd laid a few half shelves and came back to add more to them, that the books I'd just put there now looked like old classics—Dickens, Austen, and a lot of Walter Scott—instead of the leather spines and curling, illegible titles.

"Yeah, real clever," I said to no one in particular, "but some poor beggar's gunna be flamin' disappointed if he feels like reading Dickens for a change."

I looked at the shelves again, then down at the books in my hand. "Oh," I said.

It was going to be a bit hard to arrange things in alphabetical order if I couldn't see the real book spines to know. I looked down at the book in my hand and said again, "Oh."

They weren't even in English. What was it, old Welsh or something?

I didn't know; but I did know that I'd never seen this language before. The letters almost looked like English letters if you looked at them with your head on the side, but when you tried to figure out which letter was which, you couldn't.

"How the heck did I get these ones right, then?" I muttered, looking back at the book spines. I hadn't even thought about it before; I'd just put the books up on the shelf because *that* was the order they were supposed to be in. Just like I would have done if I'd been looking at books with English titles.

"Don't try so hard, Pet," advised Athelas. "You'll do yourself an injury."

"Are you telling me to work smarter, not harder, or are you giving me direct advice?"

Athelas' grey eyes dwelled on me for long, amused moment. "What do you think?"

"I think if I'm not allowed to answer questions with questions, you shouldn't be able to, either," I complained.

Athelas only said, "That is one of the joys of owning a pet. One is not required to answer for oneself *to* that pet."

"Yeah, I noticed that," I muttered. "Where did all these come from, anyway?"

There was a pause long enough to make me think Athelas wasn't going to answer that question either, but he said after a little longer, "Behind. We got them on our way back—with some difficulty, I might add."

"Had to break 'em out, did you?" I asked, but the last part of Athelas' answer hadn't been directed at me—it had definitely been directed at Zero.

"Something like that," Athelas said. "Perhaps you would be kind enough to make another pot of tea, Pet."

"All right," I said. I was happy enough to leave the books for a minute or two, and it was always good to make sure the balance was kept when it came to Athelas and payment for answers.

IT TOOK ME FIVE HOURS TO SORT THROUGH THE BOOKCASE. *FIVE hours*. It might not have taken me so long if I hadn't had to recalibrate my brain every time I looked away from the bookshelf and then looked back to see more Dickens and Austen, but there were still enough books to have taken a good few hours anyway.

And they all *did* fit in the single bookcase, too. At first, I thought it was a spell doing it, but as I worked I started to see the kind of depth to the bookcase that I usually only see when I'm Between; like the place where the human world and the Between bit meets is making extra space.

It sorta glitters. Or maybe it's more of a shimmer; like heat haze. And the more I see of it, the easier it is to see; those bits of Reality Plus, where there might be a bit more to life than you can see.

I poked my head between the shelves to see if I could see anything more there, but I heard something howl in the distance, carried on a chilly wisp of wind, and hastily pulled it out again. No use getting my head bitten off by poking it outside the house —I could have that done without leaving the comfort of my home. JinYeong was always pretty happy to talk about slaughtering me.

Athelas had long since padded away silently to do something else by then, with a passing reminder to go and buy food when I was done, and Zero had sunk even deeper into his studying.

That left JinYeong to stalk around the living room in increasingly predatory circles while I finished off the books. He was probably hungry; it was his turn to pick what we were having for dinner, which meant we would be having something I didn't know how to cook. Good thing I can search stuff online at the library, or he'd always be stalking around the house in a bad temper.

Well, he's always stalking around the house or sulking around it, anyway, but today he was worse than ever. He kept saying *kimchi* at me in increasingly irritated tones when I started making my shopping list, and when I howled "Speak English!" at him, he snarled to show off his pointed teeth.

I stomped away upstairs to find Athelas for a translation, but he wasn't anywhere in sight, and Zero was still studying his books with his most forbidding *don't interrupt* look, so I didn't dare stop him to ask what the heck *kimchi* was.

When I got back downstairs, JinYeong was leaning against the wall on the bottom landing with his arms folded, and as I passed he pushed himself away from the wall and followed me, his socks light and silent against the carpet.

He was still following me when I walked out of the house, a

step behind because he'd had to put on shoes. I turned on him in annoyance. "What?"

"*Kimchi*," he said again, and marched past me into the street.

Flamin' fantastic. I was going shopping with the vampire again.

It's really irritating walking with Jin Yeong—if you try to walk *with* him. He saunters along with one hand in his pocket, his perfectly creased trousers cutting a suave path through pedestrians and his pretty little face looking out smugly at the world. There's no one who looks as pleased as Jin Yeong does when he's out for a walk.

Might as well just say, "Here I am, ladies; look your fill!" because that's what his face says.

I like to stride it out—you do when you can't afford a bus fare around the place—because I'm used to walking; and he just *won't* keep up. Plus he likes me to walk behind him like I'm a serf or something, and that's just annoying.

I mean, I might just be a pet, but I've got my pride. We pets trot in *front*.

That morning I left him behind and stepped out at my usual pace, because if he couldn't be bothered to keep up, that was his problem. Hopefully it annoyed him as much as his smug face usually annoyed me. I went to the supermarket along Campbell Street; though I was tempted to keep going to the city one, if only to see if Jin Yeong would get lost.

Oh yeah. He's a vampire. He can smell me.

Jin Yeong's such a pain in the neck.

Literally.

Jin Yeong was still a couple of blocks behind me when I got to the supermarket, so I figured I'd better wait outside for him. I'd gotten a bit too hot with striding it out, anyway, so it was nice to cool down in the shade.

After a bit, some smokers came out and stood near me, so I moved further down, but the smoke followed me and I ducked into the garbage alley to escape it. Better garbage smell sweeping up through the alley than the smell of smoke.

It smelled pretty ripe, too; what were they keeping in there? A piggery? I wrinkled my nose and threw the closest skip bin a dark look.

It was funny, though. Something about the alley wasn't quite right.

No, something about the skip bin itself wasn't right. What was it?

I took a step toward it, eyes narrowed, but caught a flutter of movement from the parking lot.

Jin Yeong approached, one hand in his pocket. He didn't seem to see me—didn't even seem to look at me—but he sauntered toward the garbage alley without hesitation.

When he got close enough, he sniffed cautiously; gagged and said, "*Ah, nemsae!*"

"Yeah, it stinks a bit," I agreed. Today was garbage disposal day, and the trucks would be coming around soon to get the big roller bins. Most of the garbage had been sitting out here and festering for the better part of a week.

Ask me how I know that and I'll ask you if you've ever had to find food when there's no money to buy it.

And don't tell me I could've stolen it, because I couldn't.

"*Iruwa, Petteu,*" Jin Yeong said, from the mouth of the alley. He still had one hand coolly in his pocket, the other dabbing in the air to call me over as if I really was a dog.

I saw his eyes flick around the parking lot, even if his face was coolly unconcerned, and my jaw set stubbornly. I wasn't going to *come-here-Pet*. Jin Yeong thought there was something wrong here, too.

"There's something weird here," I said, taking another couple of steps toward the bin.

Jin Yeong said something exasperated in Korean, and started down the alley toward me, giving up his cool pose.

I scuttled further down the alley before he could catch me; there *was* something there, and I wanted to know what it was. It was a bit of rubbish bin that didn't look like it was rubbish bin, but I didn't know what it really looked like, either. Maybe a bit of a really big tree trunk, with giant scratches running down it that weren't from any waste removal service I'd ever seen.

They were more like...

I squinted at them. Turned my head.

I took another step forward and nearly stepped in a bit of dog poo that was cunningly concealed beneath a plastic bag.

"Yuck," I said beneath my breath, sidling sideways. Maybe I'd be lucky and Jin Yeong would step in it.

I stepped a bit closer, this time more carefully, and peered at the side of the bin.

Yeah, they were definitely claw marks; and the side of the metal bin was definitely not as metal as it should have been.

I crouched to look more closely at the scratches, but Jin Yeong's fingers wrapped around my wrist as I reached out to touch them.

"*Hajima*," he said.

"I was just gunna touch 'em!" I protested, flapping my arm to try and free it from his skinny fingers.

That was useless, of course; but I couldn't help grinning because Jin Yeong was standing really carefully, like he was trying not to stand in something bad, or *had* stood in something bad.

"What's the matter, step in something?" I asked him, but when I looked down again properly, I already knew the answer.

A pool of dark, thick liquid seeped out from beneath the skip bin, darkening more at the edges but still sticky in the middle where flies and bread flakes had caught in it.

Oh yuck.

Someone had left raw, bloody meat out.

I frowned. Looked up at Jin Yeong questioningly.

"That's a lotta blood for raw meat, isn't it?"

Jin Yeong twitched the wrist he was holding. "*Ireona, Petteu.*"

"Wait," I said, pulling back. I didn't want to get up just yet, because if it was raw meat beneath the skip bin, why was there so much blood? much blood?

And why did the bit of meat closest to the front edge of the skip bin look like it had fingers on it?

"Ah man," I said.

It was a body.

CHAPTER TWO

I MEAN, I *SAY* IT WAS A BODY, BUT IT WAS ACTUALLY JUST A hand. The rest of the body was further beneath the bin with what might have been a lot of old meat cuts, but...weren't. It wasn't exactly in pieces, but it was pretty torn up. I'd seen worse, but only *just*.

Jin Yeong crouched and peered beneath the bin. "*Ashipda*," he sighed. The hand around my wrist tightened; he pulled me away from the bin as he stood and said firmly at me, "*Nappun Petteu*."

"Thought you could smell blood," I grumbled, looking away from the skip bin and trying not to smell it as I swallowed. If I kept smelling it, I was gunna be sick. "Why'd you make—oh. You didn't want to find it, did you?"

Jin Yeong shrugged and looked away.

"What, you don't want to know about it 'cos it's just a human?"

He shrugged again and said, "*Baegopa*."

Living with a Korean vampire, that's a word I'd come to know really quickly: Jin Yeong was hungry.

"Don't eat the body!" I yelped, jerked out of my queasiness by a more normal disgusting. "You've got blood at home!"

JinYeong said something indignant at me that could have been to the effect that he didn't *eat* bodies, he drank from them, but was more likely a cross remark that he'd been talking about solid dinner and not his liquid diet. He must have had his fill of blood over the last couple of weeks fighting changelings, after all.

"How am I supposed to know when you're hungry for blood and when you're hungry for food?" I demanded.

He snarled at me, but by then I was too busy phoning the police to pay any attention. JinYeong seemed to be resigned to staying where he was, though; he picked a place against the block-work wall that was cleaner than the rest and propped himself against it to watch me in a resigned kind of way.

The radio room answered, but they knew Detective Tuatu's name straight away when I said it and put me right through to his desk. I could've just reported it to the radio room, but the detective was going to be suspicious enough about me being around another body, so it was best to get that out of the way as soon as possible. It wasn't as if the supermarket didn't have security cameras, either; he would definitely find out one way or another.

He didn't sound wary when he answered the phone with a professional, "Tuatu speaking," but that changed as soon as he heard my voice.

Maybe I shouldn't have asked, "Hey, you want a body?"

"What do *you* want?" Yeah, his voice was definitely wary now.

"Told you," I said, trying not to look at the bloody pool across the alley. "Got a body for you."

"Are you joking? If you're joking—"

"Nah, there's a body down here. Campbell Street; beside the supermarket. I found it when I came to do the shopping. You want it?"

"Do I *want* it?"

"Well, if you're bored or something. I thought you investigated murders."

"There's really a body down there?"

"Yeah."

"I'll be right there. Don't go anywhere."

He hung up on me. Rude beggar.

I told Jin Yeong, "Says he's coming. You want to scoot, or are you staying?"

Jin Yeong shrugged and pushed away from the wall. I thought he was going to stalk away down the alley and go home, but he strolled toward the sticky pool of blood and meat bits again, his nose elevated slightly.

If it had been quiet, I probably could have heard him sniffing. Why was he sniffing the blood?

"What's wrong with the smell?" I asked.

"*Da*," he said, his mouth pursed in dissatisfaction. "*Dadeul.*"

Everything was wrong about it? I thought that's what he was saying, but I'd only been trying to learn Korean for a couple weeks now. They hadn't told me to do it; I'm just a good pet who goes above and beyond.

Plus Jin Yeong always looks so offended when I understand something he says.

Oh, and the fact that I hate not knowing what's going on around the place.

"Well, it's not my fault any more if your sniffer isn't working properly. Oi! You're not supposed to tamper with murder scenes!"

Jin Yeong, who had crouched to dip one finger in the blood, gave me a look of disdain and delicately licked the blood off his finger.

"Man, that's disgusting!" I muttered, keeping a wary eye on him. Still, I suppose it was better than being left by myself with the remains.

Maybe.

Jin Yeong's pupils suddenly dilated, startling a hiss of air from me. They widened until they took over the iris, black and shiny and disturbingly reflective. More disturbing, however, was the fact that I could see...*stuff* moving in the blackness of his eyes. Stuff that definitely shouldn't have been moving there.

"What the flaming heck is wrong with your eyes?" I demanded.

Jin Yeong held up one finger, his lips compressing, and I made a small *pft* of air at him that made him freeze and then scowl.

Oh, now that was interesting! He couldn't see while he was doing—actually, what *was* he doing? I crouched in front of him, peering into those sightless, moving pupils, and waved my hand in front of them.

Nothing.

"Oi," I said, and poked his cheek with my forefinger. "Oi. You in there?"

Nothing.

I poked his cheek a couple more times, but that didn't rouse him, either. I sat back on my heels, wondering if I should let him stay like that—I mean, he wasn't frothing at the mouth or anything, and he didn't look sick—then popped back up to poke his cheek once more for good measure.

Jin Yeong's eyelids flicked shut and then opened again, dark brown and liquid once more.

Whoops.

"*Ha. Ji. Ma,*" he said, pushing me a bit further away between every syllable with the forefinger he'd used to dip in the blood.

"Yeah, but your eyes were weird," I protested, shuffling hastily backward to avoid falling on my backside. I swiped at the place his finger had touched and it felt wet, but that could have been because I was still bleeding from this morning. "Is it because you were licking blood? Your eyes didn't do that last time you fed."

"*Isanghae.*"

"Is it a different kind of blood than you usually get?"

Jin Yeong sighed deeply. "*Nan mariya!*"

"No need to get your knickers in a knot! You're the one who won't speak English."

He huffed a small, exasperated laugh and said something beneath his breath.

"Anyway, you still shouldn't disturb things at a crime scene, and you shouldn't be licking weird blood, either."

"*Kugae aniya.*"

Isn't something. Something isn't something. "Oh!" I said, as he stood up. "Do you mean this isn't the crime scene? This isn't the place he—she—heck, I dunno. But this isn't the place where that person was killed?"

JinYeong gave me the particularly offended look he gives me whenever I guess or get something he says right. "*Ne.*"

"Someone just dumped the body here to try and get it found without too much trouble?"

"*Ne.*"

I shrugged and stood up. "Makes sense. How'd you know, anyway?"

"*Pi isanghae. Nemsaedu isanghae.*"

Wait, that was the same word he'd used before, and the other word was smell. I hazarded a guess. "The blood smells weird? Is that how you know the person wasn't killed here?"

JinYeong only folded his arms and pursed his lips, shrugging up one shoulder.

Looked like I was only half right.

I swallowed a bit and looked at the mess again. I even leaned around the skip bin to look at the wall behind it, holding my breath. There wasn't much blood spatter, there; if a body was being torn to a pulp, alive or dead, wouldn't there be a bit more mess around the place? Most of it was in pools beneath the skip bin—there was only a sloppy sort of splash that went part way up the wall behind the bin, and that looked more like the kind of splash you get when you dump something into a pool of liquid.

"All right," I said. "Looks like the person was killed somewhere else. Wonder if their cameras got the person who dumped it?"

"Sangkwani obseo. Petteu—"

"Yeah, but *I* care! I'll tell the detective about it. He'll probably know anyway, but we might as well be useful."

"Uri?"

"Yeah, us. There's no point in finding a body if we aren't going to be helpful."

JinYeong said something in a particularly annoyed tone of voice that I took to mean he hadn't wanted to find a body and didn't want to be useful.

"You can go home if you want," I suggested. "Just buy the groceries first."

He snarled at me and settled back against the opposite wall of the alley, watching me balefully. He was still doing that, arms folded, when Detective Tuatu arrived.

Detective Tuatu approached us warily, his eyes flickering between myself and JinYeong a few times before they finally stayed more or less on me with occasional side-eye at JinYeong.

"He doesn't bite," I said, and then giggled. "Well, actually, he does; but Zero says he's not allowed to bite most humans."

"Chero malsum aniya! Kugol nae kkoya!"

"The heck it's not your thing! I've seen you bite more things than—"

The detective cleared his throat. "He really bites humans —people?"

JinYeong said something else, coldly; I assumed he was saying he did what he wanted to do, and that Zero wasn't the boss of him, but that was just a guess.

"Sometimes. Zero says he's not allowed to bite you."

"Thanks," said the detective, but he didn't look any more comfortable. For a bloke as dark-skinned as he was, he looked pretty pale right now. He rolled his shoulders and asked resignedly, "Who have they killed now?"

I heard a small, hissed laugh from JinYeong that made the

detective start. I said, "They didn't kill anyone. Well, they didn't kill this one, anyway; and they didn't kill the last one, either."

"Is that supposed to make me feel better?" the detective asked, his face still stiff. "Who *did* they kill, then?"

"For a bloke who's sweating as much as you are, you're asking a lot of questions," I remarked. It was nice not to be the most off-balance one at the crime scene anymore. "Don't you wanna see the body?"

"I can see the blood from here," he said, but he took the hint and crouched to see the body. He recoiled once, then peered closer. He muttered, "Fantastic. Another mess to clean up."

"Sorry," I said. "This is the only body I've found today. I'll call you again if I find a nicer one."

"Don't!" he said, and added exasperatedly, "I mean, don't go around looking for bodies."

"Never looked for a body in my life," I told him. "No one does. They just seem to find me. What's wrong with this one, anyway? You don't like blood? You should be like Jin Yeong. Jin Yeong likes blood."

Detective Tuatu threw an uneasy look over his shoulder at Jin Yeong, who grinned a sharp grin at him. "It's not that. There have been a few of these deaths over the last two years, and they've all been closed as animal deaths."

Jin Yeong made a soft, explosive sound of disgust. "*Maldo andwae!*"

"It's rubbish, but I can't do anything about it," the detective said bitterly. "Every time someone gets a case like this, it's brushed under the carpet, and a wild animal gets the blame."

I found my voice again. "A wild animal that size in *Tasmania*?"

"Exactly," he said.

"Jin Yeong says the person probably wasn't murdered here, if that helps?"

Detective Tuatu looked a bit sharper. "If there's a secondary scene to prove it wasn't an animal, they might not be able to sweep it under the carpet. Why does he say that? I'd reckon that's most of the body's blood beneath it, so—"

"For a start, what animal pushed the skip bin back against the wall after the body was dumped?" I demanded. "I dunno why Jin Yeong says it didn't happen here—he just reckons it smells wrong, but—"

"He says it *smells* wrong?"

"*Ne*," said Jin Yeong, looking particularly self-satisfied.

"But there isn't any mess on the skip bin—or the wall, either."

"All right," said the detective. His eyes were definitely brighter. "I can work with that. At least I can keep the investigation open for a while."

"Where are the rest of the cops, anyway?"

Detective Tuatu hesitated, and I got the feeling he didn't like what he was going to say. "They're coming," he said. "They're just going to take a while. I told you; we aren't encouraged to investigate these cases."

"They're hoping some evidence will be lost?"

He nodded shortly.

"*Petteu, caja.*"

"What's he want?" Detective Tuatu asked.

"He wants me to come along like a good pet," I said.

"You can't," he said. "I haven't finished asking questions. Actually, I haven't even started! When did you get here? And did you see anyone else hanging around when you did?"

"What, like a bloke with blood all over him? Nope; just smokers around the corner, and they're only killing themselves. Got here about half an hour ago."

"*Petteu!*"

"All right, all right, I'm coming!" I said in disgust.

"You can't go!" protested Detective Tuatu. "I still have questions!"

I grinned at him. "Gunna arrest me, are you?"

His lips compressed; he pinched them in on themselves and

rolled them back out. I expected him to say something about me being a smart aleck and leave it be, but he surprised me by saying outright, "After last time? I'd call that a poor use of police time."

"Yeah, me too; but you never can tell with the cops, can ya?"

One of his eyebrows went up, but he grinned. "Exactly," he said.

"Not trustworthy, the cops," I said piously. "Always hiding stuff."

"This station is, anyway," he said shortly, surprising me again. "I'd guess this thing goes pretty high, though."

"Then it's lucky I'm the one who found it, isn't it?" I told him, smiling in a friendly sort of way at him.

He looked suspiciously at me. "How so?"

"Well, we're a part of the police force now, remember?"

"*We?*"

"Well, *they* are, anyway," I said, jerking my chin at Jin Yeong, who was walking away. "Lucky, isn't it? If someone higher up is trying to hide something, maybe they can help."

"I'll remember that," he said.

I wasn't sure if he sounded relieved or annoyed. Maybe it was both, but I didn't have time to figure it out, because Jin Yeong's straight back had just disappeared into the supermarket, and I didn't want to lose him. Not when there might be a murderer hanging around. I hadn't started on my training with Zero yet, and I didn't know what I'd do if I actually met a murderer.

Well, a murderer who wasn't any one of my three psychos, anyway.

"I gotta go," I said. "Catch you later."

"Wait!"

"Can't wait—Jin Yeong'll buy up all the cologne and about six tonnes of moisturiser, and Zero only gave me a fifty."

"Give me your number," he said.

"Rude," I said. "Why should I?"

Detective Tuatu looked exasperated again. "So I can ask you questions if any more occur to me, of course!"

"Dunno," I said, pretending to think it over. "There's some weirdos around. Don't want to be giving my number to every Tom, Dick and Harry out there."

"You know I can just get it from the radio room, right?"

"Rude!" I said again. "All right, all right; gimme your phone. Don't go calling me at weird times, though."

"Why would I call you at weird times?"

"Dunno," I said again, and gave him the phone back. "Just don't."

"It's not like it's the highlight of my week, talking to you!" he said indignantly, but I was already dashing after Jin Yeong.

I bumped into him just inside the glass sliding doors, and he looked suspiciously at me. "*Handpone wae?*"

"What?"

Jin Yeong made little punching motions with his thumbs, as though he were texting.

"Oh, that. The detective wanted my number for later."

"*Wae?*"

"In case he has more questions."

Jin Yeong didn't look much less suspicious, but he said, "*Keurae. Johah,*" and grabbed a small trolley.

I heard sirens when we got to the checkout later and glanced down at my phone.

Strike a light. Detective Tuatu wasn't joking; it had taken them half an hour to respond to a dead body call.

I showed Jin Yeong my phone, but he only shrugged.

"All right, all right," I said. "But it's still weird and I'm gunna tell Zero about it."

"*Keurae, keurae; haebwa,*" he said, pushing me toward the checkout. It sounded like he was daring me; like he didn't think Zero would be interested.

"I will," I told him, putting my nose in the air.

Jin Yeong sniffed, and made a small shoving motion at me, his eyes flicking pointedly from the groceries to the conveyor belt.

"What?" I asked. "Just did your nails?" But I put the stuff up there anyway; he would only have kept staring haughtily at me until I did it, anyway.

Oh well, I suppose it's my job, after all; being the pet and everything.

That didn't stop me loading all the bags onto Jin Yeong when we got outside the store, though. He was too surprised at the sudden attack to do anything but take them; and once he had them he simply raised one brow at me and asked, "*Wae?*"

"Cos I gotta go to the library before I come home," I said. "You want your flamin' *kimchi* or whatever it is? Well, I gotta research. And if I take the bags with me, the stuff'll go off."

"*Keurae, johah,*" agreed Jin Yeong, and sauntered away without waiting to see where I went.

He must have told Zero when he got home, though; because after I'd walked past the crime scene to tilt a grin in the detective's direction, a text came through.

Athelas will bring you home in one hour exactly.

I had to stop myself from making a face at the phone. Flamin' heck! After what we'd already been through together, they still didn't trust me not to wander off and blurt out all I knew to the nearest human?

Hang on, they'd just left me alone for a couple weeks to go chasing changelings, so it wasn't that they didn't trust me not to go off and tell someone. What was going on? Or was it just that Zero was worried about me being out and about while a murderer was around?

I scowled so I wouldn't smile. It wasn't much good getting sentimental; Zero didn't like his pets dying, but that's all there was to it. I knew I could trust him that much, and that was enough. Stay behind Zero, don't die, inherit my house. That's all I had to do.

The stairs at the library felt like an effort when I got to them. I trudged up them to the second floor for the computers, wondering if I'd caught a cold or the flu since yesterday, and settled myself down in front of the least grimy one. I wanted to find out what Athelas meant by *recharging*.

The search engines weren't much use. I tried a few different iterations of *recharging fae*, but all I got was stuff about spell bags and fae that could turn into animals to recharge—though one of the results was about needing nature to recharge. That one turned out to be an urban fantasy book, and I clicked away from it in disappointment.

Still, it gave me an idea that Zero and Athelas were as out of place here in the human world as Jin Yeong was, and that maybe they needed their own form of blood to stay strong. Only instead of blood it was...water?

I still didn't really understand, but there was a glimmer of sense to it.

I followed the link about fae turning into animals to recharge and spent a good forty-five minutes trawling through blog post after blog post that got weirder and wilder as I followed the trail, but in the end my glimmer of sense was still only a glimmer, and the only thing I was certain about was that I would have to wait until they went out tonight to find out for sure.

I gave up on it and did a quick check for kimchi instead. Lucky for me, the computer actually recognised the word, and the first link under the description of kimchi was a blog post on how to make it.

I skimmed the description and snorted.

Kimchi was spicy, pickled cabbage? *Old* spicy, pickled cabbage?

Jin Yeong wanted to eat *cabbage*?

I saw a faint reflection of my grin in the computer monitor. Perfectly coiffed and snooty Jin Yeong, eating cabbage?

Yeah, I could do that.

I printed off the instructions while fumbling with one hand

for my phone, which had started to ring, and one of the librarians shot me a dirty look.

I hurried out with my kimchi-making instructions and said a bit breathlessly into the phone, "Yeah, what?"

"It's me," said Detective Tuatu, surprising me.

I mean, I know I'd given him my number, but I hadn't actually expected him to *call* me. Even Zero and Athelas usually only text me, which was why I hadn't changed the ringtone from the bog standard one—or turned off the sound in the library.

"What?" I asked. "It's only been an hour since I saw you."

"Are you trying to play games with me?"

"What?"

"They wouldn't take the case."

"They what?"

"They," said the detective, very precisely, "would not. Take the case. I called them directly to arrange it because I knew I wouldn't be able to push it through upstairs, and the one you call Zero said no."

"That doesn't make any sense. They're attached to the police force now!"

"Apparently," the detective said, and there was bitterness in his voice, "they're only interested in cases with a similarity to the one with the hanging body."

I turned onto the ramp out of the library, and the electric doors in front of me hissed open as Athelas stepped lightly through.

"I'll get back to ya," I said, and hung up.

"Admirable timing, Pet," said Athelas, doing a leisurely about-face to stroll beside me. "But it's perhaps not wise to be distracted when you step out into the street at the moment. I hear there's been a murder nearby."

That was his way of asking who was on the phone, I was pretty sure. Athelas likes to keep things balanced, and if he asks too many questions, he feels as though he has to let me ask a few, too.

"It's not like the bloke's still gunna be hanging around," I argued, ignoring the pointedness of the remark. I didn't want to answer a direct question right now, and if I was obtuse enough about it, I was pretty sure I wouldn't have to do so. "Anyone'd think you blokes were worried about me."

I didn't say it jokingly, but only because it didn't occur to me that anyone, least of all Athelas, would take it as anything other than sarcasm.

So it was a bit of a surprise when he looked briefly down at me and said with gentle pointedness, "Certainly not. Zero can't love; Jin Yeong shouldn't, and as for myself—"

"You definitely shouldn't love anyone," I muttered. I felt a bit cut, which was stupid; there was no way I should be getting fond of *any* of my three psychos, and to imagine that they were getting fond of me was just as stupid. "You'd spend all your time tallying up who owed who. That's not love."

Athelas inclined his head. "Even so. The fae are not, in general, capable of what a human would call love."

"What about concern? Not capable of that, either?"

"That," said Athelas, "depends entirely upon context. Who were you on the phone with, Pet?"

The direct question was so unexpected that I stopped and stared at him.

He waited patiently for me to think things through for a moment or two longer, a smile lingering on his lips, before he explained, "I have a responsibility to Zero. The burdens balance out, I find; and I'm willing to expend myself somewhat in his service."

Since I'd just come to that conclusion myself, I only sighed and said, "It was that detective. Me and Jin Yeong found the body, so—"

"Did you really?" murmured Athelas, his voice mildly surprised.

I knew what that surprise meant. I said, "Well, I found it; Jin Yeong was trying not to find it. I called the detective to tell him about it. Told him he should call you for help with it, too."

"Ah," said Athelas. "I see. I do wonder how it is that you made such a misjudgement, however."

"Yeah," I muttered. "I'm beginning to wonder that, too."

THE HOUSE HAD A DIFFERENT FEEL TO IT WHEN I WOKE UP THE next morning. Dunno what it was—don't even know if it was a safer feeling or a more perilous feeling—but there was definitely something different about it. If I hadn't already known my psychos were home, I would have got the idea anyway.

The dryad looked a bit perkier, too; if a little tree with a stranglehold on a pebble *can* look perky. It had been glowing a bit less every night they were away, I was pretty sure. Like it had been missing out on sunshine or something.

I took it downstairs with me when I got up to make the morning tea and coffee, wondering if a proactive spirit when it came to the dryad would mean brownie points for me. I could use them before I spoke to Zero about the body.

At the scene it had seemed natural that they would all help find the murderer for Detective Tuatu. They'd pushed themselves into the police force here, after all; and they were planning on staying in my house for a while, by the looks of things. And there had been bits of Between around the scene, too, so it wasn't like they could claim Behind had nothing to do with it, either.

I frowned to myself worriedly. After Athelas' reaction, I hadn't been able to nerve myself to bring up the subject of helping Detective Tuatu, though; Zero was already back at his studying, and he only lifted his head when I started setting the table around him for breakfast.

Maybe I'd be able to do it this morning, I thought, throwing a covert look toward the three psychos in the living room as I passed them. We hadn't gone out last night after all—I had the feeling our dead body had put a damper on things.

As I made the morning tea and coffee, I looked up dryads on the search engine of my phone. Zero had given it to me a couple of weeks ago, and it was a smart phone, but it didn't have a lot of data on the plan he'd bought so I didn't like to do too much web browsing. Pity I hadn't remembered when I was at the library yesterday.

Pity my three psychos didn't see fit to buy themselves a computer and home internet.

I mean, it wasn't like I found anything but weird Wikipedia pages and World of Warcraft references anyway, but it would have been nice to have found them in the comfort of my own home, sitting down in front of a computer, instead of at the library, or squinting at a tiny smartphone screen while the steam from the kettle misted it over.

Rats. I was gunna have to ask Athelas, which meant he would probably want to ask a few questions of his own.

A shadow fell, dark and cool, over the kitchen island.

I jumped, narrowly avoiding a nasty steam burn, and saw Zero's huge bulk in the doorway.

"Scared ten months' growth outta me!" I said indignantly.

Those cool blue eyes looked at me for a moment longer before he said, "I don't think so."

"What's that s'posed to mean?" I complained, but Zero was looking at the dryad now.

"What's that doing out here?"

"Getting some sunshine," I said. "Think it's feeling a bit cold lately."

"Dryads don't feel the cold."

"Oh. How do you know?"

"The same way I know you won't grow any taller."

I looked at him suspiciously. "You joking with me?"

"Don't move the dryad around the house," Zero said, and took his coffee.

"Hang on," I said, following him as he went back down into the living room with the tray. "What am I supposed to do with it, then? You said to look after it by the end of the month, but does that mean I'm supposed to plant it out in the yard, or what?"

"Don't plant it in the yard."

"Okay, but *why?*"

"Zero doesn't appreciate his territory being impinged upon," said Athelas.

Zero threw him an unreadable look, and said, "Exactly."

I could have been wrong, but I was pretty sure that made Athelas look surprised; like he'd been teasing Zero in his own sharp, unkind way, and hadn't expected to find himself agreed with.

"Ah, I see," he responded. "You object to anything else being given the task of protecting those things you claim as your own?"

"The dryad is protection?" I looked down at the little tree doubtfully. I mean, I'd thought myself it was helping to keep off the worst of the nightmare, but I wouldn't have thought of it as protection, exactly. More like a good luck charm, or a nightlight.

"Goodness, are you still there, Pet?" asked Athelas, sipping his tea.

Was he really surprised, or had he been trying to tell me something in his sneaky-as-all-heck way again? Not that I was complaining; it was a question I'd wanted to ask him earlier, and I was getting the answer for free, in a manner of speaking.

Zero said, "It's protection of a sort. Protection, and wisdom."

"Yeah," I said doubtfully, like it made sense. Maybe I'd still have to ask Athelas about it, after all.

"I want it gone by the end of the month," Zero reminded me.

"Yeah, I remember," I said. And then, because I didn't have

anything to bargain with but had promised the detective, I plunged ahead with, "Oi."

"What is it, Pet?"

"We gunna do something about that body?"

"No," said Zero, without vacillating. "It's a human body. It's no concern of ours."

"Yeah, but—"

"We don't involve ourselves in human affairs. When fae involve themselves in human affairs, things become complicated."

"Not to mention *very* messy," Athelas mentioned, tranquilly pouring himself another cup of tea. "Some time ago there was a self-appointed protector of the human race—"

"Made a bit of a mess over here, did he?" I asked; though I wasn't sure whether Athelas meant the fae himself had caused deaths, or that there had been deaths because of him.

"No," said Zero. "Someone made a mess of him. Go and make breakfast, Pet."

"But the dead bloke—"

"There's no connection to us," Zero said coldly. "Why should we investigate?"

"Yeah, but the detective said that there's been more than one death, and that someone's covering things up. And you can't tell me there's an animal big enough to tear someone's hand off here in Tasmania, *and* there was a bit of Between open right through to Behind next to the body, so you can't say it's not something from Be—"

"We don't investigate human deaths," Zero said; and if his voice had been cold before, now it was absolutely icy. "Pet. Make breakfast."

I bolted for it. There are times when I feel like I can push things a bit, and then there are times when I know I'm about to get my nose bitten off.

This was one of the nose-biting times.

CHAPTER THREE

I MADE BREAKFAST LIKE THE GOOD LITTLE PET I WAS, BUT WHEN I set the table and went to call my three psychos in to breakfast, Zero was gone and Jin Yeong was scowling.

"Flamin' rude," I said under my breath, but not so low that the other two wouldn't hear me. "Tells me to make breakfast and then doesn't even come to eat it."

"Believe it or not, Pet, Jin Yeong and I are more than willing to do full justice to the meal you've made."

Jin Yeong rose and swept through to the kitchen, still scowling, and brushed past me with enough force to knock me sideways.

"Oi!" I swivelled to stare at his back, and asked Athelas, "What's biting him?"

"Jin Yeong was expecting to join Zero in scouting for a suitable place to recharge, but Zero left alone."

"I don't blame him!" I said, loudly enough for Jin Yeong to hear if he chose to hear. "Why would he want to wander around Hobart with Jin Yeong?"

Jin Yeong didn't reply, but there was a pretty deadly silence from the direction of the kitchen table that spoke for him instead.

"Anyway," I said to Athelas, "it's not like that's my fault, so why's he pushing me around?"

"Jin Yeong seems to feel," said Athelas, and he didn't trouble to keep his voice quiet, either; "that Zero was in a reasonable frame of mind before you spoke with him, and that by the time he left, he was not."

"Correlation isn't causation!" I yelled into the kitchen, and this time there was the metallic rattle of a knife and fork being put back down on the table with a bit too much force. "Didn't you go to school?"

"I see that you're not in the most reasonable frame of mind yourself, Pet," Athelas said. "But do you suppose we could sit down to breakfast before it becomes quite cold? Zero doesn't care about such things, but I confess to a certain preference for eating my breakfast warm."

"I'm not stopping you," I said, but I started walking again.

Jin Yeong was still glaring at me when I walked into the dining room, but his plate was half empty and the edge had been taken off the glare. He *must* have been hungry. I sat in my usual spot closest to the kitchen side of the room, glad to avoid the worst of his dark, angry eyes, and gazed over the table with some dissatisfaction.

Athelas said, buttering toast, "Between the two of you, I'm surprised the butter hasn't curdled."

I looked at him in surprise, and Jin Yeong had the gall to do the same.

"Me? What did I do?"

"*Naega wae?*"

Athelas sighed. "I see I've upset the delicate balance of the morning. Pet, perhaps you could explain exactly what it is you expect Zero—or any of us—to do about a dead body?"

I eyed him warily, a forkful of pancake halfway to my mouth. Was this a balance question, or just a question?

Athelas saw my hesitation, and his eyes lit with laughter. "Are you becoming cautious at last? That's somewhat disappointing!"

"Dunno," I said, answering his first question and leaving the second alone. "But I thought you'd ask a few more questions and stuff, at least."

"It's a human."

"Some of the ones from your cases are human, too."

Athelas inclined his head. "That is correct. However, the majority of the victims are fae; moreover, the case has fae connections. We're certain the murderer is fae, and although we haven't ever been able to solidify a motive, we're certain that involves Behind, as well."

"And humans aren't important enough to worry about," I said resentfully.

"That is correct," agreed Athelas. "More than one hundred thousand humans die each day. Should we avenge each one?"

"You don't have to avenge each one," I argued. "Just the ones that Behindkind hurt!"

"Why should we? Did we hurt them?"

"No, but you can stop it."

"Power doesn't obligate responsibility, Pet."

Jin Yeong, very precisely, put his knife and fork in the middle of his syrupy plate, and said just as precisely, "*Neb.*"

I turned my shoulder on him and said to Athelas, "But *you* said there was someone—"

"*Ah, jjincha!*" said Jin Yeong, and abruptly left the table.

Athelas smiled into his tea. "Ah, I was curious to know if you would come back to that!"

"You said something about that person before you fixed up the problem at the house over the road," I began, ignoring for a moment the fact that my three psychos *had* actually, very recently, taken on the responsibility of righting the wrongs caused by Behindkind. Was it too much to ask them to keep doing so? I didn't think so. "And you said—well, not said, but it seemed like Zero had something to do with him."

"Did I so? I wonder if I remember?"

Right. So this was one of the balance-keeping questions. I was never quite sure which ones were and which ones weren't, because things that seemed important to me quite often didn't seem important to Athelas. *Vice versa*, too, if it came to that.

"Got nothing to trade," I told him.

"Do you not?" said Athelas, in a lingering kind of way, and went back to his toast.

Since I didn't understand what he meant—or even if he *meant* me to understand it—I shrugged and cleared the table. When Athelas was alone at the table, he asked, "What is the hurry, Pet?"

"No hurry," I said. "Thought I'd go for a walk, that's all."

"Where are you going?"

"Zero said to get rid of the dryad," I said. "I'm figuring out how to get rid of it."

Athelas' grey eyes seemed to dance. "Are you sulking, Pet?"

"I'm just a human," I said, grinning. "I'm not important enough for you to worry about whether or not I'm sulking."

"I wonder if Zero wants you walking around town on your own?"

"You can come too, if you think I'm gunna go talking to someone."

"Oh, I think not. Keep to well-peopled streets."

"If I'm not important enough for you to worry about me sulking, how come you're telling me about me keeping to busy streets?" I protested.

"Zero doesn't like it when things under his protection are damaged," Athelas replied. "I believe I told you that yesterday. Run along, Pet. Be back in time to make an early dinner, won't you?"

I would have taken the dryad back upstairs, but I wanted to be out of the house before either he could change his mind or

Zero could come back, so I skipped out with it in the front pocket of my hoodie, my fingers laced around it so it didn't get squashed.

I went to the police station first. I could have gone to the library and done a bit more internet searching, but I didn't think it would help much. There was a lot of stuff these days that just wasn't on the normal internet. Maybe there was a version of Between for that, too. I'd have to keep my ears open a bit more around the house and sort of *ninja* questions in when they weren't expecting it.

I was across the road at Maccas when the sliding security door of the copshop opened and a plain-clothed bloke walked out, his close-cut afro almost shiny in the afternoon sunshine.

Hang on. That was Detective Tuatu. He was leaving?

Under my breath, I said, "Pft. Detectives working half days? That's a bit cheeky."

He didn't get into a car, either, so I followed him. It wasn't that I thought he was suspicious or anything; you could call it nosiness, maybe. Instinct sounds better, though.

What was he doing leaving half way through the day when he'd just been attending a murder scene yesterday, anyway? Shouldn't he be busy doing murder investigation stuff and working late days?

I stayed on my side of the road and trailed along with my hands still carefully cupped around the dryad in my pocket, wondering if I was imagining the faint tendrils of Between I thought I could see lingering in the detective's wake.

"What's that about?" I muttered to myself. I already knew Tuatu was completely unfamiliar with Between, so it couldn't be him making the trails—if they were even real. They faded as I followed him, too; but I was pretty sure that the bloke in the bright green pants I'd caught sight of crossing the Maccas parking lot behind me was still there behind me.

That was more worrying than tattered bits of Between showing up around the place.

"What a pain in the neck," I grumbled, bringing out my phone from my back pocket and pretending to text with it.

Yep. The bits of Between were gone, but the bloke in the green pants wasn't. I could see him reflected in my screen. Was he following me, or Detective Tuatu?

I pretended to text for a bit longer. For a minute or two I even thought about texting for real; Zero might come to see what was going on, if I did that. On the other hand, he might just leave me to old green daks and tell me to come home over the phone in that commanding voice of his.

I still dunno whether that voice is a fae thing, or just a Zero thing. Whichever one it is, I'm not about to disobey him when he uses it. Maybe it's the pet in me.

No good texting Zero, then. I hadn't started out to follow Detective Tuatu, but now I was curious to know who was following who—and it wasn't like the bloke was a murderer, after all. Not in trousers as bright as that, anyway.

I started moving again and slid my phone into my pocket. There was a flutter of green across from me as green daks continued on his way, raising another question. Exactly how did someone with pants as bright as his, stay unnoticed? And who, I wondered, following the detective around a patch of partitioned roadwork, was so casual about following someone that they didn't bother changing into something less noticeable?

Did he want to be noticed? Or, I thought, my hand instinctively going for my phone again, was the bloke Behindkind? That would explain why Detective Tuatu didn't seem to have seen him.

I didn't call Zero, but only because while I was busy keeping an eye out for old green daks, I lost the detective. Green daks must have lost him at the same time, because after a bit of covert looking around, he mizzled off back toward the city centre, leaving me annoyed at having my trailing hijacked.

What was I supposed to do now? Just go home?

"What d'you reckon?" I asked the dryad, wandering down into a park for the heck of it, and kicking leaves as I walked. "Wanna go home? No? Me either."

I walked the length of the park along the old wall that ran down the middle, trying to decide whether to go to the library before I went home, and heard the bingle of someone's phone just beyond the gateway that led out.

A voice said, "Tuatu. Sir? I'll be back in the office in about an hour."

I felt a grin spread over my face. Where was he? It sounded like he was just on the other side of the wall. I went back to the gateway I'd just passed and poked my head into the park.

Yep. There he was; up ahead. He crossed the street as I watched, his voice carrying faintly to me, and went up a smaller side street.

"Beauty!" I said, dodging across the road after him. I was probably being a bit more noticeable now, but it wasn't like the detective had seen me. The streets were narrower and twistier here, too; high up in North Hobart, that's what happens—the streets get narrower and twistier, and the houses get higher and skinnier.

I must have scarpered down one too many of the streets without paying attention, following the sound of Detective Tuatu's voice, because by the time I could see him properly again, I was well and truly lost.

At least I could see him, now, though. He was on the other side of a residential wall that came to my knees and had an over-grown hedge for the remaining privacy, and as I stopped behind the last bit of hedge, I saw him open the gate.

Hang on. Where the heck were we?

I loitered behind the bushes and watched him follow the path around the other side of the house.

"Dodgy," I said to myself, shaking my head.

Maybe the dryad agreed; I was pretty sure I felt a tendril or a root wrap around my pinky finger. I left the hedge behind and flicked my legs over the brick wall, one after the other, and covered the front lawn at a trot. There was no sign of the detective when I peeked around the corner of the house, but when I drew back, wondering whether to follow him or wait outside the fence, someone reached around to grab the front of my hoodie and shoved me against the brickwork.

"Got you!" said Detective Tuatu, his voice thick with satisfaction.

Then he saw it was me.

He was still gaping when I kicked him in the shin. He let go pretty quick, clutching at the shin I'd kicked, and said, "Ow ow *ow*!"

"Serves you right for grabbing me!" I said indignantly.

"You were following me!"

"Yeah, but not on purpose."

Detective Tuatu glared at me, still clutching his shin. "How do you follow someone accidentally?!"

"What are you having a half day for, anyway?"

"I'm not having a half day, I'm going home for lunch. This is my *house*."

"Oh." I looked across at the brick stairway and made off for it. "What are we having?"

The detective scrambled belatedly after me. "We?"

"Haven't had lunch yet," I explained, trotting up the stairs before he could think to stop me. "And we gotta talk about the case."

"We?"

"You already said that. You leave your door unlocked all the time?"

"Of course I don't leave my door unlocked!'

I let go of the door handle and the door swung inward, sweeping lightly above the thin carpet. "Yeah?"

With one hand, Detective Tuatu dragged me back by the hood; his gun was in the other, pointed into the empty, shadowy recess of the hall.

"Bit jumpy, aren't you?" I said, but I said it quietly. I was pretty sure Aussie cops weren't supposed to go around pointing their guns at empty houses, even if the doors *were* unlocked. And apart from when he was facing my three psychos, I didn't think the detective was someone who was normally twitchy.

"Looks like I've already had a visit from Upper Management," he said, stepping up lightly into the house. "I want to make sure no one's left me a reminder about not poking my nose in where it's not meant to be. Stay behind me."

"Who's Upper Management?" I asked. Zero was the only one who could tell me to stay behind him and expect to be obeyed, but for the time being I stayed behind Detective Tuatu anyway. No point being dead before I needed to be.

"The boss' boss' boss," said Tuatu.

He wasn't trying to keep quiet, which made me think he preferred to scare off anyone in the house rather than engage them. Why?

"Why did you come to see me?" he asked. "Zero said you're not taking on the case—he said it's not the sort of case they like to look at."

"I reckon they haven't been paying enough attention, then," I said, following close behind him as he flicked the handle on one of the doors in the hall and kicked it open. "'Cos I'm pretty sure it's exactly the kind of case they'd be interested in."

Detective Tuatu put his head through the door and twitched it left and right, then went on to the next door.

"Good thing your place is so small," I said as I followed him further up the hall. There were only two small bedrooms, a tiny sitting room instead of a lounge, an even smaller bathroom, and a kitchen-dining sort of place that was poky and old and cute.

"It's called *cosy*," he said. He holstered his gun again, at last satisfied, and turned back to me. "Have your lot been here poking around?"

"What, just because you were poking around at their—at my place? Why would they? They said they weren't taking the case, remember?"

"Hm."

I looked around the tiny kitchen, taking in the rust-spotted kitchen sink and the warped window glass that faced out on a tangled old garden. "S'pose you call this *ye olde world* instead of run down, too."

The detective struggled with a grin and almost managed to win. He said, "If you want me to feed you, that's not the way to go about it."

He ducked down into one of his cupboards anyway, scrabbling for something that must not get much use, and I took the time that his back was turned to try and extricate my pinky from the clutches of the dryad.

When I pulled my hand partway out of my pocket there was a gentle glow of light, and the slight twist of pressure around my finger loosened.

That was interesting. Why was the dryad glowing again? Protection and wisdom, Zero had said, and maybe it would be protection and wisdom if it was ever planted and grew, but right now I was pretty sure it was still a nightlight.

"You trying to protect me?" I asked it softly.

"Who are you talking to?" asked Detective Tuatu, from the recesses of the cupboard.

"Myself," I said. As far as it went, it was true. It wasn't like the dryad could talk back—at least, not that I knew.

"*There*'s a surprise," the detective muttered, as he stood up again. When he turned around there was flour on one of his cuffs, and a ratty old pack of instant coffee in one of his hands. He checked the electric jug and then snapped it shut again and switched it on. "Don't you have any friends?"

"I've got you," I said, with an insincere smile.

"And that reminds me—why am I making you coffee?"

"'Cos I'm the one who's trying to make sure those three work with you," I said,

"He said they weren't interested."

"Yeah, I know," I said.

I didn't really know why I was pushing it with Zero—not *exactly*, I mean. It could have been sheer stubbornness, or the hope that he would actually help a human again, despite what he was always saying—or maybe it was just a dogged determination to make the three of them do something they said they weren't going to do.

Mostly I think it was the certainty that Zero was more human than he pretended, and that someone or something needed to remind him of that. More, it didn't feel like something I could let go—not when the three of them could do so much to help. Athelas might say that there was no responsibility that came with their power, but I was pretty sure he was wrong. And when it came to Zero and Zero's humanity, I was even more sure he was wrong.

I was also certain that this particular case went straight back to Behind, and I didn't think Behindkind should be allowed to make trouble in the human world without someone to grab them by the collar.

"I've only got baked beans and toast," said the detective, passing me a cup of coffee. "Spaghetti, too, maybe, but it's all tinned."

"Suits me!" I said, gleefully accepting the coffee. It was nice to wrap my hands around a coffee I hadn't had to make. I took a sip, slurping loudly, and said, "Not bad, for a tea-drinker."

I looked up just in time to see Detective Tuatu roll his eyes. Well, he made that quick flick of the eyes toward the ceiling, anyway.

"Thanks," he said. "Spaghetti or beans?"

"Spaghetti," I said. "Want me to butter the toast?"

"No. Just stay there where I can see you."

"You're not a very trusting person, are you?"

"Not where you're concerned," said the detective. He put two slices of bread that might or might not have been mouldy quickly into the toaster, and said, "I suppose you'll one day explain to me exactly what happened that day at the station?"

"Probably not," I said, deciding that brutal honesty was the best course. "You prob'ly don't want to know. Want some advice, though?"

"Oh, why not?"

"Keep wearing that necklace of yours," I advised. He'd been wearing it since I knew him—a gift from his grandma, who told him to wear it all the time—and even if correlation wasn't causation, my three psychos didn't seem to be able to put him under their Behindkind influence. I was betting it was that necklace. "'Specially if you're gunna be poking around in cases like this."

Detective Tuatu stopped, a piece of toast pinched between his fingers. "What do you know about my necklace?"

"Nothing," I told him, regretting the urge that had made me mention it. "Oi. You said there had been more of these cases. What cases?"

"You're not very good at the *sharing* part of information sharing, are you?" muttered the detective, buttering toast that was just a bit too black. He slid a half-empty tin of spaghetti across the bench at me, cold from the fridge and uncovered.

"Trying to burn out the mould?" I asked, but I took the plate from him anyway and peered doubtfully at the tin of spaghetti. The bits of spaghetti closer to the top were dry and stuck to the sides of the tin, but the rest looked all right; just a bit watery. I stirred it with the butter knife and tipped it out onto my toast.

I'd eaten worse.

"Why do you want those three to help, anyway?" asked Detective Tuatu, pinching the knife back from me and stirring his baked bean tin.

"'Cos stuff like this should be stopped," I said briefly. "And 'cos they can stop it, if they'll do it."

"*Will* they do it?"

"Yeah, that's what I'm working on," I explained. "So what's the go?"

"It's like I said on the day: there have been four other cases like this, all of them were found either close by this particular supermarket location, or were staff members there, all of them involved at least one body part being gnawed off, and all of them were moved from an initial scene to be dumped where we found them. Even the bloodwork is similar—there's an abnormality there in each of the profiles that we can't identify. It's similar to rabies but it isn't rabies. The sort of thing that would kill someone pretty quickly without having to worry about them being ripped apart first."

"Wait, they were all gunna die anyway?" I scowled. Jin Yeong and his weird little eye trick had definitely found out something about the blood that he hadn't shared. He hadn't been telling me —or Zero—everything. There *was* a Behindkind link, I knew it.

"The lab thinks so."

"And it's the same thing they've all got?"

"As far as we could tell. Some were worse than the others. I saw the reports before Upper Management shut down the investigations. It was something the lab had never seen before, but they said it would have killed each of the victims within a month."

"How come that supermarket?"

The detective shrugged. Around a mouthful of beans and toast, he said, "Don't know. Could be someone who works there killing people. Could be someone trying to implicate someone who works there."

"Who were the people who died? You said they were mostly employees who died."

"All but one. A tramp died nearby."

"I've heard of dangerous workplaces, but that's just mad," I said. "Oi. Your Upper Management—reckon they were trying to keep you away from the murders, or the supermarket?"

"I don't know," he said. "But it doesn't much matter. Whether someone's targeting the shop, or whether there's something going on *at* the shop, I'll probably only be able to investigate for another day or two at most. They're already putting pressure on me to close it as an animal killing, and if I stall much longer, they'll pass it off to someone else and give me punishment duties."

"Cops aren't meant to be dodgy," I said, frowning. "You should look into that."

"I'll do that when I'm feeling particularly tired of living," said the detective, grinning a bit. He took another mouthful of beans and toast before he said, "I would have thought you knew a bit too much to still think the police force is the pinnacle of human goodness."

"I didn't say I thought they weren't dodgy," I snapped. "I said they *shouldn't* be dodgy. All right. Leave it with me."

That made his mouth quirk up again, like I'd said something funny. "Thanks," he said. "You going now?"

"Yeah; they'll wonder where I am if I stay out too much longer."

"You know that's not healthy, right? Living as someone's pet?"

"Dunno," I said. He'd seen Between, but I'd seen Behind, and I was pretty sure I wasn't going to stop seeing it. More importantly, Behindkind probably weren't going to stop seeing *me*, even if I stopped seeing them. "I reckon it's pretty good for my health, staying alive. But that's just me. Catch ya."

Zero was back when I got home. I knew it before I got into the house, just like I'd known when I woke up that they were home again. It was interesting and a bit weird, and I stopped on the top step to decide exactly how I knew it.

I was still trying to figure out if it was something to do with the house or with me, when the door opened.

"Hi," I said to Zero, stuffing my other hand back into my pocket to disguise the bump made by the dryad.

He stared down at me for a minute as if he was trying to decide what to say, and at last asked, "Why are you standing on the step?"

"Dunno," I said. "But Athelas thinks I might be sulking, if that helps."

"Why?"

"Dunno," I said again. "Ask Athelas; it's his story."

"Are you—are you coming in?"

"Might as well, since I'm here," I said cheerfully. "You lot want coffee and biscuits?"

Zero said, "Yes," in a baffled kind of way and moved aside to let me in. "And an early dinner. We'll be going out afterward."

"Me too?"

There was silence behind me as Zero closed the door and thought about it. When I got to the kitchen, he padded around to the other side of the kitchen island and said, "You'll come too. Next time tell me before you go out."

Rats. Didn't look like I was going to get the chance to take the dryad back up to my bedroom before making tea and coffee. "You weren't here," I told him, filling the kettle.

"That's why I gave you the phone," said Zero; and his eyes were already on me when I turned back around.

"Oh yeah. Forgot about that." I could have said that Athelas had told me it was okay to go out, but I wasn't sure how tattling affected the balance, and I didn't think I was ready to find out just yet. "Are we doing that recharge thing tonight? Even Jin Yeong?"

"It's not recharging. And Jin Yeong doesn't need to do it."

"Athelas said—"

"Athelas said it in a way that you would understand."

That made me stop with the teaspoon halfway to the pot. "Yeah? I don't understand that, either."

"It means that Athelas, for whatever reason of his own, wanted you to understand what we were saying."

I blinked at him a bit, and dumped the tea into the pot. "Yeah, no; I understand that. But I don't know *why* he wants me to understand."

"Neither do I," said Zero. His face was still as emotionless as always, but there was a thoughtful note to his voice that made me think he was telling the truth, and that he was confused about it, too. "Try not to understand too much of what Athelas says."

"Why?"

"Because," said Zero, and the ice was back in his eyes, "it's very dangerous for you to learn too much. Don't forget that fae can remove memories, Pet."

I was just uneasy enough to nearly blurt out a bad joke about not forgetting stuff when I'd had my memories removed, but I managed to stop myself in time. Instead, I nodded and showed him the *zip the lip* mime.

That must have satisfied him, because he went away into the living room where Jin Yeong was lounging on my favourite lounge, taking up too much of it as usual. There was no sign of Athelas, but by the time I brought in the tray, a brief waft of air cooled my neck in passing as he slipped past me to sit in *his* favourite chair.

I passed Zero his coffee, frowning. Had Athelas been out, too? Where had he been?

I don't know if Zero wondered the same thing—maybe he already knew—but all he said to Athelas was, "I've found a spot. We'll go tonight."

"Very well," said Athelas, taking his tea. "Pet, it seems churlish to mention, but must you wear your hood up in the house?"

I shrugged the hood down, and it brushed the stray pieces of hair away from my forehead with it. "It was a bit nippy on the way home."

I plopped down on the couch beside Jin Yeong, causing him to hastily back away at the threat of spilt coffee on his perfectly pressed trousers, and thrust the mug at him.

"Here."

Jin Yeong made a faint expression of disgust and said something at Zero that was definitely a complaint.

Uh oh. Had he seen the dryad? I hastily tweaked the waistline of the hoodie to even out the bump that definitely wasn't my stomach, but Zero was already towering over me.

He grabbed me by the ears, lifting me right out of my seat before I could do more than squeak, "Ow, ow, *ow!*" and said, with eyes that glinted ice, "Pet. What is *this?*"

CHAPTER FOUR

I GULPED, ONE HAND INSTINCTIVELY SLIDING INTO MY FRONT hoodie pocket as if I could actually protect the dryad against Zero if he saw it and chose to take it.

I croaked, "What? What'd I do?"

Zero tilted my head. "There's a cut on your forehead."

"Yeah," I said, confused. "That's from the other morning, when I had the nightmare. Think I hit myself on the corner of the bedhead when I was coming after you."

"That was just a scratch."

An agreement came from Jin Yeong's side of the lounge. Of course he'd know—it had barely drawn blood, and had sealed quickly, but he would have known about it anyway.

"What's the go?" I demanded, trying to pull away. Zero didn't let go of me, so that just meant I scrabbled for a bit before giving up. "What about it?"

Zero turned my head this way and that, looking closely at the cut. "It's black."

"It's what?"

"Black. Did you put anything on it?"

"Nah, it's just a scratch. There wasn't any point. Maybe I got some dirt on it."

"I've a feeling it's not dirt," Athelas said, from behind his teacup. "Perhaps you should allow the pet to look in the mirror, Zero. I, too, suspect that is not the usual healing process of humans, but the pet herself will know."

Zero dropped me lightly back to the carpet, and I trotted over to the mirror.

I saw it before I was right in front of the mirror; a bit of a dark smudge on my forehead where I'd hit it on the bedpost. Nothing bad, just a bruise around the cut.

Only then I got closer and I could see that the bruise wasn't exactly a bruise. It was more of a mole—if a mole was flat, and surrounding a cut, and had...was that *hair* in it?

"That's flamin' disgusting!" I complained, looking closer. "Where did that come from?"

In the mirror, I saw Athelas put down his teacup. "Did you touch the blood at the murder scene, Pet?"

"What?" I swivelled away from the mirror. "No! Why would I touch the blood?"

"I've not noticed that you're particularly discriminating about the things you touch when you're Between," he said. "I'm not sure why you expect me to think of this matter any differently."

"Yeah, well, I didn't."

"You must have," Zero said. "Yesterday there was nothing there but a small cut; today it's black and hairy."

"Jin Yeong touched the blood," I told him. I felt a bit sniffy about his certainty. "Not me. Oh!"

"*Ah*," said Jin Yeong, at the same time.

Our eyes met; his liquid and faintly annoyed, mine accusatory.

"*You* did it!" I exploded.

Jin Yeong pursed his lips, and Zero looked between the two of us with a frown between his straight brows.

"What did Jin Yeong do?"

"Touched me with his manky, bloody finger!"

"JinYeong, why did you let the pet bring home an infectious disease?"

"It's a *what*?"

"A kind of virus," Athelas said, thoughtfully picking up his teacup again. "Lycanthropy, I suspect, judging by the hair."

"I'm gunna turn into a *werewolf*?"

"Certainly not," he said. "You're far more likely to die before that happens—or be killed by a rival pack."

"Good to know," I said, giving him the thumbs up. I felt sick to my stomach. "How long before I die?"

"You're not going to die," Zero said.

"Athelas said—"

Athelas said, "Really, Zero, the odds of survival even in humans is remarkably low; and unless we formulate an antivirus..."

I glared at JinYeong. "You did this on purpose!"

Ignoring Athelas, Zero asked JinYeong, "Did you know it was virus-carrying?"

"*Kugae aniyaeyo*," said JinYeong, and sighed. "*Hyeong, kunyang—*"

I listened to his incomprehensible explanation in annoyance, but Zero only nodded once or twice. When JinYeong had finished, he said, "It's been known to happen before. Your saliva probably reactivated it."

Athelas set down his teacup once again, this time empty, and there was a glint to his eyes that hadn't been there before. "Very well, Zero; what are we going to do about the pet now that she's infected? JinYeong may not have deliberately infected her, but he's certainly culpable if that's the way we're weighing our actions here."

"Yes," agreed Zero. "Fully culpable."

JinYeong's voice sounded sulky as he said something that contained the words *just* and *die*. It didn't take much imagination to guess that he'd asked if they couldn't just let me die instead. Or maybe he was asking if he couldn't just kill me before I turned or whatever, instead.

"No," Zero said. "You infected the pet. You fix it."

Jin Yeong suggested something else that ended with the word *die*.

"While that would undoubtedly fix the problem," said Athelas, "it would leave us without a pet—without, Jin Yeong, someone to cook your meals. And Zero seems to be of the opinion that as the pet is in our house—"

"It's got nothing to do with the house," said Zero briefly. "We have a contracted agreement and the agreement can't be fulfilled if the pet dies."

Athelas smiled dreamily. "Yes. A useful way out of many a bargain."

"Oi!"

"I was not likening Zero's morals to mine, Pet."

"Thanks a lot."

"*Ah, taesso, taesso!*" Jin Yeong said impatiently. "*Petteu, pab haera!*"

"Dunno what you're talking about," I said. Technically, it was true. I mean, I knew the *haera* meant he was telling me to do something, and I was pretty sure *pab* was rice, so he was probably telling me to cook their dinner, but beggar me if I was going to understand him while he was still talking about killing me in one breath and ordering me to cook with the next.

Besides, I was infected with lycanthropy or something, and that was his fault.

Athelas wasn't helping much, either. I sent him a sour look but he only smiled at me faintly and poured himself another cup of tea.

With any luck, he'd burn his tongue.

"*Petteu,*" said Jin Yeong, through his teeth, "*Pab haera!*"

"The pet can't cook tonight," Zero said abruptly. "Not until we know if it's still in the infectious stage. It shouldn't have been able to be infected from a dead body at all, so we'll have to be careful until tomorrow."

I plopped back down on my side of the couch and grinned at JinYeong. "Your night to pick what we're eating, isn't it? What a shame!"

"*Ah, hyeong!*" protested JinYeong again, sitting forward in his consternation. He launched into one of his flowing, long-winded complaints that had absolutely no effect on the emotionless Zero. It was surprising how much better that made me feel. It was probably mean-spirited of me, but there you are. I'm a mean-spirited pet.

JinYeong stopped arguing eventually, but he didn't stop whinging beneath his breath. As soon as he'd finished drinking his coffee, he flipped on his coat and stalked toward the front door.

"*Kalbi*," he said.

"Is that another food thing?" I asked Athelas. It sounded familiar.

"Yes and no," Athelas told me, slipping his own blazer over his shirt. "Put up your hood again, Pet. We're going out. *Kalbi* is a type of food; it's also a restaurant that just opened in North Hobart."

"You better be buying," I told JinYeong.

He didn't answer; just disappeared through the door without really opening it. There was a weakness of Between fluttering around the door, through which I could see cool stonework and green shadows, so I followed him through just to see if I could do it.

Halfway through, someone's hand seized around the nape of my neck and hauled me back.

"Bad pet," said Zero, and dropped me beside him in the hall again. Strike a light! When had he moved?

Athelas, with what I was certain was a smile, opened the door physically and slipped through, leaving it open for us.

"But JinYeong—"

"JinYeong knows how to walk Between," Zero said, herding me ahead of him. "You shouldn't be trying that without one of us there."

"Thought I was getting trained in stuff like that," I muttered. If JinYeong was going to be leaving openings Between when he walked through, what was to stop me accidentally walking into them?

"Soon," said Zero.

Kalbi turned out to be a Korean restaurant toward the North Hobart end of Elizabeth Street; it was trendy and would have felt spacious despite the small size of the shop if it wasn't already busy at just past five.

I looked around at the pale wooden tables and the pale wooden floor, then at the swathe of Korean newspapers that someone had pasted all over the inner wall as a design statement, and said, "Yeah, all right; but is the food any good?"

None of my three psychos answered me; they sat down at the last empty table pretty quickly, though, so I suppose that was telling. They'd probably been eating out here without me before.

Flamin' rude, that.

One of the three waitstaff gave us a menu each; which, to my relief, had more English letters than Korean characters. I poked JinYeong in the ribs and asked, "What's good?"

He jumped, and then glared at me. "*Hajima.*"

"What? I just wanna know what to eat."

"Don't poke the vampire, Pet," Athelas said.

"He started it," I remarked. "*And* I'm gunna turn into a werewolf, so who's the real victim here?"

"Be quiet," said Zero, and I became belatedly aware that there was already someone beside our table, waiting to take our order.

"So...what?" I asked, when he went away again. This time I was a bit quieter. "I'm really gunna turn into a wolf?"

"A wolf-human hybrid," said Athelas. Nice of him to be so informative when it was something unpleasant. It was much harder to get information I really wanted out of him. "*If* we can't formulate an antivirus, and *if* you don't perish in the attempt. Lycanthropy very rarely produces a full wolf change the first time, even at full moon."

I grinned suddenly, despite the sick feeling in my stomach. It hadn't occurred to me before that the dead bloke could be an actual werewolf. To myself, I said, "Werewolf, huh? Detective Tuatu's gunna *love* that!"

"He wasn't a wolf shifter," Athelas said. "Just carrying the virus —or so Jin Yeong says. But it certainly makes clear who—or at the very least *what*—the killer is."

Jin Yeong spoke, and Athelas nodded.

"Jin Yeong says it was an infant version of the virus, not yet fully complete—which means that whoever infected him was almost certainly the one who killed him. Wolf shifters very rarely leave their victim alive when once they have their jaws about them and the virus doesn't take more than a week or two to run its course."

I shivered, which made Jin Yeong look across at me with one eyebrow up. A week or two was *not* a lot of time. "And we need the same version of the virus to cure me?" I asked.

"Correct," said Athelas, crossing one leg over the other and leaning elegantly into the newspapered wall.

"Is that what Jin Yeong was doing when his eyes went weird? Checking out the blood like a walking lab?"

Jin Yeong shot me another look, this one slightly amused as well as arrogant. "*Nae.*"

"So what, we need to find this bloke—"

"Animal," Zero said.

"Yeah, and get some blood from him to make a vaccine—"

Athelas said, "Not vaccine. Antivirus."

"Right, to make an antivirus. Hang on, why can't we just take blood from the dead bloke?"

"Because the virus mutates as soon as it enters the bloodstream. We need the original source to counteract your version."

"So we're gunna find the werewolf that killed the dead bloke?"

"Yes," said Zero.

"Thanks!" I told him, beaming. I'd been pretty sure Zero wouldn't let me turn into a wolf or die, but sometimes it was hard to be completely certain.

"Don't thank me," he said. "Jin Yeong made the mistake; he has to fix it. It's part of the laws between your world and ours. There has to be a balance—we can't just leave things."

"Yeah," I said. I'd already begun to learn that—especially when it came to Athelas. He was very traditional in that way. "So we might as well work with Detective Tuatu, right?"

Athelas choked on his water. He gently patted his blazer with his napkin and said, "Human problems aren't our affair, Pet."

"Yeah, but—"

"We're only interested in our own cases," Zero said. "Don't offer our services to the police again."

"All right," I said peaceably, because Zero had already agreed to help, and I still felt that was a small step forward. "Only since we're both looking for the same person, wouldn't it be a good idea to work together? Sort of official? Can't hurt."

Zero's eyes dwelled on me for one deliberate moment. "Is there any reason we would need the help of the police?"

"Detective Tuatu said there had been other cases," I told him. "Reckon they're all related; they might help us find the bloke. His lot don't want it investigated, so we'd prob'ly have a hard time getting the files any other way."

"Not necessarily," murmured Athelas. "However, it will save the bother of using magic every time we want something from the station. And I believe the previous files could prove useful."

Zero nodded shortly. "Call the detective after dinner. Tell him we're taking on the investigation."

T HE DETECTIVE SOUNDED SUSPICIOUS WHEN I TOLD HIM, which was pretty rude considering how much I'd just helped him.

"What did you do?" he asked, and I wasn't sure if the suspicion in his tone was for me or my three psychos.

Since I was still pretty annoyed at being lumped with an Otherworldly disease, my voice might have been a bit snappy when I said, "You want me to tell 'em you don't want their help?"

"No," he said. "Just—never mind. Where can we meet to discuss it? Upper Management are already watching me, so I can't keep anything at the office."

I looked around at my three psychos. We were at Snug Falls— or at least, that's what Zero told me; we'd gone through Between to get here and I'd never been to Snug Falls before—and even Jin Yeong, who apparently didn't have to recharge, was reclining beneath a tree like a highborn nobleman waiting for someone to feed him grapes.

Athelas had gone even more quiet and pale than usual, his eyes closed as he sat by the water with a couple of fingers trailing in the moving stream, and Zero looked as though he'd turned to stone, all but invisible against the cool white rock he leaned against.

"When do you lot want to meet Detective Tuatu?" I asked, looking around at them doubtfully. I wasn't even sure they were properly alive, let alone awake enough to answer questions.

There was silence and stillness; then, at last, one of Jin Yeong's slender hands stirred. It rose, slowly, lazily, until one finger touched his lips.

"Yeah, all right," I said to him, "but the detective needs to know."

Zero and Athelas didn't even stir—maybe they *had* turned to stone—but Jin Yeong's eyes cracked open.

He sighed and said, "*Oneul bam. Uri jibae.*"

"Okay," I said to Detective Tuatu. "I *think* it's tonight at our place, but if that's wrong it's the vampire's fault. He won't speak English."

"What?" said the detective.

Jin Yeong showed me the smallest edge of tooth in warning and closed his eyes again.

"See you later on," I said to the detective, and hung up.

For all that Zero and Athelas didn't look like being aware, or even alive, when they started moving again an hour later, the first thing Zero said was, "Let's not keep the detective waiting."

"Perhaps we should rather say the pet," Athelas said, his grey eyes luminous and somehow reflective. "After all, we mustn't forget—"

"I haven't forgotten," said Zero, his voice as hard as stone.

In the face of that voice, I was surprised to hear Athelas continue, "Her symptoms will begin to show in a few days."

"I haven't forgotten," said Zero; and if his voice had been stone before, now it was ice.

"Yes, my lord," murmured Athelas, and his smile was luminous, too. "Come along, Pet," he said; and pinching the shoulder of my hoodie, he drew me through Between.

As we stepped lightly through green shadows that weren't quite forest but weren't quite structured, either, I asked Athelas, "What happens in a few days?"

"Just the beginning of the symptoms, not necessarily their end," he said. "Nothing to bother us unduly."

"Nothing to bother *you*!" I retorted. I was pretty bothered by it.

"Indeed," Athelas said. He was smiling again, and for all that it was a smile that could have lit the darkness around me, it left me very cold. "Why should fae worry themselves about the well-being of one pet? That is what I ask myself."

"Yeah? And do you answer yourself?"

"Not at all," sighed Athelas. "Hence my difficulty."

"What difficulty?" I demanded. "You aren't the ones turning into werewolves!"

"Indeed," he said again. "It's most perplexing."

I resisted the urge to reach out and touch the ancient stone walls through which we passed, with their moss-deepened carvings, and got the impression that, like the carvings, Athelas' words were a lot deeper than they seemed.

"I don't know what you're talking about anymore," I said.

"Do you not?" Athelas glanced down at me with the same smile, and now there was a touch of real amusement to it. He stopped me walking by pulling back slightly on the pinch of fabric he held. "I mean there's no reason for a fae—for *any* fae, Pet—to be concerned whether their pet lives or dies."

"Are you warning me about Zero again?"

Athelas blinked a little, and the amusement in his face grew. "In a manner of speaking, I suppose."

"And you're warning me about yourself as well?"

"In a manner of speaking," he said again.

I blew out my cheeks, wondering if Athelas' information would ever, like the books in Zero's bookcase, grow easier to understand without me having to work so hard at it.

"What are the symptoms?" I asked him. If I couldn't make any sense of the information he was giving me, I'd try to get some different information to work with.

"I wouldn't like to ruin the surprise," Athelas said, and pulled me out of Between and into the house with a flick of the wrist.

Zero and JinYeong were only a step behind us, JinYeong strolling past us and into the living room, and Zero reaching past me to open the front door in the face of Detective Tuatu, who had just raised his fist to knock.

The detective jumped, and I wondered fleetingly if he'd been thinking about using his picks on the door again.

I grinned at him and he went slightly pink, so he probably had been thinking about it.

"You're just in time," I said. "Coming in?"

He came in, but he still looked uneasy. "In time for what?" he muttered.

I was pretty sure he was talking to himself, so I didn't answer. I just grinned at him again, and that was enough to make him look uneasy all the way to the living room, where he sat down as far away from Jin Yeong as possible.

Zero didn't sit down, which was as little surprising as the detective moving away from Jin Yeong, but Jin Yeong didn't sit down either. I couldn't tell if they were trying to intimidate Detective Tuatu, or if it was normal for them when they met with other humans.

"All right," said the detective. He sounded pretty cool, but I could see his eyes shifting between Zero and Jin Yeong, and I knew they could, too. "First, I want an explanation."

Jin Yeong, stalking back and forth with his mouth mockingly pursed, asked, "*Wae?*"

"What explanation?" asked Zero, and now he did sit down, propping one foot up on the coffee table.

I thought at first that he was trying to make Tuatu feel better, since Jin Yeong wasn't helping, but that was silly. Athelas had just reminded me that fae like Zero didn't care about the comfort of humans, regardless of what their pets were trying to make them do. Maybe he was feeling relaxed since recharging at the falls.

"You all appeared and disappeared in my interview room without so much as a warning," Detective Tuatu said. "And that's just the tip of the iceberg. I want to know who—*what* you are, and why you're interested in my cases."

"If I remember rightly," said Athelas, "you were the one who called *us*."

"I'm told you were investigating the previous case before I was."

"We don't give explanations," Zero said. "If you want our help, we'll give it; but don't expect anything else."

The detective's lips tightened, and he pointed at me. "What about her?"

"I'm right here, you know," I complained. "Didn't your mum tell you it's rude to point?"

"She said she's your pet."

"It's true," Zero said coolly. "What of it?"

"You can't keep girls as pets."

"They can," I argued.

"It's creepy as all heck!"

"Yeah, but that doesn't mean they can't do it."

Detective Tuatu opened and closed his mouth before finally saying, "Why are *you* arguing with me?!"

"I agreed to be their pet," I told him. "Don't have a go at them!"

"They call that *Stockholm's Syndrome*," said Detective Tuatu.

I shrugged. "You can call it what you want. There's nothing you can do about it."

Maybe that was the wrong thing to say.

His eyebrows went up. "I'm almost one hundred percent sure that you're still underage," he told me. "So—"

"Actually," I said coldly, "I was born in 2000."

"It's only February."

"Yeah? Know what month I was born in?"

Another silence.

After it, the detective said reluctantly, "No."

"Yeah, well for all you know, I was born in January or February."

"Were you?"

"That's enough," said Zero, and the ice in his voice froze me as well as Tuatu. "You're not here to question the pet. Coffee, Pet."

"Right," I said. I stuck out my tongue at the detective on my way through to the kitchen, which made Jin Yeong look startled. I s'pose he's the one I usually stick my tongue out at, so it must have been a nice surprise for once. I mean, he looked offended, but he looks offended at pretty much everything I do, so that was nothing new.

I made tea for the detective, too; he was almost a part of the family now—well, if your idea of family was two twisty-minded fae and a sulky vampire. I couldn't remember if he had sugar or not, but they were talking about the case and I didn't want to interrupt them to ask about it in case they remembered I was there, listening.

If he needed sugar, he could get it for himself.

I made up the tray at the kitchen island while the jug boiled, and watched the detective pass out files between my three psychos.

"It's not much," I heard him say. "But there's a bit in there that isn't official, too. Think it's enough to get you started?"

Zero thumbed through the paperwork, his eyes thoughtful, and asked, "Who collected the blood samples?"

The detective cleared his throat, and Zero's eyes flickered back over to him.

"You collected them?"

"The results in the last two cases are from independent labs, tested on samples I gathered myself. The official ones for the first two cases kept getting mislabelled or contaminated, so I began to collect my own samples. None of them will hold up in court."

"Human courts aren't our concern," said Zero.

"They're my concern!" the detective said, a bit sharply.

"Very well," said Zero; and maybe Detective Tuatu thought he was agreeing with him, because he looked relieved.

Oh well. He'd learn better later.

I prepared the tea tray as slowly as possible, hoping to hear more, but when I looked up from the teapot, Athelas was there in the doorway. He must have wanted to speak to me, because it was suddenly hard to hear what was going on in the other room; sort of muffled and indistinct instead of clear like I was used to it being.

That was annoying, and rude into the bargain. I glared at him.

Athelas smiled and said tranquilly, "I had no idea we figured in your mind as creepy, Pet!"

"Nah, I'm used to you now."

"That's a great relief."

"Not that I can see," I told him, still trying to hear what was going on in the other room. "Since when do you care what I think of you?"

"It is always wise to care what other people think of you," Athelas said. "One doesn't need to do anything about it, of course, but it's always useful to know."

For a moment, I heard Zero's voice say, "The pet is already involved. That's our affair," and Tuatu protest, "It's a dangerous case!" but then everything went fuzzy again.

I asked glumly, "Why would it be useful to know what I think of you?"

"Say I wished to manipulate you into doing something for me," he suggested.

"Yeah," I said slowly. I was pretty sure I already understood, and I didn't like where this was going. "You mean if you wanted me to do something, it would be useful to know what I think of you and work on me from there? Like, if I thought of you as a psychopath—"

"—I could attempt to frighten you into doing what I wanted you to do. Direct, neat, and very likely to succeed."

"Yeeeeah," I said, even more slowly. Disorientingly, I heard Detective Tuatu's voice cut in— "There aren't any vacancies, but I've heard you can be persuasive, so—"

Athelas' voice continued through or around or maybe *in* it, drowning the detective's voice out again, "Now, if I were to think you thought of me as, perhaps, someone to be trusted—"

I opened my mouth to say *fat chance!* but stopped the words just in time. Since my mouth was open anyway, I said, "You mean you'd be making an effort to keep me thinking you could be trusted," instead.

Athelas inclined his head. "Having done so, I would work on those expectations you have of me to manipulate you into doing what I want you to do."

"Look, I thought you didn't *want* me to think you're creepy?"

"I've no objection to anyone finding me creepy," demurred Athelas. "So long as it suits my purposes to be thought so."

"Yeah, that's not creepy at all," I said, and gave him the thumbs up. "You lot want biscuits in there?"

"Of course."

"Oi."

Athelas' eyes rested on me. "I won't answer that question, Pet."

"You don't even know what I was gunna ask!"

"Do I not? You were going to ask me what I came in here to distract you from."

"All right, who told you to do it, then?" I demanded, feeling hard done by.

"I believe I shouldn't need to answer that particular question," Athelas said, and his voice was chiding.

"Yeah, but you do stuff off your own bat, too," I protested. "It's not just Zero you do stuff for."

"If I were you," said Athelas, and he said it very quietly, very chillingly, "I would not repeat that again, Pet."

I shut my mouth and took the tea tray into the other room. The moment I stepped down into the living room, I could hear their voices clearly again.

Detective Tuatu, his lips tight, was saying, "...and whatever it is, don't do it again! You might be running the Hobart Station from upstairs, but I don't have to obey your orders."

Good for him. Zero must have been trying out the same thing Jin Yeong had once tried on the detective and found not to work, either—that thing where they used their vampire and fae abilities to enthral or control the person they were talking to. They hadn't tried it on me—or at least, I assumed they hadn't tried it on me. I might not have remembered if they did it, but I was pretty sure they would have used it a lot of times I remembered them *not* using it.

Sometimes I'm not a very obedient pet.

I was also pretty sure I knew why the detective wasn't susceptible to their influence; that pendant of his had turned up some interesting things when I looked for it online a week ago. I still didn't know exactly why it didn't work on me. Maybe they just didn't try.

I was pretty sure they had, though.

Zero didn't exactly look startled, but he did exchange a look with Athelas. He said to Detective Tuatu, "We'll collaborate. If you need to get in contact with us for the duration, speak with the pet."

I looked from the detective to Zero. "The duration of what?"

"The most obvious place to investigate is the supermarket," said the detective. "I can't go myself, because you aren't officially with me, but if one of you can get in there using your...*skills*...it will probably be useful."

I grinned. "We're going undercover?"

"We're going undercover," Zero said shortly. "Not you."

"Yeah?" I gave him his coffee. "How you gunna convince anyone that you're checkout chicks? I'm the only normal one here. They'll sniff you out in a minute."

There was a definite glow of amusement to Athelas' soft eyes as he took his teacup from me and sat down. "The pet is not entirely wrong," he said. "And we might want to consider that a pet at home alone is potentially more trouble than a pet at our heels. Perhaps we can send her in with a handler?"

"Jin Yeong can look after it," Zero said, abruptly switching his decision without a correlating change of emotion to his face.

"*Ah, Hyeong!*" Jin Yeong said reproachfully.

Stupid vampire. It was his fault, anyway.

He didn't make any other complaint, though, and I was a bit surprised. He and Zero were always either fighting each other or fighting together against all other comers; but since they got back, Jin Yeong had been pretty civil. Usually he had a snark at Zero once every couple of days.

"Next time, don't smear blood on me," I told him, by way of testing the waters. I didn't trust his good streak, especially not where it came to me.

The detective said in surprise, "Blood? What blood?"

"All right, don't get your knickers in a knot!" I told him. "It wasn't anyone he killed, it was the dead bloke."

Detective Tuatu didn't look any less sick. "Why did he smear blood on you from the crime scene?"

"That's what *I'm* saying!" I said, in mild victory. "Who does that!"

"You can come out of here with me right now," the detective said. "I'll take you with me."

I don't think he expected me to laugh, and maybe the others didn't, either, because my laugh cut across Zero's growl of, "We *discussed* this. Leave while you still have legs to do so."

"That's pet-napping," I told the detective, and grabbed the sleeve of his jacket. "C'mmon, I'll show you the way out."

"Isn't it useful, having a pet?" murmured Athelas, as I towed the detective toward the door. "And so very amusing!"

CHAPTER FIVE

I started out to work with Jin Yeong the next morning. If it hadn't been for the fact that I was walking with Jin Yeong, it might have been an enjoyable morning; it was fresh and cool, but not too cool, and it was the first day of the first legal job I'd had.

I mean, okay, it was a job I was probably getting because of Jin Yeong's manipulative vampire wiles, but it was a real job. At least I wasn't going to get paid in cash.

Actually, was I going to get paid at all?

I stopped in the street and said to Jin Yeong, "Hang on. Am I getting paid, or what?"

He smirked at me and kept walking.

I trotted after him and asked, "How exactly are we getting these jobs, anyway? Detective Tuatu said something last night about there not being any vacancies."

This time Jin Yeong smiled a lazy, toothy smile.

"Is *that* where you and Zero went last night? You were getting rid of staff to make some vacancies?"

"*Mwoh*," said Jin Yeong, and the smile was leaner and grimmer. "*Bisutae.*"

I should probably remember to ask Athelas what had

happened to the people we were replacing; the detective wasn't gunna be happy if my three psychos were out there injuring more humans. I wouldn't be really happy about it, either, if it came to that.

I frowned worriedly. Zero wouldn't hurt humans just to get us positions undercover, would he? I was sure he wouldn't.

JinYeong must have seen my frown; he grinned a bit wider, and this time there was definitely the sharpness of canine teeth there.

"I don't believe it," I told him defiantly. "Stop smirking at me; we're gunna be late for work at this rate."

JinYeong shrugged. He probably didn't care whether or not I believed him.

"I don't believe it," I told him again; but I did wonder why they hadn't taken me with them last night. I was probably just being a jealous pet, but I didn't see why JinYeong should get to go out with Zero when I didn't get to go. I'd had to sit at home with Athelas, who, when he wasn't drinking tea, merely sat and smiled dreamily to himself. Where the recharging seemed to leave Zero bright and sharp and deep-water icy, it had left Athelas smooth, mellow, and cat-with-creamy.

I wasn't sure which one was more worrying.

JinYeong was mellower today, too though. He strolled along with his hands in the pockets of his crisply ironed suit—which he hadn't made me do over more than once—and pouted serenely at the street around him until we got to the supermarket.

When we got to the service desk we were met by a girl with big, blonde hair and a smile that appeared and disappeared so fast it could have caused whiplash.

She flashed the smile at JinYeong and said, "You're working with me today! This way!" and said over her shoulder to me as she led him away, "You wait here. Someone will come for you."

Even JinYeong's back looked smug. Most times that would have annoyed me, but maybe the recharging last night had mellowed me, too. I grinned and settled myself against the service desk to wait.

The service desk attendant, all sabre-tipped nails and eyeliner, with a name tag that read *Carmen*, said, "You're the new one, are you?"

"Yeah," I said.

"Hope you're better than the last one," she said. "He didn't even show up to his shift yesterday."

"I'll show up to my shifts," I promised cheerfully. Being undercover wasn't much good if I wasn't there. "I'll even work while I'm here. Any advice?"

She stared at me for a few seconds before she grinned back at me. Maybe she'd had a long day.

"Make sure you don't get on the wrong side of the queen bee out the back there," she said. "And you'll be fine."

"Which one's the queen bee?"

"You can't miss her," said Carmen, as an older woman in uniform powerwalked toward us. "Just watch your back, that's all."

The older woman was Rhonda, and she powerwalked me out to the storeroom like it was a race. Lucky for me, I've always been a quick walker, and I was used to keeping up with Zero's long stride now. There wasn't much in the way of training—Rhonda seemed to think I'd come from another store, so she just put me with one of the stock boys to get used to the place and left me there.

The stock boy was one of those tall, good-looking blokes that knows he's good-looking. You know: ruffled brown hair and an almost lantern chin, hazel eyes and a bit of a crooked grin. Well, I was only guessing about the last bit; he definitely didn't grin at me. He didn't really try to teach me how to do anything, either, but all he was doing was putting stuff on the shelves and it didn't look too hard. He didn't try to talk to me.

I said, "Hi," anyway.

He sort of grunted, which was rude, but I was still pretty

mellow so I just craned to see his name badge and said, "Name's Pet."

"Daniel," he said.

"Your name badge says *Scott*," I pointed out.

"Yeah," he said. "I forgot my badge so they gave me this one."

"Nice of 'em."

"Yeah. They usually give us the one that says Barbara."

"Who's Barbara?"

He looked at me sideways. "No one knows. It's one of the old badges; she probably hasn't been here for twenty years."

I straightened the cans I'd put on the shelf and looked around for somewhere to put the plastic they'd been wrapped in. Daniel nodded briefly at the shopping trolley that was hiding behind the cage of stock we were working on and I grinned my thanks at him.

At least I knew he was capable of being useful if he wanted to be.

"There were police outside," I said, going back for another carton. "When I came in, I mean."

There had been, too; though it was anyone's guess whether they'd been collecting evidence or contaminating it, if I was to believe Detective Tuatu.

"There are always police around here," Daniel said shortly. "We get shoplifters galore."

"Don't think they were here for a shoplifter," I said. "They were messing with the bins outside."

"Then it's probably another body," he said.

I stared at him a bit. "You get a lot of bodies?"

"We've had a couple," he said. "You don't have to worry about it. They'll pack up and go away soon."

"What, they don't question you at all?"

He shrugged. "What's there to ask questions about? It's got nothing to do with the store."

"Dunno," I said doubtfully. "If there were two bodies outside my house, I'd wonder a bit."

"We can't help what people throw in the rubbish bins," said Daniel. "Those are the wrong ones."

"What?"

"Those are the wrong cans. You've put salt reduced where the normal one goes."

"Oh." I looked at the cans, and then at the ones on the shelf. "There's already salt reduced ones up here."

"We can't help what nightfill does, either," he said. "Just take the wrong ones out and put 'em in the cage with the other overstocks."

"Right," I nodded. He was pretty casual about dead bodies, for someone around my age.

I mean, *I* was a bit more casual about them these days, but I'd seen a lot of bodies lately. Actually, I'd seen a lot of bodies over my lifetime, and nothing would ever be as bad as the first two I saw. Seeing your parents' dead bodies will do that to you.

What was *his* excuse?

If I'd been working harder through the day, I probably would have been sore and tired by lunch time. Lucky for me, I was working with Daniel all day. He moved at the physical equivalent of a drawl, and even if he wasn't talkative at least he didn't care when I went for my breaks, so long as I didn't mention the couple extra minutes he took on his own breaks. Hopefully I'd be working with him most days; it'd be a nice, easy way to go poking around the store without anyone noticing I wasn't where I was meant to be.

I went and looked for JinYeong when lunch came around, dodging the couple of giggling cash office girls who were asking the other women in the staff room if *they'd* seen the new assistant manager. Since there were sighs of appreciation and a general expressive exchanging of looks, I guessed he must be pretty good looking.

He *must* be, if the cash office girls were talking about him instead of their new cash office assistant.

I grinned. It would be fun to tell Jin Yeong that the cash office girls were more interested in the new assistant manager than they were in him.

Unfortunately for my plans, Jin Yeong wasn't in the cash office when I peered through the glass stripes of the two-way glass to look for him. He wasn't in the little tea-making area, either, though that didn't really surprise me; he wouldn't have made his own coffee when he could find someone to do it for him.

I found him in the manager's office, smirking.

Flamin' typical. How had he managed to come into the store to be a cash office assistant, and end up as the assistant manager? I should've known.

"What the heck?" I complained. "You've been sitting up here all day playing manager while I've been down there working like a slave?"

Jin Yeong's smirk got a couple degrees more annoying. He opened his mouth to say something—and what's the bet it would have been *"Coppi, Petteu!"*—but one of the cash office ladies knocked coyly on the open office door just in time.

"I'm going out to the shop for coffee," she said brightly. It was the woman from this morning; the one who'd taken him upstairs with her. "We always shout you your first coffee in the cash office, even if it was a mistake about you being there."

"Ah!" said Jin Yeong in satisfaction, and gave vent to a flow of words that the cash office lady nodded at every so often, like she was a waitress taking his order. I suppose it was close enough.

It was funny, though; I saw the slight blankness in her eyes that meant Jin Yeong was using his vampiric powers of persuasion, and I wondered why. She would have done whatever he asked, anyway, and as far as I could tell, he was only asking for coffee. Fancy coffee, yeah; but just coffee.

I said to her by way of a joke, "Me too. I'll have what he's having," and she gave me a confused, sideways look. I don't know if it was because JinYeong was still messing with her mind, or if it was because she wanted me to know exactly how insignificant I was, but either way, I just grinned back at her. I could make my own coffee.

I didn't occur to me until she turned pertly and left with a spring in her step, that she'd taken JinYeong's orders in Korean, without a blink. Did she understand Korean, or...?

"Waaaait a minute!" I said accusingly.

"*Petteu!*" JinYeong snapped. "*Kugol hajima!*"

"Stop what? You gotta use your mojo, don't you? Because they can't understand you if you don't use your little manipulation thing!"

"*Ah, dabdabhae,*" muttered JinYeong. He got up from the desk and stalked around it, backing me into the corner of the office.

That was annoying, but all he did was talk menacingly at me in Korean for a few minutes, and it was really satisfying to wait until he finished before I said, very slowly and clearly, "I don't. Speak. Korean. I have. No idea. What you just. Said."

JinYeong showed me his teeth, then stalked back around the desk to sit down on his chair. He pointed at the chair opposite and said, "*Anja.*"

I gave him a look. "I'm a pet, not a dog. I don't sit on command." I jumped myself up on his desk and added in a helpful sort of way, "Think of me as a cat. I might do what you tell me to do, or I might not."

JinYeong's brow went up. Questioningly now, he said, "*Chero?*"

"Yeah, I'll do what Zero tells me to do."

"*Jjincha dabdabhae!*" said JinYeong, in exasperation. He said something else, where I heard Zero's name again, and something I was pretty sure was *dog*. It was either *dog* or swearing, anyway.

"What about it?" I demanded. "I said I wasn't your dog. I can be Zero's dog if I want. Anyway, I still wanna know how come you've been sitting up here doing nothing while I've been working myself to the bone downstairs."

Jin Yeong raised a brow again and pointed at the computer screen. There were about twenty camera feeds up there in split screen; one of them showed the last aisle Daniel and I were working in. The others we'd worked were all up there, too.

"Okay," I said. "So maybe we weren't killing ourselves. Anything interesting on the cameras?"

He shrugged and tapped the screen where one of the squares was labelled *alleyway*. It was the only black square on the screen.

"Well, I s'pose we know for sure it was someone here," I said. "Or that someone here helped whoever it was. So what else have you been doing?"

He gave me a look.

"What, nothing? You've just been watching the cameras all day?"

"*Ani*," said Jin Yeong, and now he pursed his lips in a distinctly satisfied smile.

"Oh, right; you've been flirting with all the female staff members," I remarked. "I'm sure that'll be useful."

Jin Yeong lifted one shoulder carelessly and let it drop. As he did, the cash office lady came back again with three coffees in a cardboard holder and an extra sheen of lip gloss glittering on her lips.

Hang on. She really got me a coffee, too?

I looked over in surprise at Jin Yeong, who glowered at me. So *that's* what he'd been telling me to stop!

The cash office lady gave him his coffee, smiling, and took her own. Then she pushed the cardboard tray at me without quite looking at me, coffee and all.

I took it, chucking the cardboard tray on Jin Yeong's desk, and that made her jump. She turned and gave me a surprised, disdainful look that asked, without actually asking, why I was still here, breathing the same air as her and Jin Yeong. I was pretty sure she didn't even remember giving me the coffee.

I couldn't help grinning again. This was *interesting*. So if I asked someone to do something while they were under Jin Yeong's influence, they'd do that, too?

"*Petteu*," growled Jin Yeong. "*Naga*."

"All right, all right, keep your knickers on," I said, still grinning. "Gotta go have some lunch, anyway."

DANIEL LOOKED A BIT MORE BRIGHT AND PERKY AFTER LUNCH, though I didn't notice it made him any quicker at his work. It did make him look around a lot, though, so I wasn't surprised when a uniformed lady came down our aisle with a handful of tickets to put up on the shelves.

She was at least ten years older than me and Daniel, but that didn't stop his eyes lighting up, or the slight flush of red in his cheeks. I nearly grinned, but he probably would've glared at me and I wasn't in the business of making enemies at the moment.

She was a nervous lady, I thought. Pretty, but not beautiful; in her thirties, with a round chin and real gold curls like Goldilocks should have had. Her name badge said Erica, and I got the feeling that she wasn't comfortable. I'm not sure exactly why. She didn't smile at Daniel until she was nearly level with him, but when she did it was a real smile, like they were good friends but maybe she was trying to keep a bit of distance between them.

I could understand that. He was obviously fascinated with her, and at her age she ought to be able to tell. I mean, if it was obvious to me, it must have been blindingly obvious to her. She still did all the usual hello things, though, and she smiled at me as well to make sure she wasn't just singling him out.

So why did I feel like she wasn't quite comfortable?

It wasn't pertinent to the body outside, but I'm nosy and I like to know what's happening around me, so I was a bit peeved when a customer pulled me away to get them some nappies that weren't on the shelf. By rights, Daniel should have got them—he was the one who was trained and knew where stuff was. But of course Daniel was too busy pretending not to look at Erica and then watching her when she wasn't looking at him, and he completely ignored the customer.

I dunno, maybe he did it on purpose—maybe it was part of his repertoire as a stock boy.

Begrudgingly, I trotted out into the storeroom to look for the box of nappies, and felt the faint but certain stirrings of excitement around the edges of the world that meant something Behindkind was happening.

I froze, the concrete floor beneath me swirling with shadows that weren't normal shadows from the sun through the roller door. What was that? Who was playing with Between? Was something coming through?

I threw a quick look around the storeroom, but there was no one else around. I could see the nappies I needed on one of the pallets of stock that were closest to the roller door, stuck behind all the others and with no way through but to climb over. The tantalising feeling of Between opening and closing was somewhere in the middle of the stack of pallets, too; if I was to climb over the top, I could take care of both problems at once.

Another glance around at the empty storeroom, and I scrambled on top of the pallets, my hands flat against the plastic wrap around them so it didn't squeak and give me away. Lucky for me, whatever was tickling Between was also making a bit of noise itself—scratches and clacking, like a really big spider or maybe just something with a small hammer digging for it in the pallets. Up there, I could see it, too; the softening of edges that turned boxes of stock into steps climbing high up into the roof and made the emergency fire door look like a big sign with foreign writing on it instead.

And maybe it was just the lycanthropy starting to kick in, but

I could have sworn I could smell a difference, too; a clear, metallic sort of smell that wasn't the cold mustiness of the concrete in the storeroom.

I was halfway across the top of the pallets, moving slowly, when I saw a white head and broad shoulders in between pallets where they couldn't possibly have fit. It was definitely not a human thing to do—not unless that human had been murdered by being crushed between pallets.

And I mean, if he *had* been murdered, he wouldn't be moving, would he?

What was Zero doing here?

I watched him reach up and through a pallet as if it wasn't there, feeling carefully for something that looked like it was wriggling away from him.

"Oi," I said. "You can't do that."

Zero's shoulders stiffened, and he turned around. "You shouldn't be crawling around on top of the load," was all he said.

"I know. Health and safety. But a customer wants a box of nappies and I can't reach 'em so—"

The box of nappies rocked from side to side, then got up and scuttled across the top of the load toward me.

"Yikes!" I said, and fell on my backside, squashing a box of packaged noodles. I gingerly picked up the box when it got to me, and there was a little spider thing beneath it, all metal legs and bolt-encrusted body. "Thanks," I said to it, and patted it carefully where there were no bolts, just in case those were the Between equivalent of eyes.

"Go back out," Zero said. "I've got this area covered."

"Didn't think you were coming in with us," I told him, scrambling back off the pallets of stock. "Though it was just me and Jin Yeong since it's his fault."

Zero emerged from between the pallets without disturbing them by so much as a millimetre. "I wasn't."

"Got bored, did you? You weren't here this morning."

"The storeman was taken suddenly...ill."

"Bet he was," I said. "He wasn't ill in a way that Detective Tuatu's gunna worry about, was he?"

Zero looked at me for a long, expressionless moment. I couldn't figure out if he was thinking about how to answer, or what to answer, but he said at last, "No."

"All right," I said, nodding, and took the box of nappies out to the customer.

Erica was gone from the aisle by the time I got back, and Daniel was back to his laconic, inattentive self. That was okay; I didn't think there was too much more I could get out of him that was useful, anyway, and I was curious about why Zero had so suddenly appeared. I was sure he hadn't planned on coming in with Jin Yeong and me—actually, I'd got the idea he was planning something else with Athelas.

What made him change his mind?

I still hadn't come to a reasonable conclusion by the time my shift ended. Daniel finished at the same time, but he had to stop and explain why we didn't get our last cage finished before he went home.

Lucky me, I could go straight away.

I nipped off to the locker room while Daniel was still explaining to Rhonda why two people hadn't been able to finish their final cage of the day. I plunged straight into a fog of perfume as soon as I opened the door of the ladies' locker room, and someone's voice behind a line of lockers said, "No, he'll be waiting for me if I go out now!"

I wasn't trying to be quiet or anything, but by now it was habit. I slowed down and pricked up my ears.

That's just a manner of speaking. Despite the lycanthropy, I wasn't feeling *that* wolfish yet.

I put the sleeve of my shirt over my nose to protect against the fog, but it didn't do much to protect my nostrils from burning with every breath in. I would have complained, but I would have had to take away my hand from my nose, and there was no way I was gunna do that.

Someone was still spraying it, too; I heard the *shhhhh* noise behind the sound of a woman's voice. The voice stopped for a moment, and there was the chirpy sound of someone replying by phone.

"I can't!" she said, her voice hushed. "Please! Just meet me outside in half an hour!"

There was another chirpy moment while the other person spoke, then she said, "All right. An hour. *Please* come!"

Now I was *really* curious. I had to go around the lockers she was behind, anyway; my locker was on that wall. So I kept going, not taking too much care to keep quiet. Despite that, when I came around the corner, Erica and her golden curls jumped just as violently as if I'd snuck up on her.

"Sorry!" I said brightly, as she gasped and put one hand to her chest. "Just gotta get me lunch bag."

I took it out of the locker and waggled it at her, and sauntered away again. I was pretty sure that normal human interactions meant ignoring the kind of thing I'd just overheard, and I didn't want to be too weird on my first day. Not much good being under-cover if everyone thought I was a weirdo.

Still, it gave me something to think about on the way home with Jin Yeong. It was a pity Zero seemed to finish earlier than we did; walking home with Jin Yeong was just about as fun as walking to work with him. At least it was a bit quicker this time, though. When we were a few steps away from the supermarket, he pinched a bit of my sleeve between two fingers, as if I was some-thing that had been dragged into the house by a cat who liked to kill small animals, and towed me Between with him.

The bitumen beneath our feet started to look a lot spongier, and the cars around us looked a bit deader—or maybe they looked a bit more alive. They were just skeletons of metal here Between, but they were grown over with flowers and greenery, and they looked like they might still have been able to move if they wanted to. Mind you, they gave the impression that if they *had* moved, it would have been under their own inclinations and not at the demands of a driver, but they still looked like they could move. A sort of flock of free range cars.

I don't know how being Between shortens the distances between places, but I've got the feeling it involves magic. I know that sounds like it should be common sense, but what I mean is that I think it must be a more noticeable magic. I think my three psychos could shorten the distance when they're out in the regular world, too, but I reckon it's something people would notice. Like seeing the Flash out and about, you know? Here in Between, it felt like it was something that anyone who saw you kind of *expected*. The normal way to travel.

That's my guess, anyway, because none of the maybe-sentient cars paid any more attention to us when our surroundings began to blur than they had when we first arrived, and the almost-rabbit I saw foraging nearby just hopped to the side to make sure it wasn't in our way.

For a couple of minutes everything looked like an oil painting around me, nearly making sense but too blurred to discern the details of exactly what was happening, then life sharpened again. Jin Yeong still had a pained look, and a bit of my sleeve pinched between his fingers, but at least I could see Between around me properly again. Here, it was smooth and kind of bitumen-y beneath our feet, and instead of the houses that should have been on either side there were pale rocky walls divided by falling ferns at roughly house-sized intervals that grew from the top of the walls and framed a twilight sky far above us.

I pointed up at it and asked Jin Yeong, "That mean we're in Unseelie, or something?"

Yep. I'd been studying.

Jin Yeong made a contemptuous *pft* sound that got on my

nerves a lot for how soft it was, and stopped by a section of the rocky walls.

"Going through the back door?" I remarked.

That made him look annoyed, which was nice; but how he expected me not to know the bits of coloured glass that made up the top section of the back door, I don't know. They weren't glass here on the rocky wall, mind you. What should have been pieces of red glass were shimmering reflections of light from some sort of glass or crystal covered lantern nearby, and the green and white parts of the pattern were leaves that mingled with the reflections. The pattern was pretty clear, though. When I reached out to the suggestion of a bump in the pale surface of the rock, expecting to feel the coolness of the back doorknob, it turned at once beneath my hand.

"*Jaemi obseo*," Jin Yeong muttered. He tossed me ahead of him by my sleeve, propelling me back into the human world with disorienting suddenness, and sauntered in after me.

I didn't stumble, which was a nice, smug feeling to take with me into the living room, where Athelas sat in his usual chair with one leg crossed over the other, and Zero now sat on his haunches by the coffee table, making a nonsense jigsaw puzzle of the contents of one of the files Detective Tuatu had given him. He looked cool and clean, and his hair was still damp, like he'd had to take a shower to get rid of the feeling of the cold, concrete storeroom.

"*Ah, himdulotda!*" sighed Jin Yeong, and threw his tie on the coffee table where it caused two of the photos to flutter away. "*Petteu! Coppi!*"

"Yeah, it must be so hard sitting in the office all day and flirting with the cash office ladies," I muttered, but I kept going on and up into the kitchen, because I was pretty sure Athelas was also looking hopeful. I mean, it wasn't like I'd killed myself working today, either.

Zero didn't say anything, but the tie came flying into the

dining room and slid across the top of the table before slithering onto the floor. I grinned and left it where it was. Jin Yeong's mellow mood had lasted longer than I expected it to last, but it looked like he was back on his regular crusade to provoke Zero into a fight. I shuffled myself a bit faster with the tea and coffee; if Jin Yeong was going to be a pain in the neck, there wouldn't be any real discussion of our case—just snarling and unpleasantness and danger for pets who happened to be caught in the cross-fire.

"A difficult day, I take it?" enquired Athelas, from the other room.

Jin Yeong must have been sulking in silence, because it was Zero who said, "More boring than difficult. How was your hunting?"

I regretted that the kettle was now boiling at full bore; it meant that Athelas' quiet voice was harder than usual to hear.

I think he said, "More difficult than I suspected. Did you meet with the next shadow after I called you?"

"He was staying out of sight," replied Zero.

Shadow? And what did they mean by *next* shadow? Was that what Athelas had actually said?

I spooned tea into Athelas' pot and prepped the coffee pot, wondering if I'd misheard. Too late now; I'd have to ask them about it later and see if they'd tell me. Right; biscuits, coffee pot, tea pot. I had 'em all now.

I picked up my tray to go back to the interesting part of the house, and Jin Yeong, his voice sour, said something that had the word *dog* in it. I didn't know if he meant an actual dog, or if he was just swearing about something in Korean, so I called to Athelas, "Wosse say?"

"He says the whole staff area smells of dog," explained Athelas. "Hardly surprising, since we're investigating an animal attack and you were infected with lycanthropy."

"Beauty!" I said, stepping down into the living room. I put my tray on one of the spare seats instead of the coffee table, with a pointed look at JinYeong. "Does that mean he can sniff out the one who did it?"

JinYeong put his nose in the air just a fraction.

"What, you can't? What's the use of a sniffer like yours, if you can't even find a werewolf?"

"*Ya, Petteu!*"

"There are no such things as werewolves," said Zero, accepting a cup of coffee from me.

"So, what?" I asked, frowning. He hadn't said that yesterday. Mind you, I seemed to remember him talking about *wolf shifters*, not *werewolves*. "I'm infected with a figment of someone's imagination?"

"Lycanthropy is a real condition; a subset of a virus that affects a person's blood and physical makeup. Werewolves are a story told to frighten Behindkind children."

I stared at Zero. "There are things that frighten people from Behind?"

"Lycanthropes, or shifters in the vernacular, are Behindkind that were once human—"

"Like vampires?"

"*Ya!*"

"All right, settle down, I wasn't insulting your ancestors," I protested.

"Shifters," said Zero, in a tone of voice that shut JinYeong up as well as me, "are Behindkind that were once human and have now gained the ability to see and live Between and Behind. Most of them choose not to do so; they like the easy pickings among humans. They are one of the few things from this side of Between that can kill Behindkind."

"Although, technically speaking, it could be said that it's a Behindkind virus," mused Athelas. "Since it came about from bringing humans Behind. In any case, it's one effect of the changeling initiative that has been unfortunate from a Behindkind viewpoint."

"Really?" I couldn't help feeling a bit impressed. Go mutated humans! "What, they just tear out throats? Like vampires?"

Jin Yeong snarled at me, but to my surprise Zero answered the question.

"Wolf shifters are stronger than normal humans, but that's not how they kill Behindkind. The same virus that alters the chemical and metaphysical makeup of humans mutates the bodies of Behindkind past resolve. It's a long, painful death."

"*Naega andwae*," said Jin Yeong, and this time his voice was smug.

"That's because you're already dead," I told him, sitting down with the plate of biscuits. "You can't kill someone who's already dead."

For the first time since I'd met him, I saw Jin Yeong flinch. It was the briefest thing; a not-quite-snarl that wasn't smug, or angry, or threatening.

Then he stared at me for a second longer, snatched the plate of biscuits away from me, and turned his back on me to scoff them all by himself.

I was going to say *"Oi!"* at him, or maybe make a dive to get the biscuits back, but just then Athelas said, "It doesn't affect vampires because they're not Behindkind Originals either."

I forgot about the biscuits and turned to look at Athelas. "Does that mean vampires can kill Behindkind, too?"

"What a bloodthirsty little pet you are!" said Athelas, in a thoughtful sort of a way.

Surprising me again, Zero said, "There are many things that can kill Behindkind, if you know how to use them."

It wasn't until I looked at him and saw the way his icy blue eyes bored into me that it occurred to me that he thought I was planning something. I said hastily, "I'm not trying to work out how to kill you blokes! I was just interested!"

Zero held up a fist and lifted fingers one by one. "Shifter saliva, vampire tooth, true bargain, power of name. Each of them originates from this side of Between and in the right circumstances can kill Behindkind."

"How the heck do you kill someone with a *name?*"

"There are some things in which it doesn't pay to be too closely interested, Pet," said Athelas gently.

"Yeah, but—" I stopped as another thought hit me. "Hang on, what if like a shifter ant bit you? Or a shifter mosquito? Would that kill you?"

There was a biscuity sort of snort from JinYeong' direction, and Athelas' eyes shut briefly.

"Fortunately, Pet," he said, "*fortunately*, the virus has not thus far mutated to include anything other than quadrupeds and the occasional bird if the human infected has a creative enough mind. We see shifter wolves, bears, and sometimes a tiger—very rarely an eagle or hawk."

"It's the sorta thing someone should be looking into," I mumbled to myself. I didn't say it too loud, though. More loudly, I added, "So we're looking for a shifter wolf, and the breakroom smells like dog, so we know we're in the right place?"

"It would appear so," agreed Athelas. "Of course, I was not there, so I can't speculate upon the smell or lack thereof—" he paused for the fraction of a second, maybe for JinYeong to react, but JinYeong was still eating biscuits— "but one would assume as much."

"Hang on," I said again. "If shifter saliva is dangerous to Behindkind, shouldn't Zero stay away from the supermarket?"

"That would be up to Zero himself," said Athelas, with a curious little smile.

"Shifters don't typically fling their spit at their enemies," Zero said. He didn't sound particularly worried, but he never did sound particularly *anything*. "And I would have to be unfortunate enough to be wounded at the same time."

"Yeah, like a *bite?*" I asked, with more emphasis. "Me and

JinYeong can work from the inside ourselves. You don't have to be there."

There was a contemptuous spray of crumbs from JinYeong's direction, and Athelas sipped his tea with a great deal of enjoyment.

"I have my own methods of protection," said Zero briefly. "You should worry about your own symptoms."

"I'd do that," I said, "but I don't know what symptoms to expect. Athelas is being mysterious and the vampire doesn't speak English."

There was far too much about my condition that I didn't know, even if what I did know made me feel more than slightly sick. It wasn't something I could go to the hospital for—I was entirely at the mercy of my three psychos, and I didn't like it when they didn't tell me stuff. JinYeong was pretty obviously annoyed at having to help me, and I was certain he'd rather I just die, so that wasn't surprising. I had the feeling that Athelas would as easily let me die if it seemed amusing to him, too, so his lack of helpfulness wasn't really surprising, either. Lucky for me, I didn't have to trust JinYeong or Athelas.

The problem was, I thought, huddling up in my hoodie, that I could only trust Zero to a point. Zero would save me *if* he could, I was certain about that. I would trust him to fight for me, but he couldn't guarantee we'd be able to find the right bloke in time, either.

Zero's eyes rested on me, light and unemotional. He said, "Dry mouth, faintness, stronger than usual sense of smell. When your stomach begins to change you'll start vomiting up anything cooked."

"I'm gunna have to eat *raw meat?*"

"*Ne,*" said JinYeong, eyes glittering as he turned to face me. He poked the empty plate into my stomach and added, with relish, "*Mani mani mokaesso!*"

"JinYeong has an uplifting view of your condition," remarked

Athelas. "If you do indeed get to the stage of eating a great deal of raw meat, you will undoubtedly survive the condition."

"Good to know," I said. I suddenly didn't feel too good again. "Oi. There was a woman I met today."

"*Nado*," said JinYeong, looking smug and pleased. What, he'd found someone too?

I ignored him, because my lead was sure to be better. "I think there's something going on with her," I told Zero. "Like maybe someone's scaring her. When I walked in on her in the locker room today she was asking someone to come and meet her so she didn't have to walk home alone."

"There are many reasons for human women to be afraid, Pet."

"Yeah," I said to Athelas, "but they don't usually spray themselves with half a bottle of perfume before they go out of the store, do they? Reckon that's the sort of thing I'd do if I was being bothered by someone who can find me by smell."

"Wolf shifters can be territorial when it comes to a woman they see as their own," agreed Athelas. He sounded slightly more interested, and I think Zero must have been, too, because he leaned forward just a bit.

He asked, "Did she know you were in the locker room with her?"

"She nearly jumped through the roof when I came around the corner, so I reckon prob'ly not."

"I see," said Zero, and went back to sipping his coffee. "It's a pity JinYeong has only been able to confirm that there *are* wolf shifters, and not who or how many."

"He smells more than one?"

"*Ne*," said JinYeong.

"So we've found a motive, but we don't know whose it is?"

"We've found a potential motive," Zero corrected me. "The deaths could be jealous rage against people who get too close to the woman, but there are five deaths to account for, and if there were such a significant number of deaths attached to one person it would be all around the store."

"Oh yeah," I agreed glumly. It would definitely have been around the store already if all the people who had died were directly connected to Erica. I complained, "People shouldn't leave motives lying around where they could be anybody's. It makes things messy."

"Not all the links might be immediately obvious, however," said Athelas.

I beamed at him and poured him another cup of tea.

Jin Yeong made a dismissive sort of noise and said something that might have had the words *woman* and *myself* in it.

"Copycat!" I said. "Just because I've found a lead, doesn't mean you have to, as well!"

Jin Yeong showed me a bit of tooth but continued talking, which was annoying. It meant he probably did really have a suspect; and okay, I know it wasn't a competition, but I wanted to find the culprit before he did.

Zero listened to him in silence, and when he finished speaking, only said, "Interesting. Keep looking into it."

"Looking into what?" I complained. "How come you two can understand him, anyway?"

"Jin Yeong said that there is also a woman who wears a great deal of perfume in the office upstairs, and that the office itself also smells distressingly of dog."

"Oh," I said. I still didn't feel completely gruntled again, though I wasn't sure if that was because Jin Yeong had a reasonable person of interest, or because I was annoyed at Jin Yeong himself. "Oi. How come everyone has to learn Korean to be able to understand the vampire? If we're three people, shouldn't he learn English?"

"We're two Behindkind and a pet," Zero said. "If you want to understand Jin Yeong, you'll have to work it out for yourself."

"It should be added that neither Zero nor myself have learned Korean," said Athelas.

"Then how the flaming heck—?"

JinYeong smirked at me, so I stuck my tongue out.

"Outside, Pet," said Zero, standing up.

"What? What did I do?" I protested. JinYeong was still smirking, and that was annoying.

"Outside," Zero said again, and I scuttled after him, because he was using the Voice That Must Be Obeyed.

I don't know what happens if you don't obey it, but I don't wanna find out.

When we got outside, Zero reached up into one of the trees in the back yard and snapped off a branch. He didn't say anything about it, but he trimmed the ends a bit, and that was enough to make it pretty clear what it was for.

"Don't I get a real weapon?"

"No."

"Why?"

"I don't want to pick up your head from the lawn."

"Oh."

"Houses that have seen too much blood aren't good places to stay."

"Dunno why you're staying in this one, then," I remarked. "But I s'pose you know what you're doing."

"Do you?" Were Zero's eyes a bit narrower with amusement? Maybe. "You're a very yappy pet."

"Yeah," I said. "Us little ones are always yappy."

Zero grabbed me by the collar and pulled me forward to measure the stick against my arm.

"How come you're teaching me now?" I asked him, suspiciously.

Zero looked over the stick he'd snapped off, and trimmed the ends a bit more. "Didn't you want to learn?"

"Yeah—I mean *yeah*, but you've been putting it off, and—"

"I wasn't putting it off."

Coulda fooled me. I didn't say it aloud, though. "I want to learn; I just didn't think you were gunna teach me."

He handed me the stick. "Use this."

I took it, and saw the possibility in it to be either a stick or something not exactly sticklike that was quite a bit heavier than the stick. I let it be a stick and hoped Zero wouldn't notice.

"No," he said. "That's too light for practise. Change it."

"What if it doesn't want to—"

Zero's eyes narrowed by just as much as a thought, blindingly blue.

I cleared my throat and squeezed the stick until it changed into a baton, leather and heavy and slightly grippy under my fingers. "Got it, boss," I said.

"Now," said Zero, and this time the narrowing of his eyes was closer to his version of a grin. "Now—footwork."

CHAPTER SIX

I don't want to sound dramatic, but I flamin' *died*.

Felt like it by the time I got back inside, anyway. By the clock it was only an hour, but my body was pretty sure it was more like four, and I had the shakes to prove it. Maybe if I'd only been doing the lunges and dodgy footwork he was showing me, it might have been all right; my legs were a bit sore as well, but nothing like my arms. There hadn't been any comfort in Zero's body language, either; when we started our drill he was focused but relaxed, and by the end he was still relaxed, but I was pretty sure he was displeased. That made me clumsy as well as weak, and despite Zero's changing demands as we drilled, my performance didn't change.

My arms were shaking for the rest of the night, too; and it was no surprise. For all the footwork Zero had made me do, he made me drill with the baton, and none of that drill involved just holding the baton at my side, I can tell you.

The next day was worse, though. I fell asleep before my head hit the pillow, and I only woke when my phone started ringing. The ache in my arm when I reached for it made me yelp, and I might have been a bit cranky when I accepted the call.

"What?" I mumbled into the receiver.

"One of them is at the police station again!" said Detective Tuatu exasperatedly, in my ear.

I groaned, and tried to straighten out my other arm, which felt like it was frozen in a painful crook. "One of what?"

"One of those three!"

"Oh, the psychos." I groaned again. "I'm dying. I don't care."

"You're—" there was a pause, and the detective asked, "What's wrong?"

"Told you. I'm dying. Hang on."

I put the phone down and made myself sit, groaning the whole way, then stretched out my arms despite the ache. I heard Detective Tuatu's voice chirp once or twice, so I turned on the speaker mode and said, "All right, all right, keep your hair on. I'm just stretching. Zero was training me last night."

"What training?"

"Baton fighting," I said. "But he reckons it's so I'll be able to handle a sword. I dunno. He won't let me have a real sword and the baton's flamin' heavy."

"Good," said Detective Tuatu. "You'd probably cut off your own head."

"That's flamin' rude!" I said. "Zero said that, too. I'm pretty sure it's harder to cut off my own head than someone else's, anyway, so I don't know why everyone's so worried about that."

"You shouldn't be cutting off anyone else's head, either."

"What if they're trying to cut off my head?" I argued. "I should be able to—hang on. Did you say one of 'em was at the police station again?"

He sighed. "Yes. All of yesterday morning, and again today."

"Ah!" I said. "So that's where Athelas was!"

"He's Athelas? The smooth-as-cream one?"

"That's him."

"What's he doing at the police station?"

"Dunno for sure," I told him. If there was one thing I was sure of when it came to Athelas, it was that you never could be exactly sure what was going on with him. I thought about it for a bit, and said, "Oh, right. You said there was a cover up somewhere in the force. Athelas is probably checking it out."

"That's a good way to get killed," said Detective Tuatu. "They've probably got someone following him already."

I thought back to the bloke with the bright pants who'd been following the detective, and said to myself more than him, "Yeah, it's a good way to get killed, all right."

"I mean, I know they can walk through walls and everything, but—"

"You don't have to worry about them," I said. "They can look after themselves."

"Yeah," he said, but he still sounded uneasy.

I grinned at the wall opposite me. "You're a nice detective," I said. "We'll keep you."

"That's another thing," he said, after another pause. "It's not healthy, living the way you do. People can't be kept as pets, or things."

"I'm hanging up now," I said, and tapped the red circle while his voice was still protesting from the speaker. I said, "Rude!"

It was lucky he'd called, though; I'd slept through my alarm, and the digital clock on my phone showed a time of eight o'clock. Jin Yeong and I were due to start work at nine, and I hadn't even got breakfast for everyone yet.

I grumbled to myself and tried to stand up, but my legs didn't want to stretch out either, and I lost another ten minutes trying to make them bend at the knee again like they should. When that was done, I trotted downstairs to see who was still in the house. Athelas wasn't, I already knew, and there was a kind of hollowness to the house that wasn't explained until I got downstairs and found that Jin Yeong was the only other person in the house.

Jin Yeong was sitting at the table with a superior sort of

expression on his pointy little face when I found him in the kitchen.

"Where's Zero?" I demanded grumpily. I didn't like the feeling of emptiness around the place, and JinYeong's skinny carcase wasn't likely to make much of a dent in that emptiness.

JinYeong only raised an eyebrow at me and made a silent *moue* with his lips.

I looked at him in disfavour while I filled the kettle. "S'pose you want breakfast."

"*Ne.*"

"Coffee?"

"*Ne.*"

"Oh well, at least you won't talk my ear off," I said, wincing as I hefted the full kettle back over to its base. It wouldn't do him any good if he planned on it, of course, but I hadn't noticed that the lack of a listening ear stopped JinYeong from complaining. "Did Zero already go to work?"

"*Ne.*"

What a pain.

I noticed that JinYeong's *moue* was more amused than superior and demanded, "What?"

"*Petteu,*" he said lazily, "*Choshimhae.*"

"Don't you threaten me," I said. "I'll tell Zero."

JinYeong's other brow went up, and one incisor showed in a sultry half-grin. "*Petteu, iruwa.*"

"Your mojo doesn't work on me," I said. I mean, I was pretty sure it didn't, and JinYeong didn't correct me.

He just slouched a bit more, disgusted and dark-eyed. I looked at him more narrowly, and fetched a blood bag from the fridge.

"*Mwoh hanun kkoya?*" demanded JinYeong, sitting up straight in surprise.

I shoved the blood bag into his chest. "Have something to eat," I told him. "And don't look at me like that. It's creepy. I probably don't even taste that good."

"*Ani,*" mumbled JinYeong, his mouth closing around the opening of the blood bag. He said around it, with a more of a purring than a sultriness this time, "*Hangsang mashisso. Petteu do.*"

It was probably a good thing I gave him the blood bag to drink before we got to work, because if he'd been surrounded by office ladies yesterday, today JinYeong was mobbed with uniformed ladies from *every* department. At least four of them had brought coffee for him, and if he'd been surrounded with that much temptation on an empty stomach, I wouldn't have trusted him not to take a snack behind one of the pallets halfway through the day, even if Zero *was* in the storeroom.

There was no Daniel for me to work with that morning—I looked at the roster as I came through the staff room, and he wasn't scheduled on until the afternoon. Rhonda took me with her instead. I knew straight away that it was going to be harder work; Rhonda moved like a very small, very precise robot, her fluffed up hair bobbing along the aisle with a grim determination to take on the world by herself. It was a pity I hadn't been able to stomach breakfast, or even the smell of it, that morning. I was going to need the energy.

Lucky for me, Rhonda talked almost as fast as she worked and it wasn't long before I knew at least one weird or scandalous thing about pretty much everyone in the store. If the assistant manager hadn't been shanghaied by Zero and JinYeong, it was likely he would have been facing an inquiry from loss prevention—probably would be still when he got back, if Rhonda's knowledgeable look was anything to go by. Shanae from cash office had been sweet on two of the men who only had eyes for Erica from the systems office ("*...and it wasn't just Shanae, either, I can tell you that— the nice little girl we had before her was dating one of them first!*") and Amanda from the deli was using the ladies' toilet as her own personal bathroom before anyone else started work.

I didn't try to remember everything, but I did file away a few of the more interesting remarks to report to Zero later; just in case it was important to know that the cleaners had recently changed, or that someone had been urinating all around the back dock.

On my first break I followed Rhonda and sat down with the smokers in the non-bloody end of the alley. None of them seemed to be too concerned that the other end had been a crime scene, which was about as surprising as Daniel's unconcern about it. Or maybe the cops had just cleaned it all away so quickly that most of them hadn't known about it.

But it was pretty odd for a story like that not to go around an entire store, even if only one or two people knew about it to start with. People liked talking about weird and shocking things, and everyone liked to think they'd seen something.

Still, I didn't want to push things too much; none of them seemed to have noticed that I wasn't smoking even though I was with them in the smoking area, and I figured it was better not to talk too much.

When they went in, I lingered behind them. From where I was sitting I could see into the window of Jin Yeong's office; he was in there with one of the cash office girls—Shanae? I wondered, grinning—and as I glanced up, his eyes met mine.

He made a brief, paddling gesture in the air that was his way of telling me to come up to him. I pretended I didn't see him, but that made him rap sharply on the window and repeat the gesture, this time more vehemently.

I stuck out my tongue at him and folded my arms across my chest, a clear no.

Jin Yeong narrowed his eyes at me, but short of leaving his office and coming down, there wasn't any way of making me do as I was told, and I was pretty sure he was too busy with whatever girl it was he had in the office with him. She must be the one he'd mentioned last night—his best choice for suspect in an office that smelled of wolf.

Well, I had my own investigating to do, and it didn't have

anything to do with sitting in on his interviews. And speaking of investigating, I should probably get back inside. According to the roster, I was supposed to be working with Daniel this afternoon, and even if he wasn't much use to talk to, at least his work style left me free to sneak around a bit.

I got up and wandered toward the top of the alley where the body had been yesterday, and caught sight of a uniformed person coming into the parking lot. It was Erica.

A touch of breeze tickled the back of my neck, raising hairs, and Erica looked up once, meeting my eyes. She looked away again immediately, ducking her head and walking quickly through the carpark with her head down and her hands gripping the sash of her satchel like she was afraid someone was going to try and pinch it. I mean, this was the kind of area where that might actually happen, but I didn't think it was likely this close to the supermarket.

Erica, I thought as I watched her rapid pace, seemed to be the nervous sort who saw danger behind every bush. I made a face at the wall across from me, because that could mean I was barking up the wrong tree when it came to motives.

I sighed, but there was another flash of uniformed movement in the entrance of the carpark, and Daniel loped in behind Erica, his stride long and loose, his hands in his pockets and earbuds in his ears. He could have been just coming to work as normal if it wasn't for the fact that his eyes never left her.

"Creepy kid," I muttered.

So maybe Erica wasn't paranoid. Maybe she was just creeped out by the eighteen-year-old kid who was following her around the place.

I narrowed my eyes at Daniel as he crossed the parking lot and entered the store. Funny about that, though; I hadn't gotten that impression from her yesterday when she said hello to both of us. Maybe Erica was just used to hiding her nervousness around him.

The first thing I needed to do was find out whether or not he was a wolf shifter, then. What was I supposed to do, wave an uncooked steak under his nose? Hang around at full moon?

"*Hajima*," said Jin Yeong, from close beside me.

I jumped, and glared up at him. "What are you, a mushroom? Where did you spring up from?"

"*Duroga, Petteu*," he said. If I hadn't known that he meant for me to go inside, the way he jerked his head at the staff door would have given it away.

"What? I'm not late back from break."

"*Moggolae*," he explained, tugging me away from the milk crate and through the door by the collar. Just inside the door he propped me against the wall and patted at my pockets.

"You want to eat?" I batted away his hands and hissed, "I didn't bring anything with me! I can't carry blood around in public!"

Jin Yeong made an annoyed mutter about food and eating, and pointed upstairs.

"What? Why should I eat with you?" I demanded, finally understanding. "I don't wanna be part of your fan club!"

He narrowed his eyes at me and opened his mouth to say something that I wouldn't understand anyway, so I interrupted him.

"Oi. Do that vampy thing of yours and put me to work with Erica this arvo."

"*Wae?*"

"Gotta ask her some questions, that's why. You got your suspects, I've got mine."

Jin Yeong made a sniffy little laugh, but he looked more amused than disparaging, so I wasn't surprised when Rhonda came to find me a few minutes after he went back to his office and told me I was doing tickets with Erica.

"Beauty!" I said, and trotted away happily upstairs. I grinned at Jin Yeong as I passed his office, but he pretended not to see me.

Oh well. I would get the chance to have a bit of a talk with Erica, and that was all that mattered. I still had the feeling that whatever was happening around this store, Erica was the most aware of it. At least, she was the person I'd seen around the store who was the most scared. And yeah, maybe that was because she had a teenaged stalker, but there was nothing that said a teenaged stalker couldn't also be a wolf shifter, was there? And I could already smell Erica's perfume again, if it came to that; from the strength of it, she must have bathed in it.

I knocked on the cash office door and was let in by the woman I'd seen earlier in Jin Yeong's office.

I had a quick look at her name tag, and yep! Shanae.

"What are you grinning at?" she asked.

"Nothing," I said. "Just glad I'm not working down on the floor anymore."

"Whatever," she said. "But you two better not talk all afternoon while I'm trying to do the pays. Just because Cash Office shares space with Systems doesn't mean we want to hear you talk."

"Gotcha," I said, in a friendly sort of way.

Erica, who had turned her head to see who was coming through the door, gave me an expressive look behind Shanae's back, and said, "Come and sit down. I'll show you how to tear these."

She still looked a bit anxious—maybe it was the faint line between her brows that didn't quite go away even when she was smiling at me—but she didn't look downright scared in here. Maybe the office was a safe spot for her.

It didn't smell like dog to me, though, no matter what Jin Yeong said. Just a flaming nose full of perfume—two kinds.

"These tomorrow's specials?" I asked Erica, pointing at the brightly coloured sheets piled up in front of her.

Shanae shot me a reminding sort of glare, but Erica nodded. "They go up tomorrow, while the store is still closed."

"You put 'em up?"

"That's right. Here, you fold like *this* then *this*, and tear them in thirds. Then tear bottom to top: if you layer them and tear from the bottom, they stay in order."

"Right," I said. It was an easy job; lots of time for talking, if Shanae didn't go for me with her pen.

Maybe Jin Yeong was right—maybe she was a shifter. She was aggressive enough, even if she had the bad taste to go for a vampire.

Just in case, I decided I'd better wait a few minutes before I spoke again. I was all for unmasking wolves in the store, but I'd rather not do it while I was in a room that couldn't be opened from the outside without the right key if I started screaming for help.

Just as I thought I might be able to risk talking, Erica asked me, "You're new, aren't you?"

"That's right," I agreed. "Started yesterday."

"Thanks for helping me with these. The other girl had to go home sick."

I shrugged. "Beats working downstairs. At least I can sit down in here."

"Trust me," she said. "You'll want to walk around after a couple hours of this. Oh! Not like that; do it like thi—oh no! I'm so sorry!"

"It's okay," I said, putting my finger in my mouth. From how panicked she sounded, you'd think I'd accidentally cut off a finger. "It's just a papercut. It wasn't your fault."

"I'm really sorry," she said again, darting a look across the room at Shanae and away again.

There was a fed-up sigh from Shanae's side of the office. "You don't have to keep *apologising*, Erica! She said it's okay! For pity's sake!"

Erica shrank in on herself and gave me an apologetic smile.

"I've got a bandaid," she said. "Don't put it in your mouth; it's not healthy."

She wrapped the plaster around my finger for me, and when Shanae left the office to go buy herself lunch, she said, "Sorry about her. Everyone's a bit on edge at the moment."

Heck yes. My opportunity!

"Yeah, I thought so," I said. "Is it because of the dead bloke?"

That startled her, though I don't know why. "What? Oh, you heard about that?"

"Heard about it?" I asked, deciding that a bit of honesty might be the best policy. "I found it! I came here the other day to get my groceries and I saw him out in the alley. Made me feel a bit sick."

She shuddered. "I didn't see it. I'm glad I didn't. But you still came to work?"

"Yeah. Still got bills to pay."

"How...how close did you get to *it*?"

"Too flamin' close!" I told her, and had to stop myself from running my fingers over the proof of the danger of that proximity hiding beneath the loose hair on my forehead. I had to fight a shiver, too, because if we didn't find the right wolf in time, it was gunna be me that was dead next. "Who murders a bloke near a supermarket, anyway?"

She murmured something, though I wasn't sure exactly what. She'd gone back to looking like she had when I saw Daniel following her across the parking lot.

I pushed it a bit and asked, "Did your friend come to pick you up yesterday?"

"My friend?" She looked at me in surprise, and then flushed. "Oh! Yes. That was you in the locker room. I've been having a few problems; nothing too important."

"Flamin' men," I said, nodding. "Can't take no for an answer."

She ducked her head over her tickets, but she said quietly, "Yes. You too?"

"I know a few prime specimens," I agreed. "Did it help, walking with your friend?"

"Yes." She looked up again, and this time she smiled at me. "It still felt like there was someone there, but I felt safer. I was probably just imagining it."

"Someone still followed you? You should take it to the police."

"I couldn't be sure, you know? I thought I recognised his hoodie—it's so distinctive—but I can't prove anything. And now that there's been a murder at the store, I'm even jumpier."

"Yeah." I tore a few more tickets and asked her, "You know something about the dead bloke?"

She shut down immediately. "Of course not! It's just awful, that's all, and I'm scared. Why would I know anything about it?"

"Dunno," I said, shrugging. She knew something, all right; just the fact that she was dousing herself in perfume said so. Only I couldn't really bring that up without sounding not-quite-human myself. I added, "Just you seem a bit more scared than the others, and I thought you might know something about how he got killed. That's the sort of thing you need to tell the cops, too."

"I didn't see anything," she said, scrambling her tickets together. "I wasn't there, and I didn't see anything!"

"All right, all right," I said soothingly. "I didn't say you were. But you're worried about something else, aren't you? Maybe something to do with person you were talking about?"

She was scared, yeah. But it didn't look like her fear was going to be strong enough to make her speak out—or maybe it was because she was so scared that she wouldn't speak out? I'd seen a fair bit since meeting my three psychos, and it was still putting me into a cold sweat when I remembered I'd be dead or a werewolf in less than two weeks if we didn't find our man.

"It's okay," I said. "I know a cop. He's pretty nice, and if you tell him what's going on, he'll help you."

Detective Tuatu seemed to be a concerned sort of person, so he probably would, too.

"It's nothing," she said. "Really. I think I just got scared because it was dark. It probably wasn't even him."

Okay, so she wasn't speaking because of whatever it was she was hiding, which meant there was a good chance she'd seen what happened that night, too.

"I just get scared walking home alone, these days," she said. "Do you think—do you have time to walk with me this afternoon? I don't have far to go, and my friend can't do it. Please; it would make me feel less jumpy, I think."

I was going to tell her no—I knew that Zero would tell me to go straight home, and that it would probably be a good thing for her to be scared enough to push past whatever it was she didn't want to tell.

But I caught sight of her face, miserable and pleading, and found myself saying, "Yeah, okay. But you'll have to wait until I finish."

Her face lit up straight away. "Thank you! Just...don't tell anyone, will you?"

"'Course not!" I mean, I'd have to tell Zero, obviously.

"Promise," she said.

"I really won't," I said solemnly.

Somehow I actually didn't tell Zero where I was going when I finished work. In fact, I didn't even think about it until Erica and I were on Campbell Street after work, walking down toward the city centre, and a text made my phone buzz against my leg.

I fished out my phone, and it lit with the message, *What are you doing?*

"Whoops!" I muttered.

"What is it?" asked Erica, her face anxious again. "What's wrong?"

"Nothing," I said. "Just forgot to tell someone I couldn't meet him today. He can wait."

"Your boyfriend?"

"Nah, just a bloke I was supposed to meet. I'm learning some martial arts and I'm s'posed to meet up this arvo to practise."

That was true, as far as it went. It was also the reason why I was so sore just walking today—not to mention the reason it was so nice to sit down instead of walk around the store all afternoon. It wasn't far to Erica's place, though; she had a room in a shared home above someone's optometrist business right in the middle of Hobart, and walking her home only took ten minutes.

She invited me in, but whatever her roommates were cooking turned my stomach right off and I wasn't sure I wouldn't throw up if I went in. I figured it was safer to go back home.

Especially since I hadn't answered the text from Zero.

Erica had looked so scared that I didn't like to do it while she was there. Maybe that's why it felt as though my neck was crawling as I walked back down Murray Street, tapping out an answer to the text.

Or maybe, I thought, tilting the screen of the phone just a little bit to check out the street in its mirror-surface, maybe Erica's someone was following me now.

I caught a brief glimpse of something swift and grey disappearing into a street beside me, so close that I felt the breeze from its passing, then someone grabbed me by the collar and pulled me right through the craft store's front window and into Between.

I yelled and kicked, and the hand dropped me into a dark corner where wild graffiti was growing.

It was Zero.

I let out a breath that shook, and said, "Why you gotta sneak up on me like that?"

"Why did you leave after work without Jin Yeong?"

"Sorry about that," I said, looking around at the piece of Between in interest. "I kinda forgot. That woman I was telling you about—she was scared to go home alone, so I walked with her. Oi! There's people in here!"

"There are always people Between," Zero said. "Don't change the subject."

"Yeah, but—" His eyes pinioned me, and I stopped. "I'm sorry," I said again, this time a bit less flippantly. "I forgot to tell you. She was really scared, and I think she needs watching. She knows something about the body, too."

"We'll discuss that at home," he said. "Next time, tell me where you're going first. And when I text you, answer *straight away*."

"Yes boss," I said meekly. "You still got those photos out at home?"

"Yes," he said. "Why?"

"Maybe we ought to discuss that at home, too," I said, shooting another look around us.

In Hobart, I would have been right in the middle of the curtain fabric section of a craft store. Here Between, it was still some sort of a market, and there were bolts of fabric and stuff, but the clientele was kinda different. There were about as many of them as you'd get in there at sale time, though, which was a *lot*. They didn't look like the sort to put out your eye with a knitting needle if you got to the fabric they wanted before them, but they did look like they might feel it was all right to enslave you for a few thousand years. Beautiful, haughty, and dressed in flowing fabrics, they were the closest thing to Athelas and Zero that I'd seen since I'd been popping in and out of Between. Even the fae I'd seen at the Between waystation hadn't been so effortlessly arrogant and lofty.

Zero threw a look around, curious but not worried, and said, "Hold onto my strap. Don't meet any eyes and don't talk to anyone on the way out."

"Got it, boss," I said, and turned my eyes down to watch his boots. Maybe I was right. Maybe they were the sort to enslave people for a thousand years.

No one spoke to me on the way out, though a few whispers floated on the air, and we were out again in a few seconds. When we were back on the proper Hobart streets, I stuck close to Zero anyway, and shook off a bit of the graffiti that had stuck to my shoes.

"Think there was someone following me," I said. "Did you see 'em?"

"Home first," said Zero.

When we got home he didn't seem very interested in talking, though. He sat back down at his display of paperwork and photos at the coffee table, and didn't speak until Athelas got home and I came out of the kitchen with our tray of coffee and tea with biscuits. Jin Yeong, who had been glaring at me since I got home, took his coffee from me coldly and pinched the whole plate of biscuits again.

"Doesn't matter," I told him, and smugly pulled the napkin off a second plate of biscuits. "I've got another one."

He made a dart for that one, too, but I'd already started to back away in expectation of that, and Athelas caught me.

"Must you bother the pet, Jin Yeong?" he asked, in a pained sort of way, and took the second plate of biscuits to put where he and Zero could both reach them.

Through biscuit crumbs, Jin Yeong made a sharp, annoyed complaint.

"I told you to watch the pet," Zero said mildly. "Not let it run out on the streets."

"Dear me, what an exciting day you've had, Pet," said Athelas. "Slipping your leash?"

"Nah, I just forgot to tell Zero I was walking that girl home." Zero looked at me in a silent, considering kind of way, and I added hastily, "I mean, I thoughtlessly forgot to make sure Zero knew where I was and walked that girl home. Oh. And then I didn't answer his text, either."

"Dear me!" murmured Athelas. "How unlike you, Pet!"

I didn't answer that because I wasn't sure if he was being sarcastic or not. But because Zero was paying attention to people instead of just the files, for once, I took the opportunity to say, "Oi. Zero. Where are those photos of the dead people? I wanna check something."

"What do you want to check?" asked Zero, frowning.

"Really, Pet?" Athelas said, looking amused. "I had no idea that carnage was interesting to you!"

"Not the crime scene photos!" I said hastily, going cold. That was a lucky escape. Seeing one of them in real life had been bad enough; I didn't want to refresh the memory. "Them before they were killed! Why would I want to look at their mutilated bodies?"

"One can learn a great deal from a mutilation," Athelas said, sipping his tea. "If one cares to learn."

"This one doesn't care to learn," I muttered. It had been bad enough seeing Jin Yeong do his creepy blood licking thing again the other night with the blood samples Detective Tuatu had collected. "You can keep your mutilated bodies."

"There's very little use in keeping mutilated bodies," demurred Athelas. "In fact, the idea of mutilating bodies is generally to dismember and deposit them piecemeal over an area in order to dispose of them more thoroughly."

"Hope you don't go around saying that sort of thing on the job," I told him. "Humans start to get worried when people talk like that."

"They do, don't they?" Athelas said, smiling dreamily to himself. "No doubt good to remember. I'm indebted to you, Pet!"

"Yeah? Why?"

"What are you looking for, Pet?" Zero asked again, passing a small stack of thin folders.

"Some names, I reckon," I said, opening the first of the folders. It was thin because there was only a photo and a piece of paper inside. It was a woman, one with a nice face and the name of April Post. The piece of paper was a brief rundown of her life; name, age, physical description, birthplace, workplace, family, connections. "Oi. This one worked at the supermarket, too."

"The detective said most of them did," said Zero. "The only one who didn't was the one they found furthest from the store; a tramp."

"Maybe the whole supermarket is a shifter supermarket," I said. "Flamin' dodgy! How did the police get away with covering it up for so long? This woman was killed a year ago, but the first one was two years ago!"

"That is what I'm attempting to find out," Athelas said. "I fear the detective is concerned at my presence, but really, where else could I go other than the police station?"

"I told him he should watch out for that," I said, nodding.

"I'm sure he was grateful," said Zero. "Have you found what you wanted to find, Pet?"

"Yeah," I said in satisfaction, tapping the photo of one of the men. It was labelled as *Chris Turner.* "This one; I know his name."

Zero looked up. "Why?"

"Rhonda said Shanae from cash office was keen on him before he caught sight of Erica. There was another bloke, too, but he's still alive; he moved out of state."

"How refreshing!" said Athelas. "Human drama is such a delight to watch unfold!"

"We know shifters can be possessive," Zero remarked. "Jin-Yeong, is that the human you mentioned? Shanae?"

"*Ne,*" said Jin Yeong, irritatingly self-satisfied.

Oh well. It wasn't like I had a better suspect. I mean, I had one; it was just that I wasn't convinced Daniel was really the one. I bit my thumb worriedly. *One* of us had to come up with something good; I'd already begun to feel sick at the smell of food cooking, and at this rate, I'd be dead or a wolf before I got the chance to do anything with the dryad.

"In that case, you'd better have a look around her house," said Zero. "See if you can find anything. Follow her if you can do it unnoticed."

JinYeong said something in a cold, angry-eyed way that made me think he was objecting to Zero's apparent distrust in his stealth, and threw himself down on his side of the lounge.

"I'm gunna follow Daniel, too," I said.

JinYeong shot me a look and muttered something under his breath, but Zero said, "All right. We've both got the day off work tomorrow; we'll try to find out what's going on with Daniel."

That made me feel a bit better, so when JinYeong muttered again, I grinned at him.

"It's 'cos I've got a better personality than you," I said. "If you want people to work with you, you gotta be nicer."

"Shall I look in on Erica?" asked Athelas.

"No," said Zero. "We have need of you where you are."

"Even if JinYeong's suspect is the correct person," said Athelas in gentle disagreement, tapping the pictures, "it would seem that to a certain point, the deaths revolve around this woman, Erica Kroner. The first to die was a man who—"

"The first to die was a shifter," corrected Zero. "Bianca Terry. JinYeong had a look at the samples the detective collected: there were two shifters and three human deaths. I've written the information in each file."

I looked down at the file I held, the one that said *Chris Turner*, and there in the back, on the cardboard of the file itself, was a scratching in pencil.

"I can't read this!" I complained. It was more of the same script that was on the spines and covers of all of Zero's books.

"Well now, how interesting," Athelas said. "Perhaps this investigation is within our purview, after all!"

"Thought you said the last body was infected, too," I said.

Zero nodded. "Infected, but not technically a shifter. The virus is immediately effective, but there are stages before full potency, as in your case. The final stage is when the first change or death occurs. With the blood we can guess at the age of it. The body you found had been infected just before death—a direct result of an attack from a shifter. The other two humans were infected just before death just like the last one."

"Okay, so the Chris bloke?"

"Human."

"Looks like she attracts all the weirdos," I remarked. "A shifter, an obsessed kid, a jealous co-worker—and one of 'em doesn't want her to have any other kind of relationship at all."

"The female human was killed, too," Zero said. "Unless she was also showing some kind of interest in Erica, we'll need to keep investigating other lines of thought as well as this one."

I looked at the picture of April Post again. She looked like a nice person; genuine smile that curved her eyes like half-moons and a cheerful sprinkling of freckles across her nose.

"Maybe she was a friend? Maybe she warned Erica about whatever weirdo was hanging around her at the time?"

Athelas sipped his tea and returned gently to his point. "Whatever the case, Erica does seem to be our strongest point of reference, does she not? I do feel that we should keep an eye on her as well."

"I think so," Zero agreed. "Pet, does Erica work tomorrow?"

"Half day," I said. I'd checked on the roster on my way out of work. "Just the morning, putting up special tickets. We can follow Daniel in the morning and then see what Erica does after work."

"Perhaps we should give some thought to convincing Erica to open up to Pet," suggested Athelas.

Zero shook his head. "No. We're not going to Influence anyone, if we can help it."

"You should tell Jin Yeong to stop vamping women into buying him coffee, then," I suggested.

JinYeong snarled at me, but I saw the faintest smile come and go on Zero's lips, and that made me happy.

"Pet, get up," he said. "It's time to practise."

I groaned. "I'm still dead from yesterday. And I wanna know why we can't just vamp her, too."

JinYeong said something cross, but he shut his mouth on whatever else he was going to say when I refilled his coffee cup and gave him another biscuit from the second biscuit plate.

"I was using it as a general term," I said to him. "Don't get your knickers in a knot."

Athelas' eyes got that particular glow they always get when he's laughing at something inside, and JinYeong glared at him.

"Shifters are less inclined to stay under the influence of fae and vampires than humans are," said Zero, rising to his feet. "Some of them can't be influenced at all, and if we were to attempt it on someone who turned out to be the pack leader, asking very particular questions, they would certainly know we're Enforcers. Vampires, on the other hand, are free with their skills, and it's not unusual to see one exerting those skills in everyday life. I'm not willing to risk giving away our investigation just yet. I might reconsider when we're more sure of our target. Pet, *practise.*"

CHAPTER SEVEN

It might have been nice to sleep in on a day when I didn't have to work. Might have been, except that I dreamed of fur and fangs, and hot sticky blood, and something howling or screaming that turned out to be me.

Might have been, except that I woke up to see Jin Yeong perched at the end of my bed like a particularly well-dressed vulture.

I yelled and threw something at him from under my pillow, which made him duck, eyes wide, then turn to stare at the knife that was sticking out of the wall.

"What the flamin' heck?" I yelled at him. "Why are you in my bedroom!"

"*Ya!*" he snapped back at me. "*Wae gurolka? Jjincha musowo!*"

"Scary? *I'm* scary?"

Jin Yeong reached back to pluck out the knife, and waved it at me. "*Igae mwohya?*"

I puffed out a breath and ran my fingers through my hair to get it out of my eyes. "Okay, that's fair enough. I dunno where it came from. I didn't put it under my pillow."

He narrowed his eyes at me, flicking the knife down into the bed, blade first, and said something I was pretty sure was the Korean equivalent of *liar*. I would have protested against that, but I was also pretty sure he was just trying to distract me from my initial insistence on knowing why he was in my bedroom.

"Why are you sitting on my bed?" I demanded.

JinYeong shrugged one shoulder, pointing down through the floor, and said something that had Zero's name in it.

"Zero wanted me to wake up?" I scrambled my legs out from under the covers. "All right, I'm ready."

Both of JinYeong's brows went up as he took in my jeans and t-shirt.

"What? If I go to bed dressed, I'm ready straight away in the morning," I told him, scraping back enough of my hair for a pony-tail but leaving a bit to cover the obviously wolfy part of me that was dismayingly larger this morning.

It was the morning for nasty surprises, obviously.

JinYeong made a sound of disapproval and tossed my hair-brush at me.

"What? You're not the one going around town with me," I told him, but I took the band out and brushed my hair anyway. That seemed to satisfy him, because he sauntered out of my room while I was still pulling my hair back again.

He and Zero were waiting for their breakfast when I got downstairs, JinYeong with the air of a pacing cat, and Zero with his usual emotionless fortitude. Athelas had already gone, but he must have eaten the breakfast I prepared for him last night, because the dishes were in the sink, and the tea percolator was turned off at the wall.

I made them bacon and eggs, but food smelled a bit off to me again today. Not off as if it was rotten, just...not good to eat. Beggar me. I thought food was starting to smell bad, but I hadn't expected bacon to go so quickly.

While the other two ate their breakfast, I picked and poked at mine, and at last scooped it up in a huge, messy hurry when Zero said, "Eat, Pet. We're leaving in five minutes." I didn't want to be hungry while we were hunting around Daniel's house.

That turned out to be a bad idea, because I lost the whole lot of it behind someone's rose bush about fifteen minutes after we left the house. It would have been in front of the rose bush, but Zero heard me gagging and shoved me behind the bush before I had a chance to do anything except double over.

Maybe I should have tried to crouch, because what with gravity and everything, half of it came out of my mouth, and the other half came up through my nose. Let me tell you, fried egg is *not* something you wanna have up your nose. I groaned for a bit while Zero looked doubtfully at me over the bush and offered me a handkerchief.

I wanted to remark on the fact that he was carrying a hand-kerchief—I mean, who still carries a handkerchief these days?—but all that came out when I opened my mouth was a wet gurgle and another explosion of undigested breakfast. I was crouched lower to the ground this time, so it only came through my mouth.

When it stopped, I blew the chunks of egg out of my nose and spat the rest of the foul-tasting stuff out of my mouth. Great. Athelas had said I'd start to throw food up as my body started to change, but I'd expected it to take a bit longer.

"Happening pretty quickly, isn't it?" I said thickly, feeling the patch of fur on my forehead.

Zero smacked my hand away and said, "Don't play with it. Are you ready?"

"Feeling great!" I croaked, trying not to shiver. I still felt sick, but I didn't think it was my symptoms—not directly, anyway. "Here's your hanky."

He avoided that hand. "Wash it first. I don't want it."

I tucked it into my pocket instead. I hadn't really thought he'd take it, but sometimes if you do something quickly enough, it takes him by surprise. I think humans surprise him sometimes— or maybe they just remind him of things. Things like throwing up, and messes, and stuff that isn't fae-perfect. Normal things.

I suppose Jin Yeong found the address for us at work, because Zero led us straight to the right place. It was a run-down old house that was closer to Moonah than North Hobart, and Daniel was just coming out of the door when we approached, his hands shoved into his hoodie and the silver spikes on the shoulders of it catching the sun.

I suddenly remembered Erica saying something about a hoodie—*a very distinctive hoodie*, she'd called it. It was the same one I'd seen him wear to work every day, if it came to that.

"Gotcha!" I muttered.

Zero, quietly, said, "Hush, Pet. Keep walking."

That surprised me, because if we kept walking we would be face to face with Daniel. I kept walking anyway because I'm an obedient pet, and I supposed Zero did something to the way we appeared, because Daniel didn't really look at us as we crossed his path.

He did draw in a breath and look faintly puzzled when my shoulder brushed his in passing, but maybe that was just because his breakfast was disagreeing with him, too.

We kept walking for a bit, then Zero turned us around at the top of the street and we crossed to the other side.

"Slowly, Pet," he murmured. "Don't make sudden moves and stop bouncing so much when you walk."

"Can't help it," I said. "That's how I walk."

"Then you'll need to learn how to walk again," said Zero, without pity. "Otherwise you'll ruin every covert operation you're involved in."

I didn't mention the fact that pets didn't usually go along on covert operations, because I thought he might have forgotten about that, and I didn't want to remind him. I was happy being a pet who went along on covert operations.

"I'll practise when I'm not practising my sword-work," I said, a bit gloomily. "Oi, where's he going? That's not a road!"

Ahead, Daniel jumped the fence into someone's yard, his sneakers flying. His hoodie bobbed up and down and then ducked under another section of fence that imperfectly spanned a gully, disappearing into the murky depths of a storm water drain.

"He can't do that!" I said indignantly. "Flamin' rude!"

Zero's eyes flicked down to me. "Keep your voice down."

"You working a spell or something?"

"I'm dispersing notice, and it doesn't work as well if someone is making themselves noticeable."

"Yeah, but it's a spell, right?"

Zero breathed out the faintest of sighs, and pulled me Between, where the fence didn't exist. "It's not...it's similar. Spells require items and setup; I'm using my birthright. Pure magic."

"You get that sort of thing as a birthright when you're born Behind?"

"No," said Zero. "I was born in the human world. The birthright is because of who my parents are, not where I was born."

"So can I do spells?"

"No. You need a certain amount of inborn magic to do spells."

"Inborn magic is the stuff you get for being born Behind?"

"Yes." Zero stopped by the storm drain, and I heard the faint sound of Daniel at the end of the tunnel, then silence. When it was silent, Zero stepped into the storm drain.

"How come I can pull stuff from Between, then?" I asked in a hushed voice, following him.

There was a brief moment of silence, and I got the feeling that it was very grudgingly that Zero said, "We don't know. It's not supposed to be possible for a human to affect Between."

"Maybe that's my birthright," I said, very much pleased with myself. We emerged from the storm drain onto a familiar street; New Town Road, that would later turn into Elizabeth Street, or onto Argyle, depending on which way we went. Either way, it led in one direction: Daniel was going toward Hobart city centre. "Oi. I reckon this little rat is going to Erica's place."

"Perhaps."

He was going to Erica's place, though. I felt a bit smug about that; when we got to Murray Street and I was certain of it, I said to Zero, "Oi. Let's stop here for a while. Buy us some coffee at one of the cafés."

To my surprise, Zero did. He said, "Sit here. Don't leave," at the café across from Erica's shared house, and went in to order. That left me to watch Daniel, who was loitering as suspiciously as most boys his age wearing hoodies did loiter.

He didn't try to get through the locked door at the bottom where Erica had gone in last night; he mizzled along the front of the place instead, and ducked into the alleyway beside it, threading between the wheelie bins. From what I'd seen yesterday, it was a residential carpark for Erica's house and the apartments behind. Daniel kept walking through, his hands shoved in his pockets and his head swinging from side to side at a steady rate.

Daniel was sniffing around—literally, if I was seeing what I thought I was seeing. I remembered Rhonda telling me that someone had been urinating around the storeroom, and tried not to grin. Was he marking his territory, or checking on other potential visitors?

A cardboard cup settled in front of me on the table and I smelled the creamy scent of cappuccino. Nice. Hadn't had one of those in a while.

"Where's the boy?" asked Zero.

"Circling the house," I told him. "Dunno what he's looking for, but he's looking for something."

"Mm," said Zero. From him, that was almost an exclamation. Zero was very interested.

He settled himself carefully into the spindly outdoor chair, watching the house steadily. It couldn't have been too comfortable, but once he'd stretched out his legs across half the footpath he didn't look quite so cramped.

My interest waned pretty quickly, though; all Daniel did was go around the place a couple more times. When the display on my phone told me it was quarter to eleven, he turned back onto Murray Street and started to walk toward the mall again.

"What's he doing?" I muttered to myself, picking up the half-empty cappuccino. "Hang on—Erica finishes at eleven. Is he going up to meet her?"

"Not to meet her," said Zero. "I doubt he'll be in sight when she comes out."

"Yeah, he's got the creeper vibe all right," I said. Stupid kid. He was good looking enough to be able to attract girls—why was he going for one so much older than himself, who was not just uninterested in him, but possibly scared of him? "Is that a werewolf thing, too?"

"Shifter," Zero said. "Yes, quite often. The wolf side of their brain is often melded tightly with the human side, and it leads to unbalanced thinking."

"Great. So I'm gunna turn into a stalker?"

"No. You're not going to turn into anything."

"Hey, I'd be a real pet, then," I said. I saw my smile in the reflection of a store window as we passed it, and it was a heck of a lot gaunter than I meant it to be. I stopped.

We followed Daniel all the way back to the supermarket before we went home, leaving him to follow Erica back to her place. There were enough people on the streets that Zero didn't seem worried to leave Erica to Daniel's stalking, and I didn't think he'd listen if I objected, anyway.

I was starving by then, and even more so by dinner time, but the only thing that really looked good to eat was the steak I'd bought on the day I found the murdered bloke. The sickening thing about that was that I was salivating just at the sight of it in the fridge, raw and bloody. I shut the fridge with a shudder and slapped a pan on the stovetop. I was gunna cook the steak, and I was gunna cook it *well*.

No way I was going to eat bloody steak.

I cooked the steaks until the juices ran out and until I couldn't stand it anymore. It wasn't cooked as much as I told myself it was going to be cooked, but it smelled so good. The smell must have been too much for my psychos, too; they were all at the table before I took the steaks off the stove top.

"I can see you two looking at each other," I said to Zero and Athelas accusatorily, but I ate my steak anyway. I already knew things were progressing too flamin' quickly. I didn't really need them to tell me.

By the next morning, I was ravenous again, but the steaks were gone and nothing in the house smelled good to eat, so I went to work with Jin Yeong hungry, angry, and scared. He seemed amused by my moodiness; maybe he thought he was the cause of it, or maybe he just liked me being scared. At any rate, he said something in Korean that I was pretty sure interpreted as a demand to meet him for lunch.

"Whatever," I said, and stomped off through the store. I didn't know what the idea was with Jin Yeong wanting to make sure I ate around him lately, but I wasn't going to do it if I could get away with it.

I worked with Daniel again, which was just as fun as it had been the first time, though I wasn't sure which one of us was the most annoyed about it. I probably should have been trying to winkle information out of him, but I was cranky and hungry, and too busy trying to make sure I got out for lunch before Jin Yeong without making it look like I was trying if Zero asked me about it.

In the end, I didn't really have to try. Daniel vanished somewhere just a bit before lunch, and when I trailed outside with Rhonda and the other smokers to get a bit of sunshine, I could see into Jin Yeong's office. He was still surrounded by women, and I was pretty sure at least two of the girls currently in his office weren't even from the store.

He looked a bit more impatient than I was used to seeing him when he was surrounded by women, but when he looked down and saw me sitting there with the smokers, he looked amused again.

I smirked at him and his bevy and saw the brief sideways flick of his eyes that was as close as Jin Yeong got to rolling his eyes, his mouth pursed. Oh well, at least I'd have my lunch to myself; unless Jin Yeong used his manipulative powers on the whole room of women at once, he was going to be where he was for a while.

The smokers went back in before Jin Yeong's crowd of women dispersed, but I stayed where I was. I was feeling a bit raw about Jin Yeong's general, as well as particular evils, and I didn't want to spend more time with him than I had to. It wasn't like I had anything to report, anyway. Erica was still in the store, and so was Daniel—wait, no he wasn't.

He passed me at a bit of a lope, out through the lunch room and into the sunshine I'd stretched out my legs into. He gave me a bit of grunt in passing, which I suppose you could say was progress, and legged it past the grey-suited man who was just approaching across the back parking lot.

Should I text Zero about Daniel? I wondered, watching his black sneakers trot across the parking lot. But Erica hadn't left the store, and that was all we were worried about at the moment.

A cool shadow fell across my sun-warmed legs, and someone said, "Good afternoon."

I blinked and looked up. That was weird. Grey suit hadn't gone past me and through the alley to the front of the store; he was standing in front of me.

"You talking to me?" I asked.

"You're the girl who found something distressing in the alley," he said. It was hard to see exactly what his face looked like—it gave the impression of greyness, like his suit, but I was pretty sure that wasn't what it really looked like. "You're the one."

I didn't like the way he said it—that was kind of grey, too—so I said, "Yeah. A body with the hand torn off."

He crouched in front of me and asked very gently, "Are you sure?"

I pulled my legs up out of his shadow and crossed them beneath me on the milk crate. Ah, there was the sun again! I slowly folded my arms across my chest as well, and leaned back into the wall so that I could see his face better.

Grey, shadowy smudginess.

I tilted my head and looked the other way; and maybe I tricked my mind by doing that, because suddenly I saw it—the uncertainty of *Betweenness* to that grey smudge of face. I tilted my head back the other way.

Grey shadow.

Tilted my head again.

Thin, sallow face with gaunt cheeks and huge eyes and mouth. Was it just my imagination, or did he have—

Nope, he *definitely* had wings. They were bigger than he was and triangular at the top, like moth wings, all furry and soft and creepy.

I focused on his face again, hoping I hadn't gone as white as I felt, and tried my hardest to pretend that I couldn't see either face or wings.

Ah heck. I should have eaten lunch with Jin Yeong.

"You didn't answer me," prompted Moth Man, his voice just as gentle as it had been before.

I got the feeling he was used to people being a bit spacy around him. Question was, should I be going along with the vague, threatening undercurrent that suggested I was better off saying I *wasn't* sure, or should I be sticking to my guns?

Another shadow, this one in bloody ink, spread across the sunny bitumen and darkened Moth Man's lighter shadow.

"*Mwoh hanun kkoya?*" asked Jin Yeong.

I huffed out a breath of relief into my cheeks but didn't let it right out. I didn't want Jin Yeong to know I was glad to see him—how glad I was to hear him ask someone else what the heck they were doing.

"How interesting," said the Moth Man, backing away infinitesimally. "It's quite the circus at this location."

He said it casually—even relaxedly—but there were fingernail-length hairs standing up and quivering on the back of his neck, and if I'd been able to clearly see the things I was pretty sure were antennae on top of his head, I reckon they would have been quivering, too. Moth Man did *not* feel comfortable around Jin Yeong.

Jin Yeong stalked forward, smiling with eyes that glittered like rubies, and the Moth Man took another step back, then another, matching him step for step.

I grinned properly for the first time that day. That'd teach old Moth Man to try and frighten a defenceless human.

I heard Jin Yeong speaking in Korean; nothing I could understand, but just like the humans who do what he tells them to do regardless of what language he uses, the Moth Man responded to him as if he perfectly understood him. Maybe it's a Behindkind thing.

He didn't just back away this time. He spun on slender feet, a swirling confusion of grey suit and grey wings, and walked away rapidly. Jin Yeong gave a small, smug tug to the hem of his jacket and turned back toward me, smoothing back the hair that had fallen over his forehead.

"Things got a bit hectic escaping the mob?" I enquired, tilting my chin up at the office window. They must have, if Jin Yeong's hair had fallen out of place.

Jin Yeong paused in the act of fixing his hair to look at me quizzically. He considered for a moment, then said, with a tilt of his nose, "*Ne.*"

"Good thing you did," I said, willing to congratulate him on his usefulness, even if I didn't want to let him know exactly how grateful I was. "That bloke was pretty creepy. Who was he?"

He shrugged one shoulder.

"You must know who he is!" I protested. "He knows who you are!"

"*Ne,*" agreed Jin Yeong, looking very pleased with himself.

"What, just 'cos he knows you, doesn't mean you know him? Rubbish! He was asking me about finding the body. Hang on."

Jin Yeong sighed and reached out to pinch my collar between his fingers. "*Durowa, Petteu.*"

"Hang on," I said again, as he dragged me back into the store by my collar. "He's one of the Upper Management blokes, isn't he?"

He didn't answer, just pushed me ahead of him toward the storeroom.

"This is bullying in the workplace," I told him. Jin Yeong was very bad at being undercover. I suppose if I could just make people think they didn't see what they saw, I might be a bit more lax as well. "You can't go pushing your staff members around."

Jin Yeong ignored that as well, and marched me right out to the storeman's desk.

"What is it, Jin Yeong?" asked Zero, without looking up from his paperwork.

There was a spate of Korean, in which I heard the words *Pet* and *idiot*. I said, "Oi!" indignantly.

"Jin Yeong wants to know why you didn't meet with him for your break," Zero said, scribbling a fake set of initials on several pages of paperwork.

"Why would I meet with him on my break?" I protested. "I'm supposed to be poking my nose around the place."

"I see," said Zero. "Then why were you sitting outside alone?"

I wasn't going to tell him I'd been outside because it was bad enough turning into something alien and Behindkind, without having to spend my break with something alien and Behindkind.

"Spying on people," I told him.

"Don't. You're here to stay in the building and talk to anyone foolish enough to talk to you."

"Who was that bloke? The mothy one?"

"Someone who has been following you for the past two days."

Ohhhhh. So they'd been talking about *Pet's shadow*, not the *next shadow*. "That thing's been following me and you didn't tell me?"

"We wanted to see if he'd approach you. He possibly wouldn't have if he knew you knew he was following you."

I thought about that. "Oh," I said. "Then why are you slapping my wrist for sitting outside?"

"Because I prefer to be obeyed, Pet," said Zero, with a hint of ice in his voice, "and because I wanted to control the meeting."

"Sorry," I said hastily. "You want to know what he said?"

"Yes."

"He asked me if I was the girl who saw something nasty in the alley, and when I told him yes, he got a bit mothier and asked me if I was *sure*."

"What did you say to him?"

"Didn't get a chance to say anything," I told him. "Jin Yeong came out just then and scared him off."

Jin Yeong said something in an interested voice, tipping his head at me, and I thought I heard the word for *eyes*.

"Yes," said Zero, putting aside his paperwork at last and looking at us properly. "I'd like to know that, as well. You're not feeling dizzy?"

"Nope. His face made me a bit sick, but that was only because it was hard to see him with all the blurriness."

"It's not wise to try and see the face of a sandman," Zero said. "They don't like it."

"I didn't like it much, either! He was flamin' creepy."

"Go back to work," he said. "We'll speak tonight. Jin Yeong, stay and talk with me for a while. You have to sign these as well."

I left while Jin Yeong was sulkily demanding to know *why* he had to sign the papers, and went back to work.

―――――

CHAPTER EIGHT

―――――

"Hang on," I said, early the next day. "I thought you didn't want me going around by myself because of Moth Man?"

I'd been having more dreams of death and blood, and I wasn't sure I *wanted* to be going around Hobart by myself anymore. What if I turned into a wolf while I was by myself?

"That was before he attempted to make contact," said Athelas. "Now that he knows you're protected, he won't bother you again. A pity we didn't take the chance to question him properly, JinYeong."

JinYeong lazily bared his teeth at Athelas, but I got the impression he was moodily annoyed at something.

I huffed a silent sigh into the top of my hoodie. I suppose it was too much to hope that they'd actually been concerned about *me*; as soon as they needed more food, off I went to the supermarket to get groceries and walk Erica home. She'd asked me yesterday when I left for the day if I would walk her home, and I hadn't been able to give her a proper answer because I didn't think the psychos would let me out by myself.

A bit grumpy now, I asked, "Won't that give us away, though?

If they know I'm the one who found the body, and I'm working there now?"

"I don't believe so," Athelas said. "Most likely, they'll assume you were already a staff member. From what I've been able to ascertain at the police station, they don't work directly with anyone at the supermarket—they merely receive orders when there is something that needs to be cleaned up. To find the connection, I believe we need to look higher in the force."

That was both frightening and relieving, though I wasn't sure which emotion was stronger.

"So even if he thinks it's weird that there's a vampire at the store, looking after a human, he won't necessarily mention it to anyone?"

"*Kugae aniya*," muttered Jin Yeong. *That's not it.*

"What?" I snapped. "What's not right? You weren't looking after me? Tell me something I don't know!"

Jin Yeong sat up, offended. "*Ya! No demae—nol wihae—!*"

"What did you do for me?" I demanded. "Turned me into a flamin' wolf, that's what!"

Jin Yeong stared at me for a moment, then snapped, "*Ah, taesso! Petteu—*"

"He'll report back to his superiors, but there's no reason for them to report it any further," said Zero, interrupting us both without compunction. "They've done their job as far as possible; they probably don't have any orders regarding Behindkind, just humans. They'll think you're already under control; they'll concentrate on the detective, now."

"Okay," I said, slightly less grumpily, turning away from the glaring Jin Yeong. I hadn't actually expected them to let me out on my own; I'd just asked because we were starting to run out of stuff to eat. Well, we were running out of stuff that didn't make my stomach turn. Looked like I was gunna be buying a lot of steak in that week's shopping.

"What about the detective, though?" I asked Zero.

"The detective can look after himself," he said. "Don't be late going to the store, Pet. Erica finishes at noon; you can walk her home if she asks you."

"Got it," I said, and went upstairs to grab my sneakers.

It was nice to go out of the house again without an escort, mostly because I could sneak the dryad out. I couldn't do anything today about turning into a wolf, but I *could* do something about the dryad. Maybe.

So I took it with me for a walk. I had to do the grocery shopping anyway, so maybe it would take me somewhere useful when I did. I was planning on going straight to the supermarket as usual, but as I came to Elizabeth Street I caught sight of a familiar hoodie.

Daniel? Wasn't he supposed to be at work?

My plans changed faster than the lights. I watched him for a bit before I fell in behind him; there was nobody obviously following him, and Zero and Jin Yeong were now both at work, so I felt safe to follow him without getting picked up by either side.

Paranoid, maybe. But I'm not dead yet, either, am I?

It was a bright, sunny day outside, which the dryad seemed to like. I could feel it settling in the pocket of my hoodie, though it didn't actually move. It was a weird feeling; sort of ticklish and pleasant at the same time. And it didn't seem to mind me following Daniel, either, even though it had nothing to do with what I'd come out to do.

When he got to the turning at Maccas and the police station, I saw his footsteps falter. It wasn't likely that he had a desperate need for a burger, so maybe he had something to do at the cop shop?

He kept walking, though, and I wondered if I'd imagined it. It's not like the police station would be a particularly comfortable place for someone who was stalking a woman—unless he actually was a shifter and was there to talk to the people in Upper Management as the pack leader, or something. There had to be a reason the cops weren't following up on the murders, after all.

By the time I'd followed Daniel all the way from the street and up through the Cat and Fiddle Arcade, I'd started to wonder if he wasn't just out for a walk. Maybe he really was just skipping work for the fun of it.

Maybe not, though; he took the outer staircase to the parking garage, which would only make sense if he had a car, and I knew he didn't. I listened to him climb the first few levels from the bottom of the stairwell before I went after him. Maybe he was meeting with someone.

Unfortunately for me, I lost him by the time I got to the fourth level.

I leaned against the window and panted for a while. I was gunna have to ask Zero for more tips on following people. Not to mention do a bit more training so I wouldn't be so puffed out after only climbing a few floors' worth of stairs.

I could have been imagining it, but the dryad seemed heavy with disappointment—maybe it thought I could have done a better job tailing Daniel, too.

"Sorry," I panted at it. "I haven't had enough lessons yet! I wasn't bobbing, at least!"

I puffed out my cheeks and managed to catch my breath again at last. I put the dryad on the windowsill so I didn't crush it while I was flopping against the wall like a wounded dugong, and caught sight of something interesting outside the window.

I said to the dryad, "Oi. That a friend of yours?"

The window was one of the ones that are threaded with chicken wire between layers of glass, and it was pretty dirty, but I could still see through it enough to see the building opposite us. On the side of it, all mossy and drippy, was the greenish shape of a bearded man. Just the face and the beard, but it was enough to make me grin. Maybe it really was a friend of the dryad, too, because I could have sworn things felt less weighty around me.

"You playing games with me?" I asked the dryad. It said nothing, as usual, but one of its roots unfurled from the rock and settled against the dirty window. I nodded. "Got it. He's a friend of yours. You can visit for a bit, but only if I can figure out how to get over there."

A section of the concrete stairwell in the corner bubbled with old, hard chewing gum, but I knew that if I looked at it the right way, it was also tiny round flowers that grew Between. That was all right, and the damp-streaked walls were all right, too; the damp swayed in a soft breeze like the fronds of fern that they were Between, and it wouldn't be too hard to push through those, feeling the soft green tickle of them across my face and hands.

The difficult bit was getting across to the green man. There was no way up from the ground without pulling the fire escape on the other side, and I wasn't tall enough to do that. And from here, if you looked at it like a normal human, there was only a banner strung across from my side to the fire escape platform.

If I looked at it like a normal human who could see Between, things were different.

I picked up the dryad and slipped it into my pocket again. I wasn't supposed to be going Between when Zero and the others weren't with me, but there were a few things I wasn't meant to do that I did.

I blame Athelas. He's always encouraging me to do stuff I shouldn't do. I just haven't been trained right.

When the dryad was in my pocket and couldn't see anything—could it see, anyway?—I had a quick look up and down the empty stairway and brushed aside the trailing ferns that would have been damp concrete if I didn't know how to look at them. There was a cold step through concrete, or into Between, and I put my foot carefully down on the tough, twiny bough that was a banner in the human world.

It bounced a bit beneath my foot, but only enough to let me know it was healthy, and I stepped down with my other foot, too, my fingers trailing up along the ferns for that little bit of extra balance until I could feel another branch there, too.

I let out my breath in relief. Technically speaking, I could balance on a branch this broad, but it was four stories down, and I didn't really want to trust myself that much. Across from me, the green man seemed to be shrouded in more greenery than I remembered, the whiteness of the wall around him standing out in pale relief.

He moved, beard swaying in the breeze I could feel across my face, and light tendrils of fluffy moss floated across to tickle my arms and legs. I let go of the branch above me, hoping with a sudden gulp that I hadn't made a *very bad* mistake, but the moss only curled delicately around my wrists, a comforting balance on either side that felt like it held me up, light as it was.

I meant to clamber over the railing to safety when I got as far as the fire escape landing on the other side, bringing myself and the dryad back into the human world where we belonged, but somehow it felt more comfortable to sit down on the branch instead, curling my legs underneath its mossy belly.

The fluffy, clinging moss came with me and crept up my arms a bit further when I looked up at the almost-face in green moss above me.

"Hi," I said to him, feeling the flutter of breeze across my face. I reached into my pocket slowly, careful not to hurt the clinging plant life around my arms, and the dryad emerged in a happy burst of greenery. "The dryad said you were a friend, so I bought him over to say hello."

"Ah," said a deep, earthy voice, with the scratch of ancient paint to it. "I was curious to know who carried with them a dryad, and why."

I gestured at the boughs that festooned the space between buildings, deepening the green shadows around us, and asked, "Did you do this? Or did I come in by myself?"

"I let you in," he said. "This...is always this."

It probably wasn't wise to ask too many questions, but I couldn't help asking, "Did someone put you up there, or did you grow?"

"Neither," he said. "This is but one facet of me. There are others—we exist through the layers and emerge on any surface we wish."

He *said* 'surface' but I was pretty sure that when he said it, he meant something deeper than what I would mean if I said it. Like maybe he was talking about the surface of reality instead of the surface of the building.

That brought a chill to the back of my neck, but it also made me bold enough to ask another question. "Do you know what I should do with the dryad?"

"If you wish," the Green Man said, "you may leave it in the crack beneath me."

I looked down, and near my knee were a couple of damaged bricks that had left a deep cleft in the wall. It was damp and cool and probably just big enough to slot the dryad in; but I didn't think it would be able to grow much.

A tendril of something thin and alive wrapped around my finger. This time it wasn't the Green Man's moss; it was the dryad's roots, straying from their rock.

"Don't mean to be rude," I said, hoping the Green Man wouldn't push me off the branch, "but I don't think it wants to do that."

"It doesn't," said the Green Man. "Dryads are meant for protection and wisdom. Here, I am all the wisdom and protection needed."

"Do you mean it can't be happy if it's not doing what it's meant to do?"

"Nothing in life is content to do that for which it was not formed. Nor content not doing that for which it was formed."

I thought about that for a bit, and asked, "Yeah, all right, but why did you tell me I could leave it, then?"

"You are not a dryad."

"Yeah, but I'm looking after it for now. I can't just leave it somewhere if it's not going to be happy."

"You can do so," the Green Man said pleasantly.

I nearly said *All right, mum*, at him, but managed to change it to, "All right then; I *won't* do it."

"So I see. What will you do?"

"Don't know," I said, and sighed silently. "What should I do? Where's a good place for me to plant it?"

"A cleft in the wall," said the Green Man.

For a minute, I thought he was prompting me once again to leave the dryad with him. I frowned, ready to reiterate that I wasn't going to do that, when something clicked in place in my brain.

"It's supposed to fill a gap where things could fall apart, isn't it? Like when someone's in a dangerous place or needs help? Ath —my friend said it's protection and wisdom, too."

The Green Man didn't smile, but there was a sudden fragrant breath of breeze that tickled across my face as well as his, stirring moss.

"You listen well," he said.

"Been told that," I said, grinning. Mostly it wasn't a compliment, though. "So if I know of someone who's in a dangerous place, the dryad will try to protect him and make a stop-gap?"

"It is its nature. You don't mean to keep it?"

"Nah," I said. There was a heck of a cleft in the wall of my life, but there was also a pretty big protector standing there; and so long as I was a good pet, it would stay like that. Anyway, there were at least two people I could think of that needed it more. "So, what? I have to find an actual hole in a wall to plant it, or are we talking a metaphysical wall?"

"Nearby is enough," the Green Man said. "All living things need one safe space to call their own. The dryad will do best at that place."

"Okay," I said. I had a bit of an idea tickling around in my brain, and this time it didn't involve the bearded bloke. I wondered if I should say thank you and leave, or if I was supposed to wait until he dismissed me.

To my relief, he said, "If you are looking for your friend who came before you, he is directly below us. He went down by a different set of stairs."

I beamed at him. "Thank you! Reckon you can help me get down there quietly? And maybe without using the stairs?"

The Green Man didn't reply, but a slithering of vines crept around me, inadvertently pulling up the hood of my hoodie and tickling one ankle. They closed gently around me and as gently lowered me toward the earth beneath. As I got closer the mossy earth tessellated and I began to see that it was pavement again instead of dirt.

I hastily tucked the dryad back into my pocket where it wouldn't be seen, and straightened my hood. I was just in time; it was hard to tell exactly when I left the Between area for the human world, but someone saw me as I started to walk forward again and got out of my way.

I saw Daniel to my right, sitting at one of the bolted down tables in the food area, and pulled my hood that way a bit more, turning to the side. There was a café nearby, so I went and bought myself some hot chips. I hadn't dared to eat breakfast, and the chips didn't smell too dreadful to me.

Besides, I needed somewhere to sit so that Daniel wouldn't see me if we were going to loiter for much longer.

I paid for my chips and would have sat down, but Daniel got up and started walking again. Grumbling, I left the seated area with my cup of chips and sauntered along the edges of the food court, trying not to bob up and down so much.

I ate one of my chips. It tasted weird, but it didn't make me throw up, so that was nice. Even if Daniel didn't notice me throwing up, someone else was bound to, and I didn't want to lose him again in the kerfuffle. I saw him duck into the covered walkway that led to Liverpool Street and cut across the food court a bit more to keep up.

I was too late; by the time I stepped into the walkway, colourful shops to either side of me, I couldn't see him at all.

"Flaming heck!" I muttered to myself. It felt like everything was slipping away from me; Daniel, life, sanity—humanity. And it felt like there was nothing I could do about any of it.

I kept walking anyway, kicking moodily at the pavement. I hadn't got the shopping for this week yet, so I might as well go to the supermarket by going the long way around.

I made a face at myself in the shop windows as I passed, startling one of the sushi girls who looked up at the wrong time, and the next minute found myself dragged by the collar into a dark, open doorway.

"Got you!" said a voice, as the door slammed shut.

"Ow!" I said indignantly, but the hand around my throat didn't get any looser. Someone fumbled at the wall and a light flickered on, but I already recognised the voice.

Daniel looked down at me grimly and asked, "Why are you following me?"

"That's flamin' rich! I'm minding my own business, eating chips. Ah man, you spilled half of 'em!"

"Don't lie to me," he said. "I saw you near the police station and again when I went through the Cat and Fiddle."

"You're dreaming," I said.

"*And* I smelled you all around my place last night when I got back," he said. "I don't like people following me."

"Funny, that," I said. "With how much you follow Erica around. What's that about?"

"That's none of your business!" snarled Daniel, and there was wild yellow to his hazel eyes.

Beggar me. I wished, fleetingly, that Zero was around.

"You'd better start talking," Daniel said, between his teeth. "Why are you following me?"

My newly awakened nose told me something useful. "'Cos you smell good," I said.

He gave a heavy sigh, like he was used to this sort of thing, and let go of my collar. "It's not much good sniffing after me. I'm not interested."

I tried very hard not to roll my eyes. What a galah.

"Anyway," he said, "it's probably just because you're so young and I'm the first one you've smelt."

Hah! He *was* a shifter! I knew it! And he knew I knew it— more importantly, he also knew I was newly turning wolf myself.

Once the elation of a correct suspicion died away, I looked at him dubiously. Was that him trying to be kind about rejecting my supposed advances? Okay, maybe he wasn't a complete galah.

Daniel mistook my dubious look, and said, "It's true. Everything smells different before your first time; you'll find someone a lot better than me when you can judge properly with your nose. You shouldn't be eating that stuff, either."

I glanced down at my chips. "What? Why?"

"You'll just throw it up again," he said. "You should be eating meat right now. If you want to transition safely, I mean."

"Listen, Wolf Boy," I said, "I'm not eating raw meat."

He stiffened. "Don't call me Wolf Boy."

"Why not? It's true."

"I'm not a b—" he stopped in irritation, and asked, "How would you like it if I called you Wolf Girl?"

"Me? I don't care. You can call me what you want." It wasn't like being called Pet was better than being called Wolf Girl, after all. It wasn't my name, either.

Daniel opened and closed his mouth, then said, "Whatever. Don't follow me from now on!"

"You can't tell me what to do," I said to his retreating back; but I wasn't really talking to him. "You're not my owner."

Daniel, from further up the stairs, said impatiently, "Are you coming?"

"Yep!" I said, and hurried up the stairs after him. "Hang on, are you inviting me into someone else's house?"

"It's not a house," he said, and plucked the chip cup out of my hand. He threw it in the bin, disregarding my complaints, and put a frying pan on the stovetop. From the fridge, he took a very big steak, red and soft and delicious.

I nearly choked on my own saliva and coughed to try and hide it.

"It's a cooking school," Daniel said. "A friend of mine owns it."

"What are you doing?" I asked.

Daniel rolled his eyes, but didn't answer. The pan waited on the stovetop until I saw the heat shimmer, then he threw the steak in. It sizzled for about ten seconds before he turned it over and did the same for the other side.

My stomach grumbled so loudly he could have heard it from outside. I saw his cheeks curve in what must have been a grin, but by the time he turned around again with the steak on a plate his face was back to its usual sullen droop.

"Eat it and go home," he said, dropping the plate in front of me with a knife and fork. "I don't have time to waste with you. I've got somewhere to go."

I wanted to tell him again that he wasn't the boss of me, but I was too hungry. I was so hungry that when the red juices ran out from the steak, even the colour didn't put me off. From first cut to last piece, I only took a minute to eat it, and then I sat back with the satisfied feeling that *at last* I had eaten. That was stupid, because I'd mostly eaten well up until yesterday; but somehow it felt as though I had eaten bubbles all week instead, and that I'd finally been able to eat real food for the first time in that week.

"If you've finished, go away," Daniel said. He took the plate from me and ran it under the tap. "Go on; out."

I did as I was told, skipping down the stairs before he could get any more aggro than he was. I could see enough of Between around the place to guess that I could get away if he got angry and turned wolf, but there was nothing to stop him coming after me, so I'd prefer to be out on the street before I annoyed him too much.

He followed me and locked the door behind us in a pointed sort of way.

"What?" I demanded. "I didn't sneak in—you grabbed me! What's the hurry, anyway?"

"I told you; I've got somewhere I've got to be in twenty minutes."

"Funny, that," I told him instead, grinning. "I got somewhere to be, too."

He looked at me in distrust, but started off down the arcade. "Where?"

"Give you two guesses." I was pretty sure I knew where he was going, so he might as well know I was going there, too, now that we were out in the open again.

"I'm not playing stupid games with you," he said, and lengthened his stride until he was a couple metres ahead.

I followed at the same trot I use with Zero but hung back a bit more than usual. It didn't really matter whether he got there a bit quicker than me or not; we were going to the same place, and Erica didn't finish for another fifteen minutes at least.

It wasn't until I turned up Campbell Street after him that Daniel spun on his heel, glaring at me. "I told you not to follow me!"

"Not following you," I said smugly, without stopping. "I'm going to the supermarket, too."

"Are you—you walked Erica home the other day, didn't you?"

"Yep."

He stared at me, angry and baffled in equal measure. "Just go home!"

I kept walking and passed him by. "What, and let a little creeper like you follow her home? Yeah, I don't think so."

"I'm not a creeper!" snapped Daniel, striding after me.

"Yeah? You look pretty creepy to me."

Daniel grabbed my arm and hauled me around to face him. "Don't bother Erica! I'm warning you, Pet—!"

I kicked him in the shin and yanked my arm free while he was still swearing and hopping.

"You're flamin' lucky I've only had a couple of training sessions!" I told him. "Otherwise you'd be in trouble!"

"You can't kick me!" he said.

It was the shock in his voice that made me curious.

"I can, you know," I said. "I just did."

"You're younger than me!" he said, in disbelief. "You haven't even turned yet! You should be susceptible to my commands— you shouldn't even think twice about obeying!"

"Dunno," I said, "but you're susceptible to my sneakers, so I'd flamin' watch it, if I were you."

Daniel, his eyes glinting yellow again, said, "Do *not* kick me in the shins again!"

I felt a tug of acquiescence somewhere deep in my conscious- ness, faint and annoying and oddly difficult to resist, so I kicked him in the shin again.

"You're not my owner!"

Daniel gave a yelp of pain and grabbed that shin. "Stop it! If you were already with a pack, you should have said!"

"Why should I tell you anything?" I demanded. I suppose I was already in a pack, if it came to that. Zero, Athelas and Jin Yeong were bloodthirsty, non-human and deadly; close enough to wolves.

I heard him following me as I turned into the carpark, but when I looked over my shoulder at the entrance to the store, he'd stopped by the sign without coming in. Maybe he was planning on following both of us when we got out.

At any rate, there wasn't any need to worry about him; Erica and I would be in public all the way home, and it was pretty likely that Zero would be somewhere around as soon as he finished, too.

I was nearly too late to meet Erica by the time I got my groceries; as I hurried out with my plastic bags I saw her at the entrance, craning her neck this way and that, her shoulders stiff.

"Looking for me?" I asked.

Erica's face brightened straight away. "Pet! You're here!"

"Had to get some groceries," I explained, but that didn't take away the smile from her face. I felt a bit warm and pleased; it was nice to be needed. I'd probably have to watch that feeling—it was the sort of thing that made it hard for me to say no when she asked me for help.

"Thank you!" she said. "I know I asked, but I didn't really think you'd be here. It's a lot to ask from someone I've only known a week."

"No worries," I said, cheerfully. "I told you; I had to get my groceries."

Anyway, Zero had finished for the day, too; I saw him flutter past like a huge white shadow. Daniel hadn't hurt me when he had the chance, which was nice, but that looked like it was because he thought of me as a pack member. He didn't think of Erica that way, so all bets were off when it came to her. I wouldn't bet too much on him not hurting me if I got between them, either; and Zero's ghostly presence was a comfort.

CHAPTER NINE

WHEN I GOT BACK HOME, I CLIMBED IN THROUGH THE UPSTAIRS living room window for old times' sake, bags and all.

Actually, that's a lie. I climbed in that way so I could put the dryad back in my bedroom before Zero caught me coming in with it. They would probably want to debrief me as soon as I got in, and I didn't want to risk being caught with it. Of course, they'd all know I'd come in that way, but I didn't think it would occur to them to ask me why. Just a weird little thing that the pet does.

When I came downstairs, Athelas said, "Sneaking in, Pet?" over his shoulder as he selected a book from the bookcase, but he didn't bother to look at me, so he mustn't have been too worried.

"You're home early," I said to him.

"Coffee, Pet," said Zero.

I went to put away the groceries, then got the coffee and biscuits, feeling a bit miffed. I had *stuff* to tell them, and all they had to say to me was *sneaking in, Pet?* and *coffee, Pet.*

Flamin' rude, that.

Jin Yeong came home as I was carrying the tray into the living room. He didn't acknowledge me by anything more than a half-hearted snarl in passing, but that wasn't something I really cared about anyway.

He probably just hadn't had enough admiration today.

"Got stuff to report," I said to Zero, passing him his coffee and a plate for his biscuits.

"Later," Zero said, at last looking up from his knives. I expected him to go back to his knives again, but instead he continued to gaze at me, his face expressionless.

I cleared my throat. "What? I'm not late. You lot won't want dinner until later."

"Where have you been digging around?"

I blinked innocently at him, but that only made the air a bit colder. I cleared my throat again and said, "I was going for a walk when I saw Daniel, so I followed him."

"Daniel didn't do that," said Zero, pointing at my hair.

"Didn't do what?" I asked, patting the side of my head. "If those flamin' pigeons have done a number in my hair again—!"

Athelas, looking up from his book, said, "Dear me!"

Not pigeon poop, then. My fingers brushed against something cool and alive, and I snatched them away. Then I reached gingerly back up and twitched it out from between strands of hair, thin and viny and leafy.

Something was growing in my hair.

"What the—!" I muttered, tugging at it. It didn't let go.

"Did you visit the Green Man?"

"What, the old bearded bloke?" I asked, too caught up with the vine that was growing in my hair to look at him. "Yeah."

"Why?"

"Thought he looked lonely," I explained. That was mostly the truth—well, it was the truth minus the dryad, and that was as close as I wanted to get.

"*Noh*," said Jin Yeong, snabbling a biscuit and pointing at me with it, "*Paboya?*"

"I just talked to him!" I protested. I didn't like Jin Yeong calling me an idiot when I wasn't sure if I should be protesting it or not. "I didn't insult him or anything!"

"I suppose we can be thankful for small mercies," murmured Athelas.

"Is this gunna come out?"

Zero hesitated, then said. "Make dinner, Pet."

"That's not an answer!" I objected. It was gunna be murder to brush my hair if I had to brush around a vine as well. "And I have *stuff* to tell you! It's too early for dinner!"

"*Dinner*," he said.

I made dinner. I couldn't help thinking about my afternoon, though. Erica seemed scared when I came across her, and Daniel was definitely stalking her, which meant I should be looking at him as the best suspect. But I still remembered how she'd smiled at him the first time I saw them together. It had seemed like she was on pretty good terms with him.

The last couple of days, though...

I thought about that, frowning. The last couple of days, Erica had been genuinely scared of him, I was sure—too scared to walk home alone, and too scared to be backward about asking a kid like me to walk her home. No one should be that frightened.

I was just putting the steak on to cook when Athelas strolled into the kitchen with his empty tea cup.

"I take it you had an interesting day, Pet?" he inquired, leaving his tea cup on the draining board.

I nearly said, *Oh, so* now *you wanna hear about it?* but Athelas, wearing his most pleasant smile, sat down at the kitchen island instead of the table, and I didn't think his proximity was a friendly one.

"Yeah," I said, instead. "I met a shifter."

Athelas nodded, unsurprised. "You've become noticeable to them."

"Who was it?" asked Zero, stepping up from the lounge room. He didn't look surprised, either; but since Zero doesn't show much emotion at the best of times, that wasn't anything to judge by.

It was only when Jin Yeong, following Zero and sitting elegantly at the table, demanded, "*Nugu?*" as well, that I began to be suspicious.

"Hang on," I said, turning away from the stove to lean against the island. "You were using me as bait at the supermarket, weren't you?"

Athelas raised one brow elegantly. "Of course. Why else would you be allowed to work—"

"There was a good chance that at least one of the shifters would sniff you out and introduce themselves," Zero said, interrupting Athelas. "What happened?"

"He sniffed me out, all right," I said. "I was going up to get the groceries when I saw Daniel out and about. I thought he was going somewhere, but he just wandered and then I lost him. Turns out, he didn't lose me; he bailed me up in the alley out of Wellington Court."

"Are you hurt?"

"Nope, not a scratch," I said. It was stupid to feel warm at a question asked so thoroughly without concern, but I couldn't help it. "I think he was trying to warn me off. He knew I'd been chucking up and he gave me a bit of rare steak to eat; but he was also trying to scare me enough to leave him alone with whatever he's up to with Erica."

"Not exactly pack behaviour," murmured Athelas.

"No," Zero agreed, "but it is pack leader behaviour to the weak in the pack."

"You're saying Wolf Boy is the leader of the pack?"

"It's possible. Did he do anything else?"

"Nope. He told me to stop following him a couple times, but I think he thinks I'm sweet on him, so he didn't get too mean."

Zero's chilly blue eyes gleamed with the faintest hint of laughter. "It's possible," he said again. "That could be useful."

"What of your Erica?" inquired Athelas. "Do you fancy the boy could turn his eyes from her and to you?"

"Doubt it," I said laconically. Daniel was very much caught up with Erica; though I still wasn't sure whether it was obsession or love. There had been a tinge of yellow to his eyes today that worried me a bit. "He's got that same look Jin Yeong gets when he's hungry for blood and someone's bleeding. Reckon we should be watching him when he's not at work, too."

"For now, keep walking Erica home from work," Zero said. "She seems to trust you. Bring in the detective, too; he can walk her to work and make her feel safe. Do you think she knows anything about the murders specifically?"

I felt the warmth of being asked for my input and tried not to beam. "Yeah," I said. "She knows something, all right. I keep thinking if I can push her enough, she might tell me. Maybe if she trusts me enough."

"Tell her you're working with the detective," Zero told me. "Let her know you're undercover to help; it might be enough to encourage her to talk."

"What if she tells someone else?" I asked, pulling the steaks off the stovetop to cover them.

Zero leaned against the wall. "Then your part in this investigation will be finished."

"Oh," I said. They really had just put me in there as bait. Nothing would change if I had to leave. A bit resentfully, I asked, "What if no one had come up to me?"

"The leader of the pack always brings in new members," said Zero. "Even if it wasn't obvious, they would have found some way of being near you—some method of attaching you to themselves to make the transition easier. If you trust a pack leader, the odds of your change being successful are far greater. The power of the leader will also grow as the depth of trust from the pack grows, so there's benefit on both sides."

"You really think Daniel's the pack leader? Isn't he too...angry? Doesn't feel like he's trying to make me trust him."

Zero shrugged. "His relationships are more aggressive than caring, and he's antagonistic rather than nurturing, but he's a young wolf. If he's the leader, his leadership style could change over the years. He fed you, and that's something."

"Yeah, but if he's killing people, changing over the years isn't soon enough," I said. "He needs to be stopped now."

"There are shifter deaths as well as human ones," Zero said. "He'll answer for it if he's the killer."

"You're gunna hand him over to Detective Tuatu?" I asked, in disbelief. I hadn't expected that.

Athelas laughed into his tea, and Zero said, "No. He'll answer to Behind laws."

"Right," I said. That was more what I'd expected. "What time do you get for something like that? Killing shifters?"

"Ah, Pet!" sighed Athelas. "You're so delightfully young and human!"

"Yeah? Why do I feel like that's an insult, then?"

"There are very few jails Behind," Zero said.

I frowned. "So when you say he'll answer for it, he'll do what? Community service type stuff?"

Now Jin Yeong spluttered a laugh.

"No," said Zero. "He'll die. If he took the lives of his fellow Behindkind in malice, and outside of pack leadership squabbles, he'll pay for it with his own life."

"Oh," I said. I didn't know exactly what to say to that. "Then when you went after the changelings before—"

"All dead," nodded Athelas. "Did you think we were merely rounding them up to incarcerate them?"

"Dunno," I said. "Maybe? I mean, I knew you'd kill the ones that fought back, but—hang on, is that what you meant when you said that the Enforcers are judge, jury and executioner?"

"I do wonder what else it could mean," said Athelas. "I thought I was quite clear."

"I thought you meant Enforcers have a license to kill, and that sort of thing, not that they went around actually killing their perpetrators!" I protested. "I've only seen you kill people who attacked us."

"Those are the laws," Zero said. "Without reference to you or any other human. Step back now if you're not comfortable with it."

"I didn't say I wasn't comfortable with it," I mumbled. I wasn't —not exactly. But I also knew that life Behind and Between was a lot more savage, and if it meant keeping humans safe...

I still didn't know. I'd have to think about it a bit more yet.

JinYeong must have done his thing again, because I was back in the office with Shanae and Erica the next morning. Or maybe it was Zero who arranged it; to give me more time to bond with Erica and prevent Shanae being alone with her in the office for too long.

Erica was already looking a bit shrunken when I arrived. That could have been because she was working with Shanae, but it could have been because Daniel had followed her to work again this morning, too. That annoyed me, because it wasn't fair for Erica to live in fear, whether it came from being followed by a little yahoo like Daniel or harassed by a queen bee like Shanae.

More, I was restless because I didn't know which one of them it was. Time was passing so quickly, and my dreams were getting worse each night. More importantly, it was getting harder and harder to eat food. As much as I didn't want JinYeong to be right about...well, anything...I couldn't help feeling that Shanae was just as good a suspect as Daniel, and at this stage I would have been glad just to know which one of them it was.

I mean, Shanae wasn't following Erica around like a creepy

stalker, but she certainly seemed to hate her. She was full of short replies and sarcastic answers whenever Erica had to ask her a question, and when Erica went to fetch the morning coffees, she said sarcastically, "Try not to forget mine this time, won't you?"

"I won't forget," Erica promised.

Shanae's spite didn't stop when Erica had left the room, either; the first thing she said to me when the door closed behind Erica was, "I wouldn't hang around Erica so much, if I were you. You're getting pretty friendly for someone who only met her last week."

It was the first thing she'd said directly to me all day, and it sounded more like a threat than a friendly warning.

I grinned at my little corner of the room, and said over my shoulder, "Yeah? What's wrong with Erica?"

"Well, if you're interested in Daniel—"

Yeah, nah.

"—or that new manager—"

Heck no.

"—you might want to be careful. Erica has a habit of stealing men who belong to other women."

I gave Shanae an innocent look. "Really? She doesn't look like the type."

"They never do," Shanae said grimly. "That's how it works, kid. Sweet and innocent, that's the look she goes for."

Flaming heck! If this was the kind of gossip she was spreading about Erica, she obviously didn't want her to have any female friends, either. Had she said stuff like this to the human girl who'd died? April Post had looked like a nice girl—maybe she'd refused to be swayed by it, and Shanae had had to go further.

Or maybe it was still creepy little Daniel, after all, not wanting Erica's attention divided between him and other people.

Beggared if I knew.

"Try to fix your hair before you go to lunch, by the way," she said. "That lump at the side looks weird."

I patted the lump aggrievedly. The vine was still there in my hair, and although Athelas had taken pity on me and told me it would fall out naturally at some stage during the day, it didn't make it any easier to do my hair.

Lucky for me, Erica came back a couple of minutes later, panting a bit.

"You took your time," said Shanae, taking her coffee.

"Sorry," Erica said. "The new manager, Jin Yeong; he wanted coffee, too."

Shanae rolled her eyes. "Oh well, I suppose we all know why it took you so long, then! I suppose he'll be asking you out next week."

That was flaming rich. Like she hadn't been offering to buy Jin Yeong's coffee a couple of days ago herself!

Erica looked surprised. "Oh no! He wouldn't be interested in me! Anyway, I like men who are more..."

"Manly?" I suggested.

"Earthy," she said. "I like flannies and strong arms and beards."

Shanae gave us a look of disgust. "Jin Yeong is *gorgeous* and there's something wrong with the both of you!"

"Yeah, but who wants a pretty bloke?" I protested. "*And* he's dirty-livered into the bargain."

"I've never seen him lose his temper," Shanae argued. "And if you're comparing him with a boy like Daniel—"

Erica flinched, but I didn't think Shanae saw. She probably would have poked a bit more if she had.

"—if you're comparing him with a boy like Daniel, then there's definitely something wrong with your head."

"At least Daniel knows how to cook a steak," I remarked. "I bet Mr. Creased-Trousers couldn't cook a steak to save his life."

Shanae sniffed at me as if she couldn't bring herself to reply to such ridiculousness, and went back to her computer.

Later, when Shanae went to the toilet, Erica asked quietly, "Pet, have you been spending time with Daniel?"

"What?" Good grief, I'd given myself away like an idiot. I hesitated, then said, "Kinda. We met the other day while we were both in the city centre—he thought I was looking sick so he took me to his friend's kitchen and cooked me a steak."

"You shouldn't—" she hesitated, then said, "If he's looking after you, that's good. But Daniel is a very...*emotional* boy, and being alone with him isn't the wisest idea."

It must have been the day for warnings about hanging out with people.

I said placatingly, "I won't do that again. Actually, I wouldn't have done it the first time, but he kinda dragged me there so I didn't have a choice. What do you mean, he's emotional?"

"Never mind," she said quickly. "So long as you're not going to do it again, it's fine."

"Yeah, but—"

"Forget it," she said, stuffing tickets into plastic cases without being careful of the edges. "I shouldn't have said anything."

I said, "Okay," and went back to my own tickets. There was still time for persuading her to talk later in the day; still time to convince her it was a good idea to meet with Detective Tuatu.

I would have tried to persuade her over lunch, but she went all quiet and refused to leave the office. I walked out for lunch at the same time Shanae finished instead, and by the time I was in the staff room, I was happy to get away from her stiff-backed silence.

I ate lunch opposite Carmen from the front end instead, who asked me in a friendly sort of way how things were going out in the office.

"Just got safely away from your queen bee."

Carmen laughed. "What, Shanae? I wasn't talking about her!"

I stared at her. "Really? Who were you talking about, then?"

"I was talking about Erica."

"Erica? How is she a queen bee?"

"Not the nasty kind, or anything," Carmen said. "She's as nice as they come. But blokes like to do things for her, or do things around her so they can be with her, stuff like that. She's bad luck for women."

It wasn't anything I hadn't seen for myself. Daniel seemed to be the closest one to her these days, but I would have been stupid if I hadn't seen the way other men around the store watched Erica, or smiled at her, or jumped to help her before she asked. It was the biggest reason I thought Shanae was still a good suspect —she really hated the attention Erica got.

"Yeah," I said. "I saw that."

"If she wasn't so nice, it'd be easy to hate her," Carmen said reflectively. "Blokes get keen on her and girls get angry about her; 'specially if it's their boyfriend who gets keen on her. The amount of blokes who cause trouble around her is amazing."

"What blokes?"

"Well, the one that just stopped showing up a week ago was crazy about her—Daniel was annoyed about that."

"Yeah," I said, grinning. "He's crushing a bit, isn't he?"

"He's stupid, a bit," she said bluntly. "He seemed to think Chris was bothering Erica, but I'm pretty sure she liked him back and Daniel just didn't want to admit it."

"Just those two, then?"

"Nah, there were more. A while ago, one of the girls in the cash office had a boyfriend who caught sight of Erica and dropped her like a hot potato—that's what Rhonda tells me, anyway. Reading between the lines, I think it was Shanae whose boyfriend did that. She must have kicked up a heck of a stink, because he was demoted or fired or sent to another store. We haven't seen him since then."

"What was his name?" I asked. I was pretty sure I already knew, but it would be good to confirm it.

"James—James Henry, I think," she said.

Oh yeah. That was another one of our bodies. One of the shifter victims, too, if I was remembering rightly. Meaning Shanae really could be a shifter? Possible.

"And for a while there was a greasy bloke hanging around the store every afternoon when Erica finished work. Only for a week or two, mind you; she must have called the police on him, because he was gone after that."

Greasy...maybe that was the one Detective Tuatu said was a homeless bloke. Only why had a homeless man been fixated on Erica? Maybe he'd seen her walking to and from work, but it was a fairly big jump from seeing a girl you like and waiting outside the store for her every day for two weeks.

"Did she talk with him? The greasy one?"

"Not at first," the girl said. "She looked scared and pushed past him. But by the third or fourth afternoon she had an argument with him—*half* her patience, I say! I would have been screaming at him by the second day. He still kept coming after that, but he stayed at a distance."

Homeless man had been another of the humans; probably hadn't even known what he was getting himself into, hanging around a supermarket that was terrorised by a wolf shifter. That was bad luck for him.

"Sounds like she gets all the luck," I said.

"Yep," said Carmen, crushing her paper cup. "Beauty's a curse, right? You should fix your hair before you go back, Pet; it's all lumpy at the side."

I muttered about that as she went back to work, but I only had a couple of minutes to call Detective Tuatu before I went back to work, so I decided to sulk later, and went outside to call him in private.

He picked up on the second ring.

"Desperate, ay?" I said to him, combing my fingers through my hair in hopes of loosening the vine.

"What do you want, Pet?"

I picked a few small leaves from my hair. "To talk to you, of course. What do you know about a woman called Erica Knopke?"

The detective's voice sharpened. "Is she a suspect?"

"Nope. A lead. *Lots* of death around her."

"Then why isn't she a suspect?"

"Because it looks like our someone is killing anyone who gets too close to her. There was one bloke who was keen on another woman and then saw her, plus another bloke who was just keen on her, and then—"

"All right," said Detective Tuatu. "I'll do some digging and see what turns up."

"No, no!" I said hastily. "I don't need you to dig up stuff, I need you to meet us after work. Zero says I should let on that I'm undercover and that you're helping: he reckons it'll make Erica brave enough to talk. She knows stuff she's not telling, and I think it's 'cos she's scared."

"Oh." Tuatu was quiet for a while, then agreed. "All right. I'll meet you in the café on the corner of Elizabeth and Liverpool. What time?"

"Three thirty. We'll be finished by then."

"All right."

It was just Erica and me when I got back from lunch, which was nice. Not just because any office was friendlier without Shanae in it, but because it would give me a chance to convince Erica that she should really report Daniel to the police—and if not to the police collectively, to Detective Tuatu individually.

I sat down next to her and asked, "How come you didn't go out for lunch?"

"There's too much to do," she said. "I can eat in here and keep working."

"It's because of Daniel, isn't it?"

"Pet—"

"It's okay," I said encouragingly. Was this where I was supposed to tell her that I was undercover? What if she got angry? "You remember I told you I have a friend who's a cop?"

"I remember," she said. "But—"

"That wasn't exactly the truth. I mean, it's the truth, but I'm not just here for work—I'm helping to investigate from the inside. We know there's someone bothering you, and we want to make sure it stops."

Erica gaped at me. "*You're* police?"

"Not exactly. I'm just...um, helping my detective friend out. That murder outside the store—"

"I don't know anything about it!"

"I told you," I said persuasively. "We've got people who can help. What happened that night?"

Yeah, well, maybe not *people* exactly, but close enough.

"I don't know anything about it!"

"It's okay," I said. "It's okay if you don't want to talk about that right now. But you should talk to someone about Daniel. Aren't you tired of him following you home every day?"

Erica's eyes filled with tears. "What can I do about it? If I tell the police, they'll just look at him and think he's a kid. That's what I thought."

"And you might know a bit more than you think, anyway," I said. "We can work with that. I'm gunna take you to see someone today after work, all right?"

"That detective?"

"Yeah. He'll make sure there's someone watching you from home to work and back again so you feel safe enough."

She clung to my arm. "But won't you keep walking with me?"

"Yeah, of course. But there will be someone else, as well. Just in case."

"All right," Erica said, and she let out a shaky breath. "When are we going to meet your detective friend?"

"After work," I said. "We'll meet him at a café in the city centre."

She was still unsure about it after work, so I was glad she didn't see Daniel when we walked out together. I mean, he only glared at us, but for the first time since I'd met him, I felt as cold as my three psychos had made me feel when I met them. He really looked like he could happily tear out my throat.

He didn't follow us, though; or at least, if he did, he did it from a far enough distance that I didn't see him. But I still felt safer once we got to the café and saw the detective.

I steered Erica through the sliding doors and over to the table he was at.

"This is my detective friend," I said. "Erica, Detective Tuatu. Detective Tuatu, Erica."

The detective got up and shook her hand, then sat down again. Erica, a bit reluctantly, sat down too.

"I hear you've got a problem with someone who's a bit clingy," he said to her. "Let's have a bit of a talk about how to keep you safe."

CHAPTER TEN

The next day, Rhonda put me to work with Daniel as soon as I got to work.

Flamin' fantastic. Now I could toy with death at work as well as at home.

I huffed a sigh. At least the strand of vine had fallen out of my hair overnight—probably helped on by my tossing and turning—so I was feeling slightly more normal than yesterday. Still, it took a bit of energy to shoot Daniel a big, insincere grin as I approached him and the cage he was working on.

He wasn't having any of it. "Go away."

"Can't," I said. "Rhonda told me I gotta work with you. You think this is fun for me?"

"Why are you still hanging out with Erica?"

"Right to the point. Nice. Well, there's this weirdo who keeps following her around, and she's not too happy about it, so I figure I might as well."

"Erica and I are none of your business!"

"I don't care about your business," I retorted. "But Erica wants me to walk her home, so I'll walk her home."

Frustrated, Daniel kicked the cage and snatched a case of dog food out of it. "Why can't you just hang out with other shifters?"

"I don't know other shifters," I said, happily aware that this gave me a very good opening to ask him another question I hadn't been sure he would answer. "Oi. What about Shanae? Is she one of us as well?"

"There is no *us*," retorted Daniel. "You're not part of the pack. And I'm not going to play twenty questions about who is and who isn't a shifter. It's none of your business."

"It *is* my business! I'm gunna turn into a wolf soon, and I wanna know who's gunna freak out if I accidentally change in front of 'em! Anyway, you just *told* me I should be hanging out—"

"I didn't mean here! And anybody will freak out when you first change; even other shifters. It's gross."

"Well, that's rude."

"Are you still eating meat?"

As if I wasn't throwing up everything else I tried to eat. I said, unenthusiastically, "Yeah."

"Good. I'm not coming to help you out if it doesn't work out, so you better look after yourself."

Life didn't get much better when I got home, either. Zero was there before me, and he was dressed in his loose trousers instead of jeans, which meant I was in for some training again.

I wouldn't have minded, but it was flaming *hard*, and no matter how I looked at it, I didn't see myself getting better with a sword —or a stick, for that matter—that was nearly as heavy as I was.

"What are we doing this arvo?" I asked Zero gloomily, when I came back downstairs after changing. "More stick training?"

Jin Yeong sniffed a laugh and made a lazy remark at Zero that must have been about me.

"Perhaps so," replied Zero. "There's a weight and balance difference that might suit the pet. The single sword is too heavy and a smaller blade won't be enough if it's facing a larger opponent."

Another lazy few sentences murmured from Jin Yeong, along with an assessing sort of look that ended in a smirk.

"Kamikaze?" Zero's eyes narrowed slightly. "Yes, I thought so, too, judging by past experience. It should be a good fit."

"Oi!" I said indignantly. "What are you laughing at? Don't listen to the vampire. He doesn't know what he's talking about."

Zero fished out something brown and battered from his alcove, and threw it at me. I caught the scent of it before I caught the thing itself: it was a cylinder of thick leather, laced with something that wasn't leather or anything else that I recognised.

It looked like it would be good to chew on.

"Pet," said Zero, his eyes on me. "It is not food."

"Oh yeah," I said, trying not to think about how deliciously chewy it looked. "Is this a wrist guard?"

"Forearm guard. Put it on."

"Oh. What's the difference?"

Jin Yeong gave a derisive laugh, but Zero said, slipping his arm through a similar, but much larger guard and tightening it, "You'll need all the mobility in your wrist; the guard would prevent that. It needs to be high enough to leave your wrist free, and low enough to protect as much of your forearm as possible."

"Which arm?"

"Your non-dominant hand. Come out into the garden."

"Where's me stick?"

"You have to find your own stick this evening," said Zero, and strode off toward the back door. "We're doing a different kind of training today."

Jin Yeong chuckled as if at a particularly delicious joke, and I glared at him as I followed Zero. I didn't like it when Jin Yeong chuckled. There was something nasty waiting to drop on me, I just knew it.

Zero was waiting for me in the garden when I stumbled out, trying to tighten the laces on my forearm guard as I came. He wordlessly adjusted the guard down a little and pulled the laces tight. I don't know exactly what he did with the ends of the laces, but everything looked smooth when I looked down, and I might have felt a flutter of something cool against my skin beneath the guard.

"Did you just do magic?" I asked him suspiciously.

"Ready yourself," he said.

"You haven't got a—"

Zero reached into the garden and brought out something that should have been a stick but managed to turn itself into a practise sword as he withdrew it.

Hang on. Nope. There were two of them.

Zero tested the weight of them, and I saw his weight shift.

He was gunna attack?

"Hang on!" I yelped. "Where's me stick!"

"I told you," said Zero, one of his pretend blades swinging in a lazy circle. "Today you have to find your own stick. You seem to fight more...naturally...when you're scrambling."

"What?"

Zero danced forward, pretend blades sweeping in perfect union, and I ran for it. I would have run straight back into the house, but Jin Yeong was there in the door, grinning. I dodged and scampered up the closest tree, which was near enough to a taller one that I only had to make a very small leap to get there.

Zero sauntered over to the base of the tree, blades lowered, and said. "Come down, Pet."

"Heck no!" I told him. "Someone comes at me with two swords and I'm gunna run like mad. I'm not an idiot!"

"Come down, Pet."

Grumbling, I came down.

Zero waited until he saw I was really coming down, then went back to his original spot. He pointed with one sword at the spot where I'd kicked up grass in my flight, and I dropped to the ground in a shower of bark and skulked back to that spot.

"Ready yourself," he said.

He came at me again, but I felt the slither of something coming through Between behind me, and I dodged left this time. A practise sword whiffled over my head; I ducked and would have gone for my tree again, but there was a hedge of something alive and wavy and green in the way.

Beggar me.

I ran for the house again, ignoring the grinning Jin Yeong who blocked the door, and plunged right through the wall and Between.

It was a house, but it wasn't. The walls were white marble and crawling with vines, and there was no ceiling. Leaves fluttered across the floor in the gust of movement as I came through, then turned to dust bunnies as the house turned into my house again.

Kitchen. I was in the kitchen.

I needed knives.

There were no knives within reach, and I felt the whole house twitch as Zero stepped through the wall, tugging at reality.

I darted down the hall toward the front door, and there in the umbrella stand was a cane. Only one, but maybe it could be sharp if I were persuasive about it.

I snatched it out of the stand and said hurriedly, "You flamin' well better be sharp, otherwise I'm gunna get thrashed to a pulp!"

There was a small click and the cane separated between my hands, a thin crack in a circle at the centre of the cane. I saw it for what it was, grinning, and pulled my hands apart to separate twin blades. They weren't as long as Zero's blades; maybe just a little over half a metre each, but they were solid and double edged and *so light*.

"Come, Pet," said Zero.

I reluctantly joined him in the kitchen, my twin blades cautiously in front of me. Thanks to the last couple of training sessions, I had an idea of how to put up a guard with a single sword, but this was different.

"You seem to have a very particular affinity for this house," said Zero. His swords were still moving very slightly, and they were still in a position from which he could attack, so I didn't lower my guard.

I didn't know what I was doing, but any guard's better than no guard, right?

"Yeah," I said. "Lived here for a long time. And I don't like turning sticks into stuff. I like bricks and metal and city."

"Your guard isn't correct."

"Yeah? Well, I haven't done this before. Sorry pardon."

Jin Yeong gave a *tsk* of annoyance and stepped between me and Zero. With one slender hand he twitched my right wrist into place in front of me, blade forward; with the other, he bumped my left elbow into a slightly different position.

Zero moved at once, slicing at my guard. Jin Yeong leapt for cover with a bright, happy chuckle, and I fell backwards into the living room with a yell.

Somehow I turned the fall into a tumble without losing either blade and without cutting off a limb, and collided with Athelas' crossed legs.

"Not in the house!" he protested, startled out of his usual composure. "Really, Zero! Pet, if you damage my chair—!"

Zero slashed downward and I yelped, crossing blades above me by instinct. The weight of his blow sent me to my knees again, but my arms held and so did the blades.

Behind me, Athelas sat very still, and I looked up through half-closed eyes to see the edge of Zero's practise blade just an inch or two from my skull; the point a similar distance from Athelas' nose.

That would have given both of us a nice headache.

"Not too bad," said Zero, and stepped back. This time, the points of his swords lightly touched the carpet. It was the end of his attack. "JinYeong will have to give you some pointers when you get further in; his specialty is twin blades. Either Athelas or I can train you in the beginning elements. For now, we'll start with the basic attacks, blocks and defences. Outside, Pet."

I WAS DRIPPING WITH SWEAT BY THE TIME JINYEONG CAME back out to call us in. Twin blade fighting might be lighter in terms of swords, but flaming *heck* it was heavy on the cardio! And maybe Zero was right about it suiting me better; there wasn't much in the way of safety, but it was fast and frantic and if I could stop enemies from getting too close, there was a good chance I'd be able to kill someone before they killed me. If I didn't slip in a pool of my own sweat first.

We came in as called, though I didn't know why until I saw Detective Tuatu sitting in one of the spare chairs. He looked about as comfortable as he'd looked the first time he came over—well, the first time he came over to see the psychos, anyway. He'd been pretty happy picking the lock and sneaking in when they weren't home.

Anyway.

"Is there some news you want to share?" asked Zero coolly.

"One of the employees visited the police station today," said the detective. "A boy. I didn't get his name, but he went above stairs to Upper Management."

I made a small sound of disgust. "So he *was* gunna go there yesterday! He must have seen me following him from the start."

"Who were you following?" asked the detective.

"Daniel," I said. "That was the one who came to the station, wasn't it? A kid with brown hair and angry eyes, beanpole kinda look to him?"

"And a studded hoodie," nodded Detective Tuatu.

"Evidently you require a lesson or two more in tailing without being noticed," murmured Athelas.

"He probably smelled me," I said grumpily, wiping away sweat with the cuff of my hoodie. I wasn't *that* bad at following people.

Hopefully.

"He—he *smelled* you?"

I grinned at the detective. "Didn't we say? The killer is a—"

"Coffee, Pet," said Zero.

"The killer is what?" demanded Detective Tuatu. "Come back here!"

"Can't!" I called. "Boss says I gotta make coffee."

I heard him ask behind me, "What does she mean? What is it I should know about the killer?"

Zero hesitated, then said, "The killer is someone from our side of reality."

"What does that mean?"

"It means they are no longer human," explained Athelas, into the burbling of the boiling kettle. "You saw the blood test results, did you not?"

"If they're not human, what are they?"

"Something else," said Zero. "Do you know why he visited?"

"Yes," Detective Tuatu said, his voice tight. "From what a friend told me, he was signed in as a potential witness, to examine some CCTV feed from the night of the latest murder."

"A witness?" I called. "That's flamin' rich! Who brought him in?"

"I don't think anyone brought him in," said the detective. "That's the issue. Well, it's *one* issue. He's also not listed in any of the investigations as a P.O.I. in *any* way, though given the slapdash way they were put together, I'm not surprised. The biggest problem is that he came straight to Upper Management and requested to see the video footage, and they let him in without question."

I popped my head into the living room as Zero, frowning, asked, "The recording?"

"Destroyed," said Tuatu grimly. "What did you expect?"

"Athelas," said Zero. "How is it that you didn't find a security camera feed during your time in Upper Management?"

"There were one or two things I was busy with," Athelas said smoothly. There was nothing in his face or his voice, but I was pretty sure he was saying something for Zero's ears only.

"I see," Zero said. "Is there no chance of recovering the feed?"

"It's not just the recording; the entire room was destroyed," said Tuatu. "I saw the mess he made. And the only copy they had was hard copy. The original was on the store's servers."

JinYeong spoke; a short sentence, and I went back to my tea and coffee tray.

"It wasn't there by the time we checked the store's camera feed," said Zero. "We assumed it had been destroyed before it got to the police; that camera was completely out of commission."

"Why didn't you tell me about the boy?" asked the Detective, in annoyance. "I've only had contact with Erica Knopke since you went in, and she's not even a suspect! If you've got a suspect, I want to question him."

"We've got two, but I don't reckon you can talk to either one of 'em," I said, carrying out the tray. I knew the look on Zero's face; I also knew the amused glance that had passed between Athelas and JinYeong.

"Oh *can't* I? If they're suspects, I've got every right to question them!"

"Yeah? How's that gunna work out for you?" I asked him. I put down the tray and gave Tuatu his cup of tea; I'd given him Athelas' really good tea, by way of a sort-of apology that we hadn't included him more. "*I hear you've been chowing down on humans after you turn into a giant wolf. What have you got to say for yourself?* That'll do wonders for your reputation at the station."

"You—" the detective stopped, then glared at me. "That's not how I'd start out!"

"Yeah?" I said again. "Well, there's suspects, and if you think Shanae's gunna put up with you calling her a wolf, either, you've got another think coming."

"You can't question them," Zero said. "That's not your part of this investigation."

"You don't control my part in this investigation," retorted Tuatu. "I'm an officer of the law, and I'll investigate where I see fit!"

Zero just looked at him, almost as if he was Jin Yeong spoiling for a fight. "If this was only a question of human murder, I would agree. But you have no jurisdiction here apart from the human victims, and no knowledge of how to interrogate Behindkind."

"Where humans are dying, I'm *taking* jurisdiction," Detective Tuatu said, stubbornly. "There's only so much you can find out by being undercover, and if you've planted *him* in the station, the least you can do is use that to leverage an official investigation!"

Athelas, amused, passed the biscuits to the detective. Tuatu looked distrustfully at him but took a biscuit.

"I am not in your station to effect reform; I'm there to work undercover," he said. "Moreover, an official investigation wouldn't help you at all. Forms would be filed, and witnesses would be questioned, and if you were to scratch below the surface, you would see that each of them said exactly nothing."

"That's what the first investigations were like," Tuatu said. "These days, they don't even bother with the veneer; they just close the case as an animal killing."

"Exactly so," said Athelas.

"If that's so, I'm not sure exactly what you're doing there," the detective said bluntly.

Athelas' smile carried just a little coldness to it. "Amongst other things, I'm there to make sure you're kept alive long enough to close the case satisfactorily from your side," he said. "You may find you owe me something for that."

"I'm happy to pay whatever you think it costs!" snapped Tuatu.

I threw a biscuit at him, and it bounced off his temple, scattering crumbs through the tiny, tight curls there. "Don't say stuff like that!" I told him.

Athelas smiled, more of a cat-with-cream smile, this time. "I'll remember that," he said. "Don't try to wriggle out of it later."

The detective, looking uneasy, opened his mouth, but before he could speak, Zero asked, "Where are you with Erica? You both met her yesterday. What do you think?"

"She's still not telling," I said. "I thought she might talk more to the detective, but she didn't."

Back to business again, Tuatu nodded. "She's definitely holding out on us, but I don't think it'll take much for her to talk. She looked like she would have talked at any minute, but she kept pulling back at the last second. There's still something stopping her."

"Hang on," I said, frowning. "If you saw something weird—like a person turning into a wolf and killing a bloke—would *you* tell the police about it?"

"Nope," Tuatu said. "People already think I'm weird. That'd just give them the opportunity to kick me out of the force."

"Exactly," I said. "You said I could tell her I'm with the detective, and maybe she feels safer, but she won't feel really safe until she knows she can talk about the weird stuff, too. There's no way she doesn't know it was a wolf, with how much perfume she's been spraying around the place."

Athelas' eyes crinkled. "Yes. Jin Yeong may have mentioned the inconvenience once or twice. It makes it difficult for him to differentiate scents."

"Tell her about us if you must, but tell her as little as you can," Zero said. "What's her schedule tomorrow?"

"She's got the day off. Daniel's working, and so is Shanae."

"You?"

"I'm meant to be working."

"Forget work—"

"Heck yeah!"

"—and go visit Erica. Take her out somewhere with you, if you can; somewhere with a lot of people and a normal look. Detective, you'll keep an eye on them, won't you?"

Detective Tuatu sighed. "All right. But *call* me if you discover anything that's pertinent to the case!"

I KNEW DANIEL WAS AT WORK. I KNEW HE WAS AT WORK, AND that Zero and Jin Yeong were both there, too. I knew the detective was somewhere around even if I couldn't see him.

But I still had that crawling feeling like someone was watching me.

And okay, yeah; the detective was watching me. He was meant to be watching me. It still felt like someone else was watching me, though. Maybe the bloke in green trousers was out there as well, less visible this time.

Still, no one tried to attack me, and I didn't see the Moth Man again, either. Before long, I was outside Erica's house, and a flutter in the window drew my attention. Erica was there, gazing out on the street, and she saw me just as I saw her.

She looked so happy to see me that I forgot about the discomfort of being watched.

"Pet! Isn't it your day off?"

"Yeah," I said. "But I figured you might be stuck inside here, so I've come to drag you out to coffee or something. What's wrong?"

"Nothing. Today has been lovely; it's just that I don't...I don't go out much by myself these days."

"Figured. C'mmon, let's go for a walk down to the waterfront and throw some fish at the seal."

"We've got a seal?"

"Yeah, he pops in to be fed every now and then. We can get ice cream down there, too. It's nice and sunny, so we might as well."

"All right." She disappeared from the window, and a couple of minutes later turned up at the door. She locked it behind her, pulling both doors firmly until they clicked.

I didn't blame her.

We wandered down toward the waterfront, and for a while we just talked about her dress (it was new) and her neighbour across the road (he was new, too) because I knew I was going to have to bring up the night of the murder again, and I wasn't much looking forward to it.

She looked so uncomfortable and scared when I tried to get her to talk about it, and I didn't like making people look like that.

I was going to have to steel myself to it, I thought determinedly. Because Erica wasn't safe, and she would keep being unsafe as long as she didn't tell me everything. My psychos could only fix the problem if they knew what it was.

So I waited until we'd had a nice walk and a coffee; and I waited until we were dangling our legs off part of the pier with an ice cream each.

I didn't eat mine—just sort of watched it dribble and drip into the water as I said, "You know, you wouldn't have to be scared to come out on a nice day like this if you told the detective what really happened that night."

Erica jumped and nearly dropped her ice cream. Maybe her stomach was as queasy as mine, because she hadn't eaten much of it, either. She recovered herself, and said in a small voice, "I don't want to talk about it, Pet. I've already told you I don't know anything."

"Look," I said, "I know you saw something weird that night. I know it probably makes you feel like an idiot to say it aloud, but since I've been walking you home, something has started following me. I want to know if I'm going to be murdered. I've got some friends who deal with weird stuff—"

"More friends," said Erica, and there was a wan smile on her face. "Oh, Pet! I'm so sorry! I didn't mean to drag you into this, but I was so scared!"

"I know you're scared, but they can really help."

"I don't think they can help with this," she said. "It doesn't even sound real to me."

"They helped with something involving face swapping and a house that vanished," I said. I felt a bit exasperated, which wasn't fair on Erica; she was just a human who hadn't been around big scary stuff before.

Her eyes got huge. "With—with *face swapping?*"

"Well, sort of. Anyway, there's something following me around after work, and they don't like it. I don't like it either. They want to do something about it, but they can't do something about it until they know what they're looking at."

"If it can keep you safe—" she began hesitantly.

"And they're not gunna be too happy to help you out if you don't help them out, either," I added, a bit more sternly. There was no way I was going to leave her to Daniel's stalkerish little ways, of course, but she didn't need to know that now.

We needed to know whether it was Shanae or Daniel responsible for the murders, and soon. I hadn't been able to eat breakfast this morning, again, and there was a cold pit of hunger in my stomach that felt a lot like fear. If Erica didn't talk soon, there was a good chance that I really was going to end up as the latest victim, Zero or no Zero.

I asked again, "What happened that night?"

Erica drew in a deep breath. Let it out.

"You saw Daniel?" I prompted. "Or was it Shanae?"

"I can't say it was him for certain," she said urgently. "Or her.

You have to remember that. I saw the hoodie, but there has to be more than one of them around Hobart. And the—the *thing* that took Chris wasn't wearing a hoodie by the time it came after him. It wasn't—it wasn't even *human*, Pet! I thought it was a dog at first, but it was so, *so* much bigger!"

I looked at those wide, unfocused eyes, and the fingers that were white around her bag's strap, and said, "Not there. Don't start there. Start at the start; you were at work and it got to the end of the day."

"Night," she said. "It was night time. Shanae and I were on the late shift to put up the displays again after the floor was polished, so we didn't finish until midnight. We went out with the nightfill team, but I forgot to get my lunchbox, so I went back. Everyone was gone by the time I came out again, except for Chris."

"He stayed to walk you home?"

She nodded. "Yes. We talked for a while, and then he tried to kiss me. I liked him, so I let him. Only then, something collided with Chris and knocked me into the wall. At first, it looked like a person, but it...it *changed* into a wolf. A *really* big wolf. I suppose I fainted, because the last thing I remember before I woke up on the tarmac in the alley is the screaming as Chris was dragged away."

She stopped, shuddering. "I know it sounds crazy, Pet, but I swear that's what happened! When I woke up the light in the alley was out and all I could see was the moon at the end of it. I got up, but it took a long time. And it felt like—it felt like I was being *watched*."

Almost definitely Daniel, I thought. I asked her, "Was there anything in the alley beside you?"

She shivered. "You mean Chris? There was something dark near the skip bin, but I didn't want to look at it, so I ran for the parking lot. I saw the person when I looked back over my shoulder—I mean, I saw the hoodie. The moonlight caught on the metal spikes, so it was easy to see. I ran all the way home, and when I got inside I locked both my doors and checked all the windows."

"Good job," I said. "You did good."

"I couldn't say anything," she said, sniffing. "No one would believe me that a giant wolf came and murdered a man. And I thought—I thought if I said anything about it, he would come back and kill me, too."

I nodded. "I understand. The perfume was a clever idea."

"And then there was Daniel, and I couldn't help feeling they were *connected*, even though that's impossible, too. But I can't say it wasn't a woman, either."

"All right," I said. "I understand."

We were getting somewhere at last. It was time for Erica to properly meet the psychos.

CHAPTER ELEVEN

I brought Erica to Detective Tuatu's house after work the next day. I would have brought her back to our house, but Zero had said "No" in his most expressionless, implacable way; and even the detective, who looked like challenging him as much as JinYeong sometimes, had taken one look at that face and agreed to have Erica at his place.

"She's familiar with me, Pet," he said. "We don't want to frighten her more than we need to. Bring her to my house."

I was tired and weary after a night of tearing out throats in my dreams (which gave me a new dislike for JinYeong that only seemed to amuse him) and I didn't try to argue. That must have surprised Athelas, because I saw his brows go up.

I also saw the way he and Zero looked at each other, but I didn't have the energy to complain about that, either. I just went to work like a good pet and took Erica to Detective Tuatu's house when we finished.

I was pretty sure it was Athelas following us there at a safe distance, and when we got to the door I knew Zero and JinYeong were already there, too. I could smell them there with Detective

Tuatu; Zero like icy rain in the offing, Jin Yeong all salty and almost but not quite human.

Maybe Erica had something of the same sense, even if she couldn't scent it like I could; she hesitated on the doorstep and said, "I don't know, Pet! It seems ridiculous now; I'm sure it was just a misunderstanding."

"Don't give up now," I told her "My friends are gunna make sure no one hurts you again."

She didn't seem too sure about that, but she let me shoo her into the house and the living room, where Zero and Jin Yeong stood behind one of the couches like a pair of bodyguards while the detective tried—and failed—to wipe off something that had set on the coffee table before we got there.

And behind us, Athelas slipped through the door and padded silently into the living room.

Erica stared at them; from Detective Tuatu, to Zero and Jin Yeong, to Athelas, and back again. "All five of you—you're all working together?"

She looked terrified.

I didn't blame her; with his height and extreme whiteness Zero was intimidating, and Jin Yeong's eyes were liquid and dangerous tonight; something I thought Erica would recognise, if only from Daniel. Not to mention the fact that this newly alien duo had until yesterday been just a couple of other staff members where she worked, and that she was probably wondering how long they'd been spying on her. If I didn't know my psychos, I'd probably be freaked out, too.

Actually, I did know them, and I was still creeped out by them at least half the time.

"It's okay," I said to her. "They're the friends I was telling you about. They're trying to help catch the person who murdered Chris and the others."

"I thought the detective—"

"He's my friend, too," I said. "These guys are...kinda detectives. They help with this sort of thing, anyway."

Erica almost smiled. "Weird, impossible things?"

"Exactly."

"Coffee, Pet," said Zero. "We need to have a long discussion with Miss Knopke, and a hot drink will help matters."

He wasn't wrong; coffee helps *everything*.

Erica still looked pretty terrified, but she didn't plead with me to stay with her, so I trotted away into the kitchen to make tea and coffee. Hopefully the detective had more in the way of tea and coffee than he'd had last time I was here.

Zero's voice, just a little above a murmur, followed me. I wondered if Erica knew how calming he was being with her. He was never like that with me, trying not to scare me and trying to make me feel at ease.

I huffed at the kettle and set up the tea and coffee tray. Lucky Erica. Still, I thought, opening a new packet of biscuits, it wasn't her fault that Zero didn't appreciate his pet. I would just have to practise my swordsmanship and Between skills until I was a more exemplary pet.

It seemed to be working, too; I heard Erica's soft voice rising and falling as she explained to Zero all that she'd explained to me earlier, pausing to listen to questions and stopping and starting when she became too upset.

Oh well. At least Erica would be safe with them. I'd been afraid they would be as brusque with her as they'd been with me at first, and that wouldn't have worked with Erica. It didn't make sense to get hurt feelings because they were treating her *too* nicely.

I'd already filled them in on Erica's story last night, so I wasn't surprised that they were nearly finished asking her questions by the time I came back with the tea and coffee.

"Erica can wait for us here in the living room," said Zero, taking his coffee. "Make sure she's comfortable, Pet. We'll talk in the kitchen and come to a decision before you walk her home."

If I hadn't been looking at him when he said that, I might not have seen the way his eyes met Athelas' eyes.

Right. So even though I was the one who was supposedly walking Erica home, Athelas would be trailing behind again. Good. I wasn't so comfortable with the thought of being approached by Daniel at the moment. There was just a bit too much animal rage in his eyes for me to think I'd be able to hold him off if he chose to attack—and that was just the human version of him.

I'd already seen the damage the animal side of a shifter could do. More, I was afraid of what would happen to me if the wolf that had been growing in me was threatened enough to come out like it did in my dreams.

I sat with Erica while the others left, and until it felt like something muffled the voices I'd been listening to as they faded down the hall.

Rude. They were doing something so I couldn't listen from here.

I waited just a bit longer, then left Erica with a comforting smile, and trotted up to the kitchen. Much to my joy, Zero didn't tell me to go back when I perched myself up on the detective's kitchen bench.

He asked me, "Is she calm?"

"Yeah, not too bad. She's less frightened now than when she first saw you."

"Good," said Zero. "She'll have to trust us enough to sit still and be protected without running into a panic."

"If I stay with her, I think she will," I said. "What's the plan? What are we gunna do?"

"It seems evident that Erica thinks it was Daniel that night," said Athelas.

Jin Yeong complained, and I heard Shanae's name in there.

In the interests of fair play, I said, "Yeah, it still could have been her, Zero. She was there that night."

"She was also in the vicinity the night April Post and Bianca Terry died," said Tuatu. "Bianca Terry died outside a work party, and April Post was killed in the parking lot before her 4 am Monday shift. Shanae was at the party and claimed she left early, and she was working the same shift as April Post."

"I mean, I still think it's Daniel," I said. "But that woman's flamin' terrifying and if she's a shifter, she's got as much ability as Daniel to get nasty."

"I agree," Athelas said. "Zero?"

"We can't discount her."

I sank my chin on my palm. "So, what do we do?"

"Set a trap," said Athelas, smiling dreamily. "Nothing too convoluted, since we're dealing with shifters. A message, perhaps, Zero?"

Zero nodded. "We need full cause before we administer judgement."

"Judgement?" demanded Detective Tuatu, looking more alert. "What judgement?"

"It's part of our job," Athelas said. "It's a requirement for Enforcers that they find Intent, Initiation, and Act all present before they act in judgement as Enforcers."

"What do you consider as Intent, Initiation, and Act?"

"The offender must be present with the intent to commit the crime, have initiated the crime, and be in the act of the crime before we can proceed with infield justice."

"So we've gotta get Shanae and Daniel to go somewhere they *think* Erica's at with her new friend, and they'll go there to kill—hang on. You're going to use me as bait again, aren't you?"

"We'll use the promise of you as bait for them," said Zero. "That's all we'll need for them."

"Yeah, but how do you get the Act, if that's how you're gunna do it?" I asked, frowning. "If Daniel goes haring off to where he thinks I'm being a bad influence or whatever on Erica, he might have Intent to hurt me, and he might even Initiate that by changing to his other form, but how does that give us the Act?"

"That's *your* legal system," said the detective. "I just have to see them there before I can question them. Nobody gets hurt."

Zero nodded expressionlessly. "Jin Yeong, give Shanae a message for Erica tomorrow. Tell her that Pet will be waiting at the City Theatre at ten o'clock tomorrow night; they're going to see a show together. I'll make sure Daniel knows they'll be at the Botanical Gardens for a late-night performance at the same time."

"Will that be impetus enough, do you think?" asked Athelas.

"It will be, if it's Daniel," I said. "He's been glaring at me for the last few days whenever he sees me with Erica."

"And if it's Shanae, it will probably be enough to get her there, just to see what's going on," Zero said. "Jin Yeong and the detective will watch for Shanae. Athelas will wait for Daniel. Pet and I will be at Erica's house to make sure nothing happens to her while the exercise is ongoing."

"I'm with *him*?" Detective Tuatu looked doubtful.

"That's what *I* keep saying," I confided. "I don't know why we keep him; no one wants to work with him."

Jin Yeong showed me his teeth, but Zero ignored both that and my remark.

"Go walk Erica home, Pet. You can tell her what we've decided; make sure she understands she needs to be at home all day tomorrow if she can, and to definitely be out no later than 9pm tomorrow night if she must work."

"Got it," I said, and went back to the living room.

As soon as I got there, Erica jumped up from her seat.

"What's happening? What did they say? Are they going to help me?"

"They've got a pretty good idea of who it was," I told her. "So they're setting a trap. Don't worry; you'll be completely safe the whole time. You'll be with me and the big white bloke."

"Is he actually a detective, too?"

"Well, sorta."

"What do I have to do?"

"Nothing," I promised her. "You just stay snug at home all tomorrow night while everything happens. We'll come to meet you at nine or a bit before, and guard you while they spring the trap elsewhere."

"You're not—you're not going to use me as bait?"

"Nah," I said. "Not actual you, anyway; just the promise of you being somewhere. We'll be safely at your house while everything's going down somewhere else."

Erica looked down at her bag, then up at me, and her eyes were luminous with tears. "Thank you," she said quietly. "Really. I'm ashamed of myself for being such a coward, especially when you're so brave. But after the second one died..."

"It's okay," I said. I jerked my head toward the kitchen. "They're the ones doing all the dangerous stuff; I'm just following along and doing the housework. They're good at what they do, so you don't have to worry."

"Thank you, anyway," she said. "I still think you're the bravest one. Don't go meeting with Daniel again, will you, though? It's not safe."

I probably wouldn't have met him again anyway, but I found myself saying, "I won't. I might see him at work, but—"

"Don't even talk to him!" she said urgently. "Not if they're—not if they're making plans about him. I don't want him to find out."

"They're making plans about Shanae, too," I said. I didn't think it was Shanae, and I was pretty sure Erica didn't, either. She might not like Shanae, but she didn't act as though she was scared to death of the other woman, either. "Don't worry about it. I'll walk you home now."

"Ready?" asked a voice from the doorway.

Detective Tuatu was there, slipping his keys into his pocket.

They must have sent him to walk Erica home as well, which was pretty rude considering that everyone was camped out at his house.

"That mean I'm staying?" I asked the detective gloomily, but I didn't expect him to say yes, and he didn't.

"They want a bit more coverage," he said. "You're meant to come, too."

"Fine," I said. Flaming Behindkind. They wanted to talk without me there. What were they up to now? "But someone better be buying me dim sims or something."

I slept in late the next day, and I suppose Jin Yeong must have been hungry, because when I woke up he was perched on the end of my bed again. Lucky for him, I was awake enough to recognise his figure as him instead of the wolf-Daniel figure I had been leaping for in my dreams.

He looked poised to duck, but I just flailed at him a bit and groaned, "Why are you in my room? What is it you don't understand about privacy?"

"*Irona, Petteu,*" he said. "*Pab haera.*"

Then he stalked away and out the door. Left by myself, I groaned a bit longer and made myself get up. I didn't want to get up, and I definitely didn't want to cook anyone's breakfast. My stomach was already lurching from the smell of vampire in the room.

I went downstairs and made toast, which didn't smell exactly good, but at least didn't stink to my nose right now.

"How come Athelas is at work?" I asked Jin Yeong, putting a plateful of toast in front of him. These days there was a lazy susan in the middle of the table, full of jam and honey and other spreads, so at least I didn't have to run back and forth to fetch stuff.

Jin Yeong just shrugged one shoulder at me—which meant

either he didn't know and didn't care, or knew and didn't care to tell me.

And yeah, maybe I wouldn't have understood him if he told me anyway, but his attitude was still annoying.

Zero came in after Jin Yeong started eating, and I knew right away that it was going to be a hectic morning, because he was dressed in his training clothes. He sat down and ate a mountain of toast with raspberry jam, then said, "Get dressed, Pet. We'll practise in the house this morning."

"Athelas didn't like us practising in the house last time."

"Fortunately for us, Athelas isn't the master of this house. You seem to do better with a more urban training ground, so we'll start in here. You'll have to find your own weapon again."

"I'm gunna change into a werewolf before much longer," I complained. "How come I still have to do training?"

"You're not a wolf yet," said Zero. "And the skill of drawing things from Between is useful whether or not you're human. You need to be able to draw on anything in an emergency. You need to practise until you can put your hand to anything and bring its other form from Between into your reality."

"Yeah, but do I have to be running around and trying to dodge swords while I do it?"

"Yes," said Zero. "There's no benefit in being able to access Between while you're safe and calm. You need to be able to do it when you're bloody and beaten and dying."

"Oh," I said. "But doesn't it make more sense to be able to access stuff before it gets that bad? Then I won't have to be bloody and beaten and dying. Also, what if I accidentally shift?"

There was the faintest breath of a laugh as Zero rose. "I thought you wanted to be trained, Pet."

"Yeah, that was before I found out you were going to make me dodge from one end of the place to the other while you chased me with two flaming big swords," I said. "*And* my legs feel like they're going to fall off, *and* I might lose my arms."

"The more you train, the stronger you'll get."

"Yeah," I said again. "That's what you say, but I don't think my legs got the message. The other day you had me starting from a squat and dodging between markers, and at my age my knees shouldn't be clicking. They are."

"You're wasting time," said Zero. There was a movement of stuff coming from Between as he drew two swords from nothing.

"*And* I have to work today."

"Prepare yourself, Pet."

"And how come your swords are bigger than mine?"

"You choose your own weapons," said Zero. "You fight with whatever you take from Between."

"I gotta pee."

"You already went."

"You've only shown me how to guard and stuff; I haven't had enough practise!"

"This is the practise," said Zero, and began to move forward, blades lifting and sweeping into position. "All I ask of you is to seek your own weapons and turn to fight."

"*All*, that's flamin' rich!" I muttered, but Zero was already surging forward. I turned and ran.

THE HOUSE WAS EMPTY WHEN I GOT HOME FROM WORK THAT night, which was weird and unsettling. Funny how quickly I'd gotten used to coming back and feeling that certain *something* that meant one of my psychos was at home.

I hung out in the kitchen for a couple of hours, trying not to feel nervous about the night ahead and drawing random things out of Between to see what they were, or if I could affect what they came out as. It was nerve-wracking doing it when Zero was charging after me with his weapons, but by myself it was pleasant, even calming.

After a while I lost my nervousness, and I'd almost forgotten I was going out again that night until Zero called me and I realised I was going to have to jog for it to make it to Erica's place by the agreed time of nine o'clock.

"Pet," said Zero's voice, jarring even by phone. "You haven't started yet."

"All right, all right, I'm going!" I said. "Just gotta get me hoodie."

I hung up on him before I could feel guilty about not telling him that my hoodie was still in my locker at work from my shift earlier. He probably would have told me not to bother getting it, and I felt weird without it. I only had two of them, and it was my favourite one. If I was going to be on a stakeout with Erica, I wanted my good hoodie.

Lucky for me, the last of the nightfillers were only just leaving when I arrived, and they let me sneak back into the store. That surprised me, but the last one out said, "Erica's in there; she'll let you both out. Make sure you don't leave without her, though; you'll set off the alarms."

Hang on, Erica was *here*? She was meant to be at home right now, meeting Zero.

"Flaming heck," I said.

I dodged a few scattered milk crates and the piece of freezer cladding some long-gone workman had left open to expose the innards of the freezer, and jogged for the locker rooms. I must have been moving more quietly than I thought, because when I came around the corner of the last aisle and met Erica, she nearly jumped through the roof.

"Pet? What are you doing here?"

"Forgot my hoodie," I said. "What are you doing here? You were meant to be home all day; Zero's expecting you to be there when he arrives at nine!"

"There was—my locker was—someone has been going through my locker. I came back tonight to get out my watch. I took it off for tickets yesterday and forgot to put it back on. I only just remembered it now, and I thought it would be safe for me here if nightfill was still around."

"I'll call Zero and let him know where we are."

"Don't!" she begged me, and I hesitated. "He'll be so angry, and I know I shouldn't blame him, but don't, Pet!"

Zero had said to call or text if anything went wrong, but with Erica looking at me like that, it was hard to say no to her.

Ah heck. I should really say no. Why wasn't I saying no? I struggled to lift my phone, and eventually put it back in my pocket.

"We'll be right there," she said. "I promise. We can leave as soon as I find it."

"Okay," I said. "But you'd better hurry up. If we hang around here too long, Zero will call first. He was expecting to find you at home when he got there."

"I will," she promised. "I just—I couldn't leave it there for *him* to have. It's precious, you know?"

I would have hung around outside the locker room while she fetched her watch, and texted or called Zero anyway, but Erica pulled me in with her.

"Stay with me," she said.

So I stayed with her. I couldn't really do anything else, not now that I was here. But it was *hard*, hanging over her shoulder and waiting while she went through every piece of rubbish in her locker with more and more frantic reiterations of "It's got to be here! It must be! I know I left it in here!"

Actually, I was surprised she could find anything in the mess of old mouldy food and scrap paper—by the looks of it, she hadn't eaten any of the lunches she'd brought to work this week or the week before that.

I jiggled up and down beside the locker, taking out my phone every five minutes to check the time and wishing the detective or Zero would call first; but although Erica's search grew more frantic, she wouldn't leave.

It took nearly half an hour before she found it, a tiny gold thing that was small enough to fit beneath a badly stained bowl without making it sit sideways, and by then I was so relieved that all I said was, "Good, let's go!" without complaining about the wait.

"I'm coming, I'm coming," promised Erica. "I'm really sorry, Pet! But I couldn't leave it, especially not tonight!"

We hurried toward the side of the store and the door out, the store empty and ghost-like around us. I was feeling antsy now, prickles up and down my back where I might have had hackles if I was...you know, a wolf. I would have jogged all the way across the fridge and freezer section if it hadn't been for Erica trailing behind me.

Oh yeah, I was *very* antsy.

It was such a relief to see the door that led out into the alley that I didn't see the person standing by the end of the freezers until he moved, black hoodie separating from the display of black labelled frozen yoghurt behind him.

Metal studs caught the yellow light above.

"Ah heck," I said.

"Found you," said Daniel, through his teeth.

CHAPTER TWELVE

ERICA WHIMPERED, AND I TRIED VERY HARD NOT TO SIGH IN irritation. If she hadn't waffled around for the last twenty minutes, we would already have been safe at her house.

"Go home, Daniel," I said. "You shouldn't be around Erica."

He laughed, but it sounded almost like a sob, and there was a feral yellow gleam to his eye when he said, "That's funny. I just came to talk."

"Yeah?" I edged sideways a bit. Here in the store it was hard to see Between, but I could see the yellow in his eyes, and that was enough. I didn't know whether it was because I was getting so close to being wolf, or because of being able to see things like Between, but I knew he was close to turning wolf.

"Why are you here?" he demanded. "I told you to go home!"

"Left my hoodie here," I told him. Good thing I had, or Erica would have met Daniel alone—and that would have been a mess I didn't know how to clean up. "You know there's a whole lotta cameras in here, don't you?"

"I don't care about cameras!"

"Yeah, I figured," I muttered. "C'mmon, Erica. Let's go home."

"I—" Erica looked around wildly and grabbed at my arm. "I —I can't!"

"Exactly; she can't," said Daniel. He looked broader and taller today; less like a boy and more like a man. "We're going to talk."

"You can talk with her when the others get here," I said. Flaming heck, I wish I'd been able to call Zero.

"I'm going to talk with her now! Mind your own business and go home!"

"Yeah, I don't think so."

Daniel let out a sound of frustration that was almost a growl, and Erica began to cry.

"I killed a man for her, you know?" he said.

"Yeah, I know," I said, huffing a sigh.

"I didn't...didn't *ask* you to do that!" sobbed Erica, clinging to my sleeve.

I twitched my sleeve away from her. "Look, can you stop crying on me?"

She hiccoughed on a sob. "What?"

"It works on the blokes, but Wolf Boy already knows you were playing him."

"What?" she said again—bewildered, lost, helpless.

"And I'm not a bloke."

The frightened helplessness dropped from Erica's face like a snakeskin.

"What a pain in the neck," she said, carefully dabbing away the tears. "I'll have to work myself up to tears again later."

"Not on my account," I said.

"Not on yours," she agreed. "You were so helpful and caring before—really useful! What gave me away?"

"I didn't realise it earlier because I wasn't used to feeling a pack pull from anyone, but it must have been working away in the back of my mind, because as soon as you used your pack leader pull on me to not call Zero, I knew. You've been trying to steal me from the start, haven't you? What am I, a replacement idiot for him, or just someone to make you stronger?"

Erica snorted. "Steal you? You're rootless; open to anyone who wants to bring you in."

Daniel, still through his teeth, said, "I *warned* you, Pet! Why couldn't you mind your own business and stay away!"

"What warning?" I demanded. "All you did was glare at me and snarl at me!"

"I was warning you to stay away from her!"

"Use your words next time, you flamin' galah!" I told him. To Erica, I said, "I'm not rootless, you know. I'm already part of a pack, so your pull doesn't work on me." I thought about that, and added, "Well, it doesn't work properly, anyway. When I didn't know what it was I went along with it by instinct, but now that I've recognised it, turns out I can refuse it."

"A pack? With a vampire and two Behindkind fae?" Her voice was only amused, but her face was contemptuous. "It gave me a shock, I'll admit; seeing them all in the same room together. I knew what you were up to, but I didn't realise Behindkind were investigating as well. They certainly won't come to the aid of a human, if that's what you're thinking. They have their own reasons for investigating, I'm certain."

"It's a temporary pack," I said, frowning. "And it's not like your pack is looking like a flamin' healthy place these days. At least we're not killing each other."

Well, not yet, anyway; Jin Yeong certainly didn't mind the idea of killing me, and I was pretty sure Athelas was ambivalent about my death.

"Anyway," I said, "that's how I knew you were lying about being scared of shifters and stuff. You couldn't be scared of 'em if you were one of 'em, and since you were able to sway me into doing small stuff, I reckoned you had to be the boss. Is that how you made Wolf Boy kill that bloke for you as well?"

Daniel squeezed his eyes shut and opened them again. "Stop calling me Wolf Boy," he said to me. To Erica he said, "You told me Chris was trying to take over the pack! He wasn't even a shifter!"

Erica laughed. "He certainly would have been by the time you were finished with him, sweetheart! I thought he would agree to starting the change when there was no other option, but he fought it right until the end."

"Are you trying to die?" I asked her. Daniel's face was very red, and he was so angry he was almost crying. Almost crying, and almost, but not quite, wolf.

"He can't kill me," she said. "Not unless he's trying to challenge my leadership, and then we'll just see how strong his will is. Bianca couldn't do it, and she was fighting for her mate—Daniel couldn't even kill the human. I had to finish the job myself."

"You killed Chris because he didn't want to be a shifter?"

"It's a non-negotiable part of being with me," said Erica simply. "I thought he was just being coy, but it turns out he really wanted to be human. I told him he'd die if he didn't turn wolf, and he still refused it."

"What about the other ones?"

"How many of those do you know about?" Erica stared at me for a moment, then laughed again. "Sweetheart, if your friends know what's good for them, they won't meddle with Upper Management. Upper Management has a way of tidying away problems, and they're already following your detective friend very closely."

"Good friends of yours, are they?" I asked, unsurprised. "You scratch their back, they scratch yours, that sort of thing?"

"I explained to them that the incidents were matters of pack succession, and they stepped back."

"I don't think it was pack succession," I said. If I could string this out a bit longer, there was a chance—just a slight chance—

that Zero would realise something was wrong and come for us in time. If I got out of this alive, Zero was gunna kill me for not calling him—again. And I couldn't blame it on the pack leader pull, because once I'd recognised it, there had been a minute or two where I could have resisted. I only hadn't because I hadn't wanted to give myself away while it wasn't safe. "Bianca Terry, yeah, maybe, if you want to call it that. But there were three human victims and only two shifters. What were the humans doing wrong—apart from not wanting to turn into wolves?"

Erica sighed. "They got in the way. I don't have to answer for the deaths of a few unimportant humans."

I thought back to the photo of the single female human victim, April Post, her face bright and young, and then to Bianca Terry—the shifter fighting for her mate. "They were too attractive, weren't they? They were taking away the attention and trust of the other shifters—even the unimportant human one. What about the other human male—the tramp? What did he do wrong?"

"She said April wanted to join us," Daniel said, his face suddenly white. "She said it didn't go well and that James went wild with grief and attacked. He had to be put down."

He would have believed that, too. I'd thought it was just a normal crush on an older woman, but he must have been influenced by Erica as the pack leader as well.

"That's why you broke up the room at the police station, isn't it?" I said suddenly, to Daniel. "You were suspicious because of something—"

"Yes," said Erica. "I thought he might be more useful to me angry, and it looks like I was right. I gave him a hint of what really happened before he got there that night, and he went after the footage just as if I'd told him to do it."

"You figure he was going to get rid of the footage as well?" I asked, with one eye on Daniel's face. It was redder than before, and I wasn't sure whether he was about to burst into tears or into a rage.

Gotta keep her talking, I thought. Zero must be wondering why we weren't safe at her house; he'd told me to text or call if things went wrong. I just had to keep her talking until he came looking for us.

"No, that was just a nice extra," said Erica.

I ticked them off on my fingers. "So there was a human who was too attractive; dead. The shifter who was too keen on her; dead. A female shifter who was too attractive and maybe too ambitious, dead. One human bloke who didn't want to be turned into a shifter, even if it meant being with you—also dead. Seems like a pattern to me."

"Leadership carries certain perks with it," said Erica. "If I give myself for the good of the pack, I should expect to receive the benefits of that sacrifice. And the more trust my pack has in me, the stronger we get—it's a symbiotic relationship. The tramp, though; he actually thought he could blackmail me—he saw what I was capable of, and he still tried to blackmail me! If he'd been able to turn, I would have kept him."

I tried very hard not to roll my eyes. "I'm pretty sure that the sole attention of every male in the pack isn't one of the perks of being a leader."

Erica shrugged. "I don't expect to be the focus of every male in the pack; just the ones I pay attention to. And I don't appreciate other shifter women trying to undermine my authority, either; the pack is mine, and will remain mine. Sometimes a heavy hand is needed. Fortunately, I think your friends see things my way."

"Maybe," I said. It would have been nice to give vent to the angry negative that had sprung to my lips, but I wasn't sure it was true. "But killing other shifters is gunna make a difference if there weren't any legitimate challenges to your leadership."

"Perhaps," said Erica, "but I don't suppose they know about

that. I think you only just figured this out for yourself. They still think I need protection, and I'm quite certain they don't know I'm a shifter. I've been spraying enough perfume around the place to confuse the nosiest vampire."

Ah heck. I'd been hoping she didn't think of that. "Wouldn't bet on it," I told her.

"That's a shame," Erica said, smiling. "I think your three Behindkind will be willing to be persuaded when they find me crying over your dead body, having killed the shifter who attacked you. You're both so delightfully predictable—*he* came here without even thinking about it. It makes my job much easier. It won't be too hard to convince the Behindkind, I think."

"Yeah? How are you gunna do that? Wolf Boy—"

"My name is Daniel!"

"—he's pretty strong, from what I saw of that body before Upper Management tidied it away, and if you turn wolf, you're going to have Zero and Jin Yeong on your tail so quickly—"

"Can you please spare me the creative threats?" she said, and pulled out a gun.

"Flamin' heck!" I muttered.

What kind of a werewolf brings a gun with them? I mean, yeah, I know there's no such thing as werewolves and that she's a lycanthrope, but what kind of lycanthrope brings a gun along with them to a pack fight?

Erica smiled at me. "What? You don't think I got to be pack leader by letting my animal side run things, do you?"

Great. We were definitely going to die. From here, I could see two bits of metal piping in the exposed section of freezer that might be persuaded to turn into knives if only I could get to them; but I was too far away.

I said, "So, what? You're going to shoot Wolf Boy—"

Daniel stormed over to me, pushing me back a few steps, and snarled in my face. "My *name* is *Daniel*!"

"Do you really think that's important right now?" I demanded.

I managed to fall over one of the milk crates, which was pretty useful in two ways.

One, it made Erica sigh and look away for a second in a pained sort of way.

Two, it put me right in reach of the two bits of metal piping that only needed my hand on them to convince them that they were actually knives made of some kind of slick, dark metal.

Erica, this time numbly, said, "What?" and belatedly began to bring her gun back in line with us.

I threw one of the knives. Just chucked it at her like it would do some good, without planning anything except to wish it would cut off her hand or something. Somehow it hit the gun instead, and something went *crack* and then *thunk* so quickly that it was impossible to tell the sounds apart.

The gun landed behind Erica and she moved as if she would have dived for it, but Daniel was a wolf faster than my eyes could make sense of, huge and white, and already leaping.

"Ah heck!" I said, scrambling to my feet with my remaining knife. I didn't know how to do anything except footwork, and I hadn't been trained with knives, either. That might have been survivable, but my knees didn't seem steady, and I wasn't sure how much I could trust them.

Erica turned, growling, and fur rippled all over her, sprouting dark and thick.

White fur collided with dark in a snarling, toothy ball of furious energy, blood and fur flying.

"Ah heck!" I said again, and fumbled for my phone with my left hand, my right wrapped tightly around the hilt of my blade.

Gotta call Zero.

It wouldn't unlock, but then it didn't matter, because something hefty and full of teeth knocked me into a fridge door, shattering glass and shocking every bone in my body. For a moment I couldn't breathe, unsure if it was me or the glass that had been shattered into a thousand pieces.

Then everything *hurt*.

Blood mingled with the glass around me. I tried to push myself up to face the thing that had hit me, but wolf Daniel was between me and it, snarling. I couldn't find my knife but that didn't seem to matter to my body.

My body said *teeth* instead of *knife*, and instead of climbing to my feet to fight, I pulled myself up on all fours. Claws and paws scrabbled against the glass, knocking me over again as Daniel threw himself at Erica a second time.

Teeth, teeth, TEETH! said my brain.

And below that, deep and primal and hot, something sizzled into my being. *Pack leader*, it said. *Protect the pack leader.*

Ah heck. My body was trying to turn me into a wolf, and I didn't think I could stop it.

"Zero!" I screamed, trying to make sense of fingers and arms that wouldn't stay still. "*Zero!*"

Wolves yelped, sharp and sudden, and there was a breaking of glass somewhere nearby. I pushed myself onto all fours again, and saw a slim figure rise beside the prone body of a wolf. Dark fur; the wolf was Erica.

I was so focused on that that I didn't see anything else until Zero's boots stopped right in front of me. A blade touched the slick tiles beside his feet, clean and shiny, and a dim, still-slightly-human part of my brain said, *gloves*. Zero had on gloves, and full sleeves of something dark and shiny, and there was a similar shininess to the distant figure that must be Athelas. They were fully prepared for fighting wolves, and they had arrived in perfect time for the Act part of Intent, Initiation, and Act.

Flaming heck, said the human part of me, a bit more strongly. *I wish they'd tell me when they're using me for bait.*

"What are you doing?" snapped Zero. "Stand on your feet!"

I staggered to my feet, and they were still feet because he'd told me to stand on them and I didn't dare disobey. My head was still human when I turned it from side to side to see what was happening, too.

Erica was down in a furry mass behind Athelas, who cleaned a slim, short blade, eyes bright. Detective Tuatu stood between me and Zero, and the still-standing Daniel. Daniel snarled at him, eyes glowing yellow, but there was a film of disorientation over those eyes.

Detective Tuatu lifted his gun, hands shaking, and I threw myself at him.

Something strong and implacable wrapped itself around my arms and avoided my kicking as I struggled to get to Daniel, the wolf-thought still there in my brain that this was now Pack Leader, and Pack Leader must be defended. Human brain knew the human pack, but wolf brain was hot and hurt and confused.

"Put your gun away," said a voice, distantly; and my thoughts cleared enough to realise I was being passed from Zero's arms to the detective's.

I would have bitten the detective to get to Daniel, but he jerked away just in time.

"Ow! Stop it!"

I tried to snarl *let me go!* but all that came out was an actual snarl. Detective Tuatu went white, and his arms tightened around me.

"Just a moment, please," said Athelas' voice, though I couldn't see him now. "There's really no need to be so overwrought; in just a moment—yes, there he goes."

Daniel collapsed by the door, a matted mess of blood and fur, and shrank again until he was a human, now white and bloody in patches.

"Jin Yeong?" asked Zero.

"Coming; the last I saw, he was dealing with the couple of loiterers outside who wanted to ensure their pack leader's privacy. Should I take blood from the male or the female?"

"Both, if Jin Yeong doesn't arrive soon," Zero said.

I wriggled furiously to get free, but although the detective panted with effort, he didn't let me go.

"*Yogiya, yogiya*," said a familiar voice.

"At last!" said Athelas.

"*Ah!*" said Jin Yeong, his eyes narrowing on Daniel, who lay in a swiftly widening pool of his own blood. "*Chajada!*"

"It's the boy?" Zero said sharply. "It's his blood?"

"*Ne.*"

Athelas knelt swiftly beside Daniel, and there was a disturbance in the blood pooling around him. Did it lift up or did it dance? I didn't have the chance to figure that out, because Athelas moved further over, until I couldn't see anything but Daniel's closed-eyed face.

Athelas asked Zero, "Do you want him to live or die? With this kind of blood loss he'll be dead in minutes."

I tried to shout at them that of *course* we wanted him to live, but all that came out was a snarl, low and wild. Daniel twitched, his head turning blindly toward me.

"*Hold* the pet!" Zero snapped. "Pet, do not shift!"

"I'm *trying!*" retorted the detective, and that was almost a snarl, too.

Wildly, I tried again to bite him, scrabbling at the floor with my feet to get to Daniel. Detective Tuatu yelled, and a vice-like hand closed around my neck.

"Bad pet!" said Zero's voice, with that commanding tone in it. It cut through some of the compulsion to go to Daniel, and the teeth that had begun to grow longer and rounder thinned out again.

I choked a bit, and said hoarsely, "Save him!"

"Take the blood we need," said Zero. "Make sure there's enough. Then save him. I'll take the pet home."

Jin Yeong asked a question, his voice a garbled blur, and Zero answered, "Bring them both. That one will die Behind."

"Wait!" said Detective Tuatu, his voice panicked. "You can't kill her! I didn't call you in to kill people!"

"You didn't call us in," Zero said. "Our purposes aligned for a brief time and we worked alongside you. You have no jurisdiction here."

"But the law—!"

"I told you when we began," said Zero, his voice utterly terrifying in its calmness, "that we care nothing for human courts. This shifter is Behindkind and under Behind law she will die for her crimes."

Detective Tuatu took two steps forward, putting himself between Zero and Erica. "You can't kill her!"

My eyes were clouded, but I saw Jin Yeong sigh. He was behind the detective before I could blink again, one arm slipping around Tuatu's throat in a way that could have been affectionate if it hadn't been for the way it made the detective's eyes bulge. The other snaked down to seize Tuatu's right wrist.

Detective Tuatu fought for air, his mouth opening and closing, and I began to struggle again, forgetting that it was Zero's implacable hand that held me.

"Don't you kill him!" I yelled at Jin Yeong.

Jin Yeong raised one brow at me and forced the detective's arm back toward himself, wrist upward.

I screamed at him, or maybe I snarled again, and Zero's hand tightened around the nape of my neck. Both of Jin Yeong's brows went up this time, his eyes bright, and he grinned at me. Then he bit down on the detective's wrist, a single, brief puncture; and let go.

Detective Tuatu's eyes rolled back and he collapsed onto the floor.

Athelas, who was crouched over Daniel, hiding him from view, said over his shoulder, "The pet is very combative today."

There was a warning in his voice. I didn't know if the warning was for me, or for Zero, but I didn't care. I made an inarticulate growl and kicked out at Zero again, my eyes fixed on JinYeong.

"I've noticed," said Zero, holding me further away. "Do not bite me, Pet."

JinYeong licked the trace of blood from his lips slowly, mockingly, and asked another question of Zero.

"Leave him where he is," Zero told him. "He'll wake up soon?"

JinYeong shrugged and spoke again.

"Can you be finished within the hour?" Zero asked Athelas.

"I'm nearly finished," murmured Athelas, without turning his head. "And JinYeong will attend to the old pack leader. You can take the pet home."

"*Ne*," agreed JinYeong. He gave me one last, exultant smile; and if I was nearly beside myself with rage and the urge to tear myself out of my own skin, I saw what he in his complacency didn't.

Erica staggered to her feet behind him and stood on all fours, swaying. She saw me dangling in Zero's grip, her eyes clouded but vicious, and Zero snapped a warning at JinYeong that was just too late.

Bloody, rage-filled, and savage, Erica shot past JinYeong, leaping over the detective's prone body and right for me.

Maybe she was blinded with rage. Maybe she thought I was the easiest way through, or that Zero would be so occupied with making sure I didn't bite him that he'd have no time for her.

Maybe she knew she was going to die anyway, and just wanted to take me with her.

She leapt, snarling, and I saw teeth. Zero pivoted, wrenching me sideways and thrusting upward with his sword hand at the same time. Shocked and unable to see, I heard the liquid patter of something hit the floor, my legs dangling against Zero's thigh. A reflection glittered on the freezer doors, broken into a triptych of myself, Zero, and Erica.

I dangled from Zero's right hand in one freezer door, my

hands clinging so tightly to his wrist that the glove pulled away from the skin, and my teeth too close to that exposed wrist for his safety. Zero, side-on, filled all of the middle freezer door and extended past the frame of it; and in the third was the wolf form of Erica, gutted and impaled on Zero's sword like some kind of grisly standard, her own teeth just a foot from Zero's face. There was a spatter of darkness on his face and neck in the reflection.

"Did she bite you?" I panted, shocked out of my haze—or maybe it was just because Daniel was unconscious. Somehow my teeth and my face were my own again instead of struggling to tear through my skin and turn me wolf. "Did she get you?"

Zero turned his head, catching my eyes, and said, "Don't bite me, Pet."

"Not gunna," I said, coughing. "Did she get you?"

Zero's other shoulder went down a bit, and something in the reflection in the corner of my eye slid to the floor with a heavy *smack*, like wet concrete.

"Don't bite me, Pet," Zero said again, but this time it felt like that wasn't what he was really saying. It was hard to look away from his eyes. "She didn't touch me."

"Okay," I said, but one of my hands was stretching out to wipe away the blood anyway, just in case there were teeth marks there.

Zero twitched me away from himself and put me down gently, facing the front of the store, with his hand still around my neck. "I'm taking the pet home," he said again. "Bring the blood as soon as you can."

He pushed me in front of him, and it was no use trying to turn around and see what was happening behind him, because he was too big, and his hand was too strong. He marched me from the store with that hand. I don't remember doors opening for us, or alarms going off, so I suppose we wandered Between at some stage before we reached the front doors. I was used to it by then, and I didn't notice exactly when the freezers faded and we began to walk through an icy maze of smooth, glassy Between walls that eventually brought us back into the house in the bathroom.

"How many ways can you get Between from this house?" I asked. It was a stupid question; an inconsequential question, but my mouth wanted to talk because if it didn't, my teeth might start chattering instead. "What if someone wants to come in?"

"They can't come in without killing me," said Zero. "Keep walking."

"But I've got some stuff in the bathroom," I protested, pushing back ineffectually at the tidal wave of forward motion that was Zero. I'd been buying stuff like bandages and antiseptic wash while they were gone; figured we'd need them sooner or later. "We've got to clear up all that blood and make sure she didn't get you."

"I'm not injured," Zero said, without acknowledging my futile attempts to stay in the bathroom.

"Yeah, but—"

"I'm not injured."

He lifted me right through the door and across the hall, then down into the living room and dropped me on my side of the lounge.

"Just...sit there," he said. "Don't move. Don't chew on anything. Don't shift."

"I'm not gunna shift," I said, moving uncomfortably. There was glass all through my clothes, and even though they were big pieces, I didn't like them there. Glass, and blood. "Not anymore. It was just that Daniel was—and then Jin Yeong—anyway, it doesn't feel like my skin is crawling off anymore."

As though I hadn't spoken, he warned, "Once you shift for the first time, the change is complete; you'll never be human again."

"I said I wouldn't shift," I told him, scowling.

"I said I wasn't injured," he countered.

I shivered a bit. "What?"

"Never mind. Clean your face."

"That's what I was *trying* to say in the bathroom," I muttered. "That's where the stuff for cleaning is."

"Stay," said Zero warningly, and went back to the bathroom himself. He came back with a small bucket of warm water, two flannels, a towel, and the antiseptic wash. He threw one of the flannels at me, dipped his own in the water first, and said again, "Clean your face."

I didn't realise how much blood there was on my face and hands until the water turned red and the flannel still came away sticky. Zero finished before I did, and that made me wonder how I hadn't seen the state of my face in the same reflections that had shown me the splatter of blood on his. Maybe it was just because he was so white that it showed up more clearly.

I went to the mirror to make sure I'd gotten the rest of it, and there was a wound along my chin. The glass door must have cut me after all. I grimaced and dabbed it down with antiseptic wash, which made me grimace a bit more.

"Use the butterfly strips," said Zero, without looking up at me. "Your face is still messy."

While I had been busy cleaning my face, he was busy setting out something on the coffee table. It wasn't photos and stuff this time; it was something that looked like it could have been a lab set with a beaker and a tiny vial. Instead of a network of tubing and a Bunsen burner, there was a silver wire with a flat-bottomed pendulum at either end, one each in the beaker and vial, and beneath the beaker was only empty space. I couldn't see what was holding it up, even when I blinked at it a couple of times, so I looked away again and stuck butterfly strips across the cut on my jawline.

It didn't help with the pain, but it did make my face look a bit better. I sat down on the lounge again and leaned forward to point at the glass beakers.

"What's that?"

"Don't touch."

"Yeah, but what is it?"

"Something for making the antivirus," he said.

"Ah," said Athelas, slipping from Between at the same time as his voice, "I see you're ready to go. Very good."

"Did you get enough?" asked Zero, his eyes running over the red-filled bottle that Athelas was holding with a professional sort of assessment.

"Where's Daniel?" I demanded, at the same time.

Athelas, ignoring me, answered Zero. "I believe so. Are you ready for it?"

"You can begin. Try not to disturb the pendulum. It's a delicate balance in this house."

Athelas poured blood into the beaker carefully, and it looked like so much that I couldn't understand how Daniel was still alive.

"Where is he?" I asked Athelas, suspiciously.

"Somewhere safe," he said easily, holding the bottle over the beaker to allow every last drop to drain.

I scowled at him. "Yeah, that's what people say when they've killed someone."

Much amused, Athelas asked, "How shall I convince you, then, Pet? When I left him they said I'd gotten him to them just in time; any more blood loss would have been fatal."

"Who is *they*?"

"Daniel is somewhere Behind," Zero interrupted. He set something bubbling and coiling below the suspended beaker of blood; something that was invisible but somehow still seemed to make movement in the air. "Somewhere like a hospital with some of the pack members. He'll survive."

"All right." If Zero said it, I would believe it. I sat back on the lounge, wrapping my arms around my legs, and watched them over the torn, bloody knees of my jeans. "What are you doing with the blood?"

"Extracting what I need from it," Zero said. "Be quiet, Pet."

Zero was worse than Athelas when it came to answering questions without really answering them, I thought glumly. To add to the fun of the evening, I smelled the stench of vampire as something tickled the edges of Between, and Jin Yeong strolled into the room, his clothes and face as clean as if he'd checked himself in at the dry cleaners.

I opened my mouth to remark on his general lack of person-hood, but Zero said again, "Be quiet, Pet."

Jin Yeong grinned at me and said a brief something to Zero.

"The detective is at home and sleeping off the small amount of vampire saliva he was injected with," Zero said.

"*Injected?* He was flamin' well bi—"

"Be quiet, Pet."

I glared at Jin Yeong over my knees as well, and he made a mocking air-kiss at me. That was even more annoying, and I felt my skin begin to do the same, itching, crawling thing it had done before. I looked away from him and caught Athelas' eyes; saw the amused comprehension in them.

"Shall I make you coffee, Pet?" he asked.

"Can't afford it," I said. "Oi. What's that?"

From the beaker of blood, a single drop rose along the silver wire, travelling slowly, and grew smaller as it followed that wire. It sank into the pendulum in the smaller beaker like the first three or four drops had done, and I saw a small, velvety drop burgeon at the bottom of the pendulum.

"Antivirus," said Athelas.

"It looks like blood," I muttered.

"The appearance is similar," Athelas allowed. "However, the composition of it is entirely dissimilar. When it comes to rest in the vial through a combination of magic and alchemy, it is something else entirely."

Unconvinced, I watched the passage of blood drops across the silver wire until there was almost half a vial of dark red stuff that wasn't blood but looked exactly like the blood from which it had been taken. It looked so much like it, in fact, that I glanced back at the larger beaker to compare the colour, and was surprised to see it empty.

"Oi! Where'd it go?"

Athelas, smiling faintly, didn't answer.

Zero said shortly, "Athelas told you." He lifted the pendulum in the vial by the wire until it was clear of the glass, then took it swiftly away and let it drop into the original beaker with a soggy sort of *clink*.

The vial, he picked up and stoppered with a glassy top, then shook.

I giggled, which made them all look at me, and said, "*Shake before use* works for everything, I s'pose!"

Zero looked at me in silence for a moment or two, then leaned across to give me the vial. "Drink it," he said.

"It still looks like blood," I said doubtfully, pinching the glass stopper out.

Jin Yeong hissed a disparaging laugh, but Athelas only smiled.

"Oh well, here we go," I said, and upended the vial in my mouth.

It was bitter. Bitter and salty and tarry. I swallowed, shuddering, and complained, "How come I have to swallow it, anyway? Why can't you inject it? Won't it work slower this way?"

"I don't know how to administer an injection," said Zero. He leaned forward and pinched my chin carefully between two fingers, avoiding my cut, and twitched it one way and then another. "And Behindkind don't usually use them."

"The goblins do," I muttered.

Zero tilted my head back to peer at my eyes and didn't answer. He was frowning.

"Behindkind have a swifter method of delivery," Athelas explained. "If the antivirus was merely chemical, administered to your bloodstream, it would be quicker to give you an injection."

"Yeah, bet you know how to give injections, too," I mumbled to myself.

Athelas' eyes crinkled slightly at the edges. "Since, Pet, the antivirus is both chemically *and* magically derived, it is quicker to administer orally, where the magic can sink in more quickly."

"How quickly?" I asked him, going cross-eyed in my attempts to see him. "When's it gunna work?"

"It should already be working," said Zero.

CHAPTER THIRTEEN

"Yeah, but *is* it working?"

But I could tell from Athelas' faint frown and Zero's utter stillness that it wasn't working—and worse, that they had no idea why not.

JinYeong, muttering to himself, plucked the antivirus vial from my fingers and sniffed at it. He offered it to Zero, who tapped one finger to the lip of the bottle.

The residue collected and melded together into a single, small drop, lifting until it floated right out of the bottle and hovered in the air in front of Zero.

I hugged my knees to my chest and watched the drop slowly revolve in the beam of Zero's icy blue eyes. JinYeong watched it, too, though that was probably because he was getting hungry again and it looked a lot like blood. In his eyes I saw reflected the moment Zero sent a spark of what must have been magic through it.

I couldn't help gasping a little bit, because it was so sudden and bright.

"Perhaps you should consider looking away when Zero

employs his magic," suggested Athelas, as the drop sank back into its vial. "You'll find yourself a little more sensitive at the moment. Zero, shall I fetch more blood from our young friend?"

"We can't take any more," I said, and there was a feeling of sharp sickness in my stomach. Next time the crawling of my skin began and my teeth tried to force their way out of my mouth, I wouldn't be able to stop it. There was no time to wait for more—and no way I was going to let them take more right now. "You said he'd die if we did."

As if I hadn't spoken, Athelas enquired again of Zero, "Shall I?"

"*No*," I said.

To my relief, Zero put the stopper back in the bottle and said, "No."

"I see," nodded Athelas. He was smiling. "All very heartening, but that is our last drop of antivirus. What is missing?"

Frowning, Zero said, "There's nothing missing. It's fresh, it's activated, and it's the same strain that infected the pet. It should have worked."

I huffed a small sigh. "So I'm gunna die."

"*Ne*," said Jin Yeong, more cheerfully than usual.

"You're taking an unusually grim view of things, aren't you, Pet?"

I glanced over at Athelas and saw the glitter of amusement in his eyes. If there was anything I knew about Athelas, it was that he could be amused at the idea of people dying; but I didn't think that was why he was amused. I'd seen him like this before.

When had I seen him like this?

"Ah!" I said. "Got it!"

Jin Yeong made a *pft* sort of noise and stuffed his hands in his pockets, but Athelas, whose eyes flashed up to meet mine, looked startled.

I grinned at him, and the startled look faded back into amusement again.

"What is it, Pet?" asked Zero. He hadn't reacted; his voice wasn't particularly interested, either.

That was all right. Zero never sounded particularly interested in most things, but I'd come to understand that it didn't stop him noticing them.

"Reckon Athelas has an idea," I said.

I remembered that look—that quiet amusement, with an edge of superiority. Athelas had looked the same way the day Jin Yeong dragged me out of my hidden room—he'd known I was there all along, and he hadn't told, just for the sheer fun of knowing what no one else knew.

"I'm afraid you won't care for the idea, Pet," Athelas said now, and this time there was a malicious note to his voice.

Ah heck. Whatever it was, I was *definitely* not going to like it.

Zero's eyes rested on Athelas. "What do you know?"

"I suspect."

"What do you suspect?"

"I suspect that if Jin Yeong were to volunteer his saliva once again, it would make a difference."

"*Heck* no!" I said, trying to scrabble away.

Zero's implacable hand at the nape of my neck stopped me.

"There's no reason why that should be true," he said. He didn't let me go, though; he was thinking about it. "There are no special considerations when a human contracts lycanthropy. Source blood antivirus should kill it."

"Then there's no reason why the antivirus shouldn't be working," pointed out Athelas. "All I'm suggesting is that we should consider again—perhaps take into account Jin Yeong's saliva."

"Wasn't that what started the virus working again in the first place?" I complained. I still felt pretty aggrieved about that.

"Indeed," said Athelas. "It's very interesting!"

"Well, I'm not drinking his spit!"

Jin Yeong gave a small sniff of laughter and I glared at him, but he only pursed his lips in one of his more smug looks.

"It can't hurt to try," Zero said, thoughtfully; but he surprised me by letting me go. He watched me in an evaluating sort of a way, like he was waiting for me to be reasonable about this.

Forget being reasonable.

"I'm not drinking his spit!" I yelled again, dodging away from him and nearly colliding with my lounge in my haste to put the coffee table between us.

"Would you prefer to die in the throes of lycanthropy?"

"Yeah!" I said to Athelas. "Yeah. I'm gunna die. That's okay, but I'm not drinking his spit as well as Wolf Boy's blood!"

"I believe I've already explained that it is no longer blood," began Athelas, "but in fact—"

I saw JinYeong roll his eyes, but somehow I didn't see him move again until he plucked the vial of antivirus from Zero's hand, even though he was across the room from Zero.

"What the—"

JinYeong was *there*, in my face. I jerked away, feeling too late the hook of his sharp shoes behind my ankle, and went over backward.

I'm not proud of it, but I shrieked.

A mad flapping of arms did me no good; my back hit the couch seat and JinYeong's hand closed silkily around my neck before I could pick myself up again.

Leaning over me with one knee perched coolly on the couch seat, he removed the stopper from the vial with his teeth and spat it to the floor, then tipped the single remaining drop of the antivirus onto his tongue.

"Zero!" I yelled. "Help!"

Lightning fast, JinYeong touched his finger to his tongue and stuffed that finger in my mouth. I bit down on it, but I could already taste the sharp acidity of the antivirus, and when he wrenched his finger away I didn't try to spit the antivirus out.

JinYeong inspected his bitten finger, baring his own teeth, and pushed away from the couch. I don't know what he said, but he can't have been feeling more hard-done-by than I was, so I only glared at him and tried to sit up again.

My arms didn't want to let me push with them, and there was something weird about my legs as well. Like static on the telly, only warmer.

"I really wouldn't bother trying to sit up, Pet," Athelas said. "You'll only pass out again in a few moments, so it hardly seems worth the trouble."

"Why am I passing out?" I complained, but already my voice sounded as warm and staticky as my arms and legs felt. "I didn't pass out when…"

My voice faded away, and maybe someone said, "You didn't swallow Jin Yeong's saliva the first time," but I wasn't sure if it was Zero or Athelas, or just my own annoyed inner voice talking to me.

After that was warmth, and the sound of rushing water—or maybe blood—and I floated away somewhere voices didn't make sense any longer.

I suppose the good thing about waking up the day after someone has shoved vampire spit down your throat is that it gives you *really good* reflexes for a while. I didn't expect that.

Didn't expect to be able to see so much stuff, either. Little stuff I'd never usually see, like the ants crawling on the leaves outside the kitchen window from all the way across the room while sunlight warmed the green to yellow so vibrantly that I could almost smell it. It made the world feel more alive but less touchable, and I wasn't sure I liked it.

And Between was *really* easy to see. It made patterns around the edges of the living room, as if the house was halfway Between in a way I'd never realised before, and kaleidoscoped around Zero like some kind of psychedelic signpost that he definitely wasn't just your normal bloke. Athelas was less spectacular; I gazed at him as he sat in his chair opposite me, and if it wasn't for the fact that he had a bit of a pearly gold glow to him, or that his shadow didn't quite sit right, he might have looked nearly the same as usual.

Hang on. The glow and shadow weren't what made him different today. It was that here, inside, he shouldn't have *had* a shadow. Not one quite so dark or silky, that seemed to sink into the very fabric of the house itself.

"You're really scary sometimes," I told him, sitting up.

Athelas tipped up his head to look at me and his shadow did the same, just a little too late. I shivered, and he smiled.

"Well, Pet?"

"Yeah, I'm all right. You want tea?"

"I think not," he said. He put a bookmark in his book and set it down on the coffee table. "Try not to bite Jin Yeong, won't you?"

"Why would I bite Jin Yeong?" I asked blankly, but Athelas only smiled again.

From his alcove, Zero said, "Jin Yeong won't be back until later. I sent him out."

Typical. Zero probably just wanted to make sure I couldn't get Jin Yeong back for shoving his spit down my throat. He probably thought by the time Jin Yeong got home, I would have forgotten about it.

Well, he was gunna be flamin' surprised, I thought darkly. I had a few ideas, and none of them involved letting smug-faced vampires get away with making me swallow their spit.

"Sit up, Pet," said Zero, crossing the room. He crouched by the lounge as I did so, and grabbed me by the ears, sudden and gentle.

"Oi!" I protested, because even if it was gentle, it was still surprising.

"Sit still, Pet," he said, and tilted my head this way and that. I suppose he wanted to see if there was still yellow in my eyes, because it was definitely my eyes he was looking at. When he was satisfied with that, he pushed away the hair from my forehead and tipped my head down to stare at the patch that had been furry yesterday.

"It's gone," I told him, but I didn't expect him to let go until he was satisfied himself, and he didn't. "How's Daniel?"

"Alive."

"Yeah, but is he okay?"

"He's alive, for now. If that changes, I'll tell you."

I wasn't exactly satisfied, but at least I knew he wasn't dead, and I could check on him later—if I could find him. I sat still and let Zero study my forehead until at last he let me go.

"Don't bite Jin Yeong," he said.

"Athelas already said that," I remarked. "Why would I bite Jin Yeong?"

"I should have thought the prospect was more particularly attractive today," murmured Athelas.

I narrowed my eyes at him. "I only bit him yesterday because he shoved his finger in my mouth."

"Exactly my point," agreed Athelas.

"Enough," said Zero.

I wasn't sure if he was talking to me or Athelas, but I shut up anyway.

"Don't let him feed you blood, either," he added. "There could be more unpleasant side effects than those you had with lycanthropy."

"Yuck," I said. "I had enough blood with the steaks I've eaten lately. I'm not gunna drink the stuff."

Zero looked me over once again. "You're not hungry?"

"Nah. Why? You want some breakfast?"

"No," he said, and this time he seemed to be satisfied. "Just an early dinner."

I made a face. "All right, but I'm not having steak."

I heard a deep rumble that could have been a chuckle, but when my head snapped up to look at Zero, his face was as dispassionate as always.

"As you please," he said. "It's Jin Yeong's turn to choose tonight, in any case."

"What you want me to do, anyway?" I asked him. "I can make lunch in an hour or two, and we could work on my footwork or—"

"I don't think so."

"But I've been—"

"I don't have time to train you today," Zero said. "And I don't have time for lunch, either."

Yeah, he looked *real* busy; flipping through bits of newspaper and photographs. I sighed, but he ignored that, so I mizzled away into the kitchen to do the dishes someone had made when they did dinner last night and breakfast this morning.

"Don't do that," said Zero's voice, and Athelas' gentle laugh floated through from the living room. "It's too noisy. Find something quiet to do."

So I spent the morning profitably instead. And when I say profitably, I mean that I went around the entire house and made every picture on the walls just a *little* higher on the right. Not much. Not even so much as an obsessive-compulsive human would notice. Maybe a millimetre. If Jin Yeong was going to shove his spit down my throat and be smug about it, I was going to make a nuisance of myself, too.

After that, I went quietly around the house and took off one curtain ring from every set of curtains to make a single section sag slightly on each one. That didn't seem like quite enough, but I didn't want to risk Jin Yeong coming home and catching me at it, so the only other thing I did was to pinch Athelas' cologne and put the tiniest drop of it in the carpet of Jin Yeong's wardrobe.

With any luck, it would drive him crazy, the suspicion of someone else's scent in his clothes.

It's the little things in life, man.

THE DAY PASSED SLOWLY, WITHOUT ANY LESSENING OF THE extra senses or reflexes I'd gained from Jin Yeong's saliva. If it wasn't for the bits of Between I could still see dancing around the house, I might have found it a boring day. I tried to read one of Zero's books from the bookshelf and he didn't object when I took it, so I supposed he didn't mind. I couldn't understand it anyway, even when I skim-read it without letting myself pay too much attention, and Athelas had left earlier to go somewhere mysterious as usual, so I couldn't ask him about it. After a little while it ended up face down on my chest while I gazed up at the slowly moving ceiling.

It wasn't really moving, of course; but whatever it was Between, or Behind—that version of it was moving. What was it? Water? Sky? I didn't know, but it was strangely calming to watch it.

Late afternoon drew on, but neither Athelas nor Jin Yeong returned home, and at last I turned away from the lazily flowing ceiling to flick my legs up and off the couch.

"I'm going out!" I called to Zero.

"For how long?"

"Dunno. 'Bout an hour or two?"

"Take your phone."

"Gotcha, boss," I said, and went upstairs to grab my hoodie. The phone was already in the big front pocket, but I slipped it into the pocket of my jeans instead: there was something more important that needed to go in that big front pocket.

I didn't tell Zero where I was going, and he didn't ask. He might have expected me to go to the supermarket to get stuff for dinner, and I *was* planning on doing that, so it wasn't that I was being a bad pet.

I just wanted to do something else first.

This time I made sure the detective wasn't hanging around the other side of the house before I sneaked into his yard. There was a light on inside the kitchen, but he shouldn't be able to see me if I stayed behind the bushes, so I found myself a nice quiet, sheltered part of the garden with a bit of shade and a bit of late sunlight, and started to dig a hole. The dryad seemed to watch me do it, and I found myself slowing down until finally, I stopped.

"What? What's the problem?" Its branches shivered slightly, and I asked, "Too cold for you?"

Another shiver.

"You're a plant. How can you be cold?" I looked at it again and sighed. "All right, all right. I'll take you inside where it's warm—but he's gunna look at me like I'm mad, and that's your fault."

As usual, the dryad didn't reply, but it felt like if it could have spoken, it would have said *thank you*.

I wasn't sure the decrepit-looking doorbell would work, so I knocked on the door, the dryad sitting happily in the palm of my other hand.

There was a small click from the little view-hole, so I gave it a grin. The door swung open.

"What do you want?" demanded Detective Tuatu, without opening the door the whole way. "If you try to bite me again—"

"Yeah, sorry about that," I said. "Came to apologise."

"Did you."

"Yeah. Brought you a house plant." I held up the dryad, and the roots that had unwound from the rock swayed, then reached for the detective.

"That's not a—" he stopped, and blinked once or twice. "That's weird. It didn't look like a plant before."

"Too much stress," I told him. "You're seeing things. And if it looks like a tin of cat food sometimes, just remind it that it's a plant."

"If it looks like—"

"Gunna ask me in?"

Detective Tuatu looked suspiciously at me.

"Promise I won't try to bite you again."

He sighed, and opened the door wider, standing aside. I slipped past him gleefully and carried the dryad through the hall.

"You'll have to clean the muck off your windows," I said over my shoulder. "It'll want more light than that."

"Why can't it go outside?" he demanded. "I don't want a house plant."

"It's easier to talk to if it's inside."

"I'm not going to talk to a house plant."

I shrugged and cleared aside peeling paint and a kitchen scrubber so that the dryad would have the whole windowsill to itself. "Suit yourself. I'm pretty sure it'll grow faster if you talk to it, though."

"It's going to get bigger? I thought it was a bonsai. Am I supposed to water it?"

"Didn't say it'd get bigger," I told him. "I said it'd grow faster."

"I never know if what you say makes sense to you, or if you're just talking out of your hat."

I grinned at him. "It's a pain in the neck, isn't it? That's what those three do to me all the time. I think it's catching."

"Those three," began Detective Tuatu. "What did they do to me?"

"Wake up with a headache, did you?"

"No," he said. Dark and frustrated, his eyes went rapidly from the dryad to me, then back again. "What did you do with the boy?"

"He's fine," I said, answering the question he hadn't asked first. "He might turn himself in when he's recovered a bit. Dunno if you'll be able to do anything with him, though. Not unless you've got a special department in the Police Force that I don't know about."

The detective gave vent to a frustrated laugh. "I could charge him with accessory after the fact, or assault and battery, but I couldn't prove it. What about *her*?"

"You don't need to worry about her."

"Did they kill her?"

"Sort of," I said, trying to edge him kindly into it.

"How can you *sort of* kill someone?!"

"She got loose and tried to kill me. Zero stopped her."

He sighed. "All right."

"All right?" That was surprising. I'd expected him to be a lot more upset about it, especially since Erica was dead.

"I don't like it, but at least there's a reason for it. Pet—"

"Yeah?" Funny, that was the first time he'd called me that. I wasn't sure whether it was weird or nice.

"They've finished their investigation, haven't they?"

"Yeah. Why?"

"Nothing much," he said, absent-mindedly touching one finger to the dryad's branches. I wondered if he could see how the roots reached out to him. "But Athelas is still at the station."

I frowned. I'd wondered where he'd gone this morning after I woke up. "That's weird," I said. "He didn't say anything. Wonder what he's up to."

"So do I," Detective Tuatu said grimly. "A friend of mine said he'd been pulling some old case files."

"What sort of case files?"

"He said he'd talk about it with me later. Am I supposed to water that?"

"Probably," I said. "I mean, I'm pretty sure it's normal like that."

"Well, that's something, anyway. Don't blame me if it dies— I'm a bad gardener."

I grinned. "You'd have to do a lot more than be a bad gardener to kill this one."

Something like dying, I was pretty sure. That stopped me grinning.

"Good," said the detective. "Because I don't have time to look after houseplants."

"This is a houseplant that looks after you," I said.

"What?"

"Never mind. What are you doing?"

"I'm going out," Detective Tuatu said, sliding his keys into his pocket.

"Cool. Where are we going?"

"*We're* not going anywhere. I have someone to meet—you're going home."

"Who are you meeting?"

"Someone who messaged me last night."

I gave him a sceptical look. "Sure that's safe?"

"He's a friend of mine," said the detective. "Of course it's safe."

"Sometimes people who look like your friends aren't your friends," I muttered. I still remembered the changelings my psychos had dealt with a little while ago.

"What?"

"Nothing. Is that the friend who told you about Athelas?"

"Yes."

"I'm gunna walk with you."

Detective Tuatu grinned. "For my protection, or yours?"

"Neither," I said. "Just Zero gave me two hours, and I've still got about an hour. Can't hurt."

"They still only let you out of the house for a few hours at a time?"

"Remember how I tried to bite you?"

"Ah."

"Yeah. They're just making sure I don't try to bite anyone else."

"What was that about, anyway?"

I looked across at him. "You really wanna know?"

"Oh well, maybe not," he said, sighing. "You're not coming in when we get there."

"All right," I said agreeably.

I followed him up the stairs when we got there, anyway, even though he glared at me.

"Don't reckon he's home," I said. The day was starting to darken, and most people would have had a light on somewhere around the house by now. More than that, there was a sense of emptiness to the place that I was putting down to my currently heightened senses.

"He probably hasn't finished work yet," Detective Tuatu said. "I have a key; I'll wait."

Maybe there was a slight stressed accent on the word *I*.

"Trying to get rid of me?" I asked, grinning. I wasn't going anywhere; I still had forty-five minutes before Zero expected me back, and I wanted to make sure JinYeong had a chance to get home and uncomfortable before I got back. I didn't trust myself not to snigger in his face.

"Why are you interested in my friend's house?" asked the detective suspiciously.

"I'm not," I said. "But I'm interested in why you're trying to get rid of me."

"I'm not trying to—fine. You can come in. But if you start making trouble, I'll kick you out."

"What trouble?" I protested, as he unlocked the front door. "What trouble am I gunna start in someone else's house? I've never even been here before."

"You can have a cup of coffee before you go home," said Detective Tuatu.

It sounded like he was trying to be stern, so I gave him an encouraging grin and trotted through the door and down the hall.

"I don't like it when you grin at me like that," he said, following me down the hall and into the kitchen. "Boil the jug; I'll find the coffee."

"Oi," I said, with one eye on the faint steam that was still rising from the spout of the kettle. "Thought you said this bloke wasn't home yet?"

"He isn—" he saw the steam and frowned. "He must have gone to the shops for something—or maybe he's out the back."

"Maybe," I muttered. I popped my head back out of the kitchen and looked suspiciously down the hall.

The wallpapered vines tracing along the hallway moved.

Uh oh. Maybe I should have taken the dryad along with us—only I didn't think it worked as well portably as it did when it was planted, so to speak.

I kept an eye on the vines, and heard something scratching away further down the hall.

"This bloke have a dog?"

"No."

"Cat?"

"No. Why?"

"What about really big rats?"

"I'll make you wait outside if you don't start talking," the detective warned me.

I was gunna say *Yeah? You and whose army?* but this time when the vines along the hallway moved, it was because a fresh, stirring breeze moved them. Behind those vines, suddenly so leafy and concealing, something scratched or dragged or rattled.

"Oi," I said to Detective Tuatu. "Reckon we'd better get out of here."

He didn't move; hadn't seen the vines, or heard the scratches. Even his voice sounded reluctantly amused when he asked, "What are you talking about?"

"We gotta go," I said, and grabbed him by the sleeve.

It wasn't my new instincts that made my heart beat fast, or the hairs on the back of my neck stand up. Nope. That was good old human fear.

"There's something coming, and I'm pretty flamin' sure we don't wanna be here when whatever it is gets here."

"Something coming from where?"

There was a thump, this one loud enough that even Detective Tuatu heard it, and a limp body came tumbling through the vines. It hit my leg on the way through, startling a yelp out of me, which made the detective grab my collar and haul me back with him out of the way.

"'S'okay," I said, panting a bit. "It's dead."

"How is that okay?" snapped Detective Tuatu. "Don't touch it!"

"I wasn't gunna touch it!" I snapped back, leaning over the body. It was face down, and there was no movement to show it was breathing. "I was just making sure it's properly dead."

Detective Tuatu said tightly, "I really don't want to know about bodies that aren't properly dead. Where did it come from, and who is it?"

"Between," I said, gently touching the vines on the wall. They were utterly still again, and I couldn't hear the scratching any longer. "And I dunno who it is. You know where your friend is?"

At least we weren't going to be attacked, I suppose. But there was still the matter of the body someone had chucked at us, and I was pretty sure that the sound I could hear outside, that wailing in the distance, was—

"Sirens," said the detective, who had reached for the body's shoulder to turn it, despite what he'd just said to me about touching it. His face was grim, his eyes chips of amber.

"Don't look at me," I said. "I never called the cops."

"Neither did I. You'd better sneak out the back."

"Can't," I said. Jin Yeong's saliva must still have been doing its thing, because I could pinpoint exactly where the cop cars were coming from, and exactly where each one of them stopped. "They're out there, too. Someone must have given 'em a really good tip."

"Get up in the ceiling, then," said the Detective, crossing the hall to look carefully out the window. "Stay quiet. If you're quiet enough, they might not find you."

Gloomily, I pointed up at the high ceiling. "No recess."

Detective Tuatu rolled his lips together, and back out. "Sorry," he said. "I shouldn't have brought you with me. I knew they could do something like this, but—"

"Hang on," I interrupted. "It doesn't matter about who brought us here. The important thing is that I can get us out."

"There's no way," he said, nodding at the window. "It's like you said; there's a dozen cars out there. No way we're getting out of here through any of the windows or doors—they're expecting us. Expecting me."

"Never said we were gunna go through the doors or windows," I said happily. Zero said I wasn't meant to go Between by myself, but this had to count as an emergency, right?

"What are you talking about?" Detective Tuatu's voice was uneasy, and there was the slightly white-eyed look of the startled horse about him.

"Gimme your hand," I said, grinning. "We're gunna take a bit of a detour. This lot can have the body, but if I'm not home soon, my psychos will want to know what happened to dinner."

He looked at me suspiciously. "Are you going to drug me?"

There was a shockingly sudden *crash* of splintering wood, and the front door snapped in half.

"Flamin' heck!" I said, and grabbed Detective Tuatu's hand. "Run for it!"

I dragged him back up through the hall and through the door of the second bedroom, and right through the mossy wall into Between, the green wall paint sticking to us like tar as we pushed through it.

"What the heck?" I panted, struggling to pull us both through. What was wrong with Between?

Whatever it was, it wasn't proof against my continued wriggling, and even as I heard the muffled sound of policemen running through the house, we were through. Through into a copse of silent trees and mossy hollows that was so lined by ferns and moss that every sound was deadened, even the sound of our voices.

"What?" demanded Detective Tuatu, his eyes still wild and white around the edges. "What's wrong? Why did it take us so long? Why are there bits of—of—is that the *wall* sticking to my arm?"

"That's flamin' rude!" I told him. "I haven't done this very often, so sometimes it takes a bit longer. You in a hurry or something?"

I wondered if he knew he was clinging so tightly to my hand that it was going numb.

He swallowed, and said, "All right, then. How do we get out of here? Where is here?"

"Not a clue where we are," I said, peeling off the bit of wall that seemed to be bothering him. We were out of immediate danger, but it wasn't like I really knew where I was going—I didn't have a lot of solo experience with Between. And most of that was accidental, too; like the way I got out of each situation.

I huffed a breath at the dark green shadows around me, then fished out my phone. No signal. Yeah, that was about right. It looked like JinYeong was going to miss out on his choice for dinner tonight, too.

"Who did you annoy this time?" I asked the detective, slipping my phone away without telling him I had no way of contacting my psychos. He already looked a bit overwhelmed. "Looks like someone's still got their eye on you."

"I don't know," Detective Tuatu said tightly.

"Was that your friend back there?"

"I don't know that, either. Didn't get the chance to see his face."

"Bet it was."

"What—Pet, what are we going to do?"

"First? Get home. Zero might start looking for us if we're too long, I s'pose, but we can't depend on it. After that, we'll have to figure out who's trying to frame you, but first of all we gotta get out."

The detective looked around us, his eyes darting toward shadowed hollows and ferny corners. "How? What do we do?"

"Follow me," I said to the detective. "Don't let go of my hand. Watch out for goblins and don't touch stuff."

www.ingramcontent.com/pod-product-compliance
Lightning Source LLC
Chambersburg PA
CBHW070451120726
47910CB00003B/1003